RE

The places, titles, businesses and names contained within this work may be real, but the views are not necessarily the views of them. The names, places and events used by the Author are for purely fictitious purposes.

First published in Kindle Direct Publishing in Ebook October 2020

First published in Kindle Direct Publishing in Paperback October 2020

For Ber, for all her patience

Index

Preface

The author started writing this novel as the pandemic COVID19 took a hold in the United Kingdom and lockdown rules were applied, alongside severe travel restrictions both domestically and internationally. It had originally been assumed by the author that the pandemic would viciously decimate the population in Ireland and in the Bergamo vicinity of Italy, but not the rest of Europe. As a result of this supposition travel through the rest of the European Nations mentioned in the novel were largely unaffected. Whilst we can all reflect on the rules and regulations regarding movement around the globe, which would have prevented some of the characters from their various and lengthy travels between locations, the author had to believe that the pandemic was over and that certain restrictions did not apply. With hindsight some of the occurrences described in this novel must remain fictional but they nevertheless gave the author a start to an ending that had been in his head for decades.

1 Road to retribution

Ardavan Kamandi was livid, absolutely seething. Months of work had just been blown apart and it was all down to the deliberate spoiling tactics of the three members of the British delegation. He was aware that the military attaché in the United Nations delegation was also British and also that some collusion was at hand. The three delegates from the French hosts and the other two from the United Nations had all voiced their favour during the whole process, backing the three from The Kurdish Regional Government in northern Iraq.

The conference had been set up to discuss the setting up of an autonomous homeland nation for the Kurds. Now it was all in disarray, thanks to the British.

Ardavan Kamandi, Brigade Commander of the Kurdish forces vowed to exact retribution. He would seek out and destroy the British, the two politicians and the two Generals. He would do this at any cost.

As his stony face looked down on the departing delegates he reflected on the events of the last two weeks of December. His face was hard and severe, fully shaven, with little humour and lined forehead, with deep vertical grooves above his beaked nose and bushy black eyebrows which came together as his furrowed brow closed. His large, athletic frame quivered in anger and frustration. A man to be reckoned with, people thought.

He had been the first to arrive on that cold December day. He had looked down from his selected vantage point on the first floor, behind the fronds of a small potted palm at the end of the wrought iron balcony and surveyed the French group, wondering what the real reason was for supporting the Kurds. They had initially proposed the Kurdish homeland, which would be internationally recognised, firstly in Northern Iraq, where the Regional Government existed. Then a further extension into southern Turkey, effectively returning the lands to those mapped out centuries before. The Turks could be accommodated, with entry to the European Union. The Iraqis really didn't have much of a say in their own destiny since the overthrow of Hussein. The Kurds would be assisted by the British, due to their union in the fight against Daesh and all that they did to help the cause in the First and Second World Wars. It always came down to politics or trade. He had wondered if the lovely atmosphere of this beautiful new hotel, with its marble floors, the grand piano playing in the lobby, the gym, sauna and outdoor pool and the chosen Executive Suites would soften the hard edges of the people who would be attending, or could the meeting have been just as easily held in a hot tent somewhere in the desert and still get the same outcome? Time would tell.

The cool pastel shades of the marbled Reception greeted the French, the first to arrive, led by Jean Paul Girard. A porter took their cases from him and his two colleagues, but they kept a hold of their briefcases and laptops. He had heard them arranging to meet in the lobby bar within the hour as they checked in and were shown up to their rooms on the first floor. Their accents had been unmistakably French.

He had imagined Jean Paul stacking away the contents of his cases in the drawers and in the wardrobe, stripping off, showering, and lying down on the quilted cover on the large bed. He would have set his alarm and napped for fifteen minutes, then dressed casually and gone out, along the wide corridor towards the head of the grand sweeping staircase to the lobby.

The bar, intimately lit in blue hues, with contrasting yellow recesses adorned with artefacts, had been below Ardavan's vantage point. Jean Paul's two colleagues had beaten him to it, sitting at the bar in the pools of light cast by the round red lamps. He had seen Jean Paul go down the marble treads, shouting to greet them, sticking to the form of a casual businessman. 'Hi guys, you're all settled I see. What's that beer you are drinking? Is it local or one of our usual ones?'

'No Jean Paul,' was the loud reply 'it's one of those German ones, Weizen, in a half litre. It's quite tasty, as most would be right now if I'm honest.'

Jean Paul had caught the attention of the girl behind the bar, pointed to his associate's beer and asked for another. The three of them had sat chatting about the hotel, commenting on the fact it was too cold for the pool at this time of year. 'It would be a bit like the Blue lagoon in Iceland. We'd be swimming in warm water with a fur hat on. Icicles would be forming on us as we dried off' Jean Paul had loudly joked.

Ardavan had looked around the bar, searching for the others who would be at the meeting. There were tables of Germans, Italians, Norwegians and locals, either Iraqis or Kurds, all obvious in their forms of dress. Not their national costumes, but the creative modern style of each country, which marked out most nations from each other. He wondered if the Germans and Italians were selling equipment, as well as beer and coffee machines and if the Norwegians were off duty members of the Norwegian Forces, who were training the region's Kurdish soldiers. They certainly looked fit enough, he mused, but most Scandinavians look fit enough normally.

Over the weekend all the players had flown in to Erbil International Airport in various executive jets, dressed in civilian clothes. To the man in the street they were all likely business people from the host of international companies vying for lucrative contracts in the region. There were no hangers on, just the players to be around the table, so that discussion could be earnest and frank. The need to find a resolution was of paramount importance in order that the situation could be stabilized smoothly and quickly.

The five star hotel had been chosen, as anyone watching would see that a more private location would be out of keeping with a business group, but the security issues could not be discounted. The transport from airport to the hotel was in Volkswagen minibuses with blacked out windows, quite a common sight on the roads, hotel and airport. Their route from the airport had been quick, around twenty minutes to cover the ten kilometres, taking them alongside Sami Abdulrahman Park, past the Kurdistan Regional Government parliament building on the right, then in along Zagors and cut through to the hotel on Meter Street.

The hotel had also been conducive to a high-powered meeting and the place of choice for top company executives. There was a private meeting room which had been built to exacting standards for noise control, with an ante room to further separate meetings from the corridor. There were no windows, a solid floor and a solid ceiling with no void above. It was a very secure space and large enough to squeeze in twenty at a push around a square table.

He had noticed another group arriving at the Hotel Reception, as the French supped at their beers. From the look of their attire they were certainly British and one of them had the upright swagger of a military man. So that's the famous General Douglas, he had thought, and noticed Jean Paul catching the elbow of his colleague and indicated with his head towards the Reception. He in turn had nudged the third and they had all looked over surreptitiously, turned to each other and had concluded that the group was indeed the British. The small and wiry dark haired Defence Secretary and the fair haired, balding, tall, but portly Foreign Secretary had been well known to the French. The lean figure of the General was a new cog in the wheel. Short dark hair, tanned complexion, about two metres in height and broad shouldered. He looked as if he could still run a 5k with ease. The British group had moved off towards the elevators, porters in tow, for their adjacent rooms on the second floor. Jean Paul had resumed his chat with his colleagues.

The next to arrive were the UN delegation, a truly international trio, Ardavan recalled. The three delegates were also herded from the front door of the hotel towards the front desk clerks by the concierge. The tall blonde chap with the goatee beard in front had been the Danish cultural representative, the petite olive skinned girl behind had been the Malaysian financial representative and the tall nondescript guy at the back had been General Russell Murdoch, on attachment from the British army. He had been the one weak link in the chain, as his masters may have had first call on his reasoning, rather than the United Nations. A weak link, but a formidable person to have as a foe. He had seen active service in Northern Ireland, The Gulf, Iraq, Afghanistan, Bosnia and had been Director of Special Forces before his secondment.

As they had moved past the bar Ardavan had noticed Murdoch's eyes sweeping over the French group at the bar, their Gallic movements showing them up. He didn't miss a trick. Definitely one to watch he had thought.

The remaining delegates, the Kurds, had arrived in the last of the minibuses, strode straight up to the desk and had been greeted by the hotel manager, before by-passing all the formalities of check in. They had been taken straight to the Service lift and whisked up to their top floor suites, the three largest in the hotel. The French didn't see them, but Russell Murdoch did.

Ardavan had seen what lay ahead and a first glance at personalities from afar could tell him more than the carefree but false smiles across a table.

At that particular table, representing the British had been General Sir Patrick Walsh Douglas as their military advisor. To his immediate left had been the Secretary of Defence. To the Secretary's left had been the Foreign Secretary. On the opposite side of the table had sat the Foreign Minister of KRG, the Prime Minister of KRG and himself. Between them, at right angles, to form a square, to the left was the delegation from the United Nations and to the right the French representatives, the sponsors of the meeting.

They had been sitting in the small conference room within the Erbil International Hotel, in Erbil, Northern Iraq, the centre of the Kurdistan Regional Government. They had been brought together to discuss further moves towards an autonomous country of Kurdistan, sequestrating in effect a large region of Northern Iraq, ending the PKK involvement, easing relations with Turkey and expanding the boundaries of the European Union, into Northern Arabia and Western Asia at the same time.

There had been a lot to discuss in the Agenda tabled by Jean Paul Girard, the head of the French delegation. Prior notification of the agenda had not been transmitted to any party, to avoid sectarian discussion and allow some free thinking between the various policy makers around the table. The idea had been novel, but fraught with difficulty at the same time. The scheduled time frame had been two weeks, made up of two, four hour sessions daily, for six days. It had allowed for a discussion forum, with only one of each side of the table representing each party, of two whole days and two final days to ratify all the work that had been agreed.

The United Nations military representative had been General Russell Murdoch of the United Kingdom armed forces on secondment to the UN as overall commander of UN military combined forces in Northern Iraq. This had perhaps been unfortunate but the leader of the UN delegation, a Dane, had stated that, at no time in the discussions would their military advisor and the British military advisor be free to discuss matters of importance to the United Kingdom as such.

Ardavan had expected the group to be extremely fair and willing to suggest finer points, which would have smoothly lead to the passing of the resolution. The French had been pushing it, likely to get more influence within the European Union, as a founding member. The Kurds had of course been bargaining for more than they would eventually expect to settle for. The British would have been expected – before they had arrived at the table - to see the Kurds finally get national frontiers, but had always been known to drive a hard bargain to get the final deal. Most of the work had been discussed by each of the three groups before coming to Erbil. The next fourteen days had turned out to be interesting.

There had been an unseasonable chill to the weather the following day. Clouds had scudded in, over from Turkey in the north and a few light flurries of snow had sprinkled the hotel grounds, but did not lie for long. The groups had breakfasted, the Kurds in their Prime Minister's largest suite, the other three in the breakfast room. The UN and French delegates had exchanged pleasantries and the British had selected a round table in the corner, away from prying eyes and listening ears, discussing a point with concerned looks on their faces.

The first meeting had been set for 09:00 and the UN delegation were in first, followed by the French and British and, at five past nine, the Kurds.

Jean Paul Girard had opened the proceedings, declaring that all words spoken would, by necessity and open honesty, be conducted in English, as decreed in the invitations. All present had voiced their agreement and he had continued by reading out the agenda, noting that no other agenda points could be added at that stage, as all parties had had enough time to resolve issues before this final set of discussions. Again, all around the hollow square had been in agreement. Jean Paul had gone on to state that each individual around the table should be in a position to voice his or her opinion, without the necessity of passing the question to another member of their delegation. Again they had been in agreement.

The conference had continued, mostly in subdued conversation, sometimes in raised voices, in consternation and indeed anger, much to the disdain of the French and United Nations delegations.

At every opportunity Ardavan Kamandi and Russell Murdoch had silently viewed the animated or calm faces of the individuals around the oak table, with the green leather writing pads, white notepaper and black Erbil Hotel pens. At times their eyes had met, but mostly moved on, sucking up information, in the way they had both been trained.

A week into the process an impasse had begun to build between the Foreign Secretary of Great Britain and the KRG Foreign Minister and both Ardavan Kamandi and Russell Murdoch had wondered where this had been going, but both had kept their powder dry.

The discussions came around to the subject of what military weight the new nation would have. The non-military representatives of the UN had both suggested that a neutral stance would be best, like Switzerland, Sweden, or Ireland. The French thought that a force based upon a common bond between Europe and the new nation would have been best, with the French playing a leading role.

The Kurds had wished for a better supply of arms than they had been receiving, to defend themselves against a threat, from the air especially. Their Defence Minister had asked for an increase in ground to air combat facilities, as they could hold their own, as could be seen from history, against ground based troops. The threat would come from air strikes, from fighter jets, bombers and missiles.

The British had argued that, for world peace to be certain, there needed to be the ultimate strengths of the more advanced players, so that other less powerful nations could be policed.

Ardavan Kamardi had known that the British had been talking bullshit. They were always interested in trade and wealth and the control of smaller nations, just like the Americans, Russians, and French. They were all keen to get you to spend money on their arms, but just not the most recent variations. Those they would always keep for themselves. He had thought that Russell Murdoch had taken it all in.

By the end of the second week, the only issue open for debate had been the sticky subject of arms. All other business had been concluded fairly and had been signed off by all parties around the table. Only the last afternoon session had remained, to reach an agreement. They had broken for lunch in their respective groups, the Kurds left, followed by the French, then the British ministers with the UN delegates.

He remembered, as he'd left the room he'd seen, in the reflection on the glass covering of the picture on the wall in front of him, General Douglas signalling to General Murdoch to hang back, in the full knowledge that he was not allowed to do so under these particular rules of engagement, and had whispered something to him. With that they had both exited the room. As he had made to turn the corner, he glanced right and saw the two military men clearly saying something to each other. His eyes narrowed, but he walked on with his two colleagues leading the way.

By three in the afternoon, the decision had been voiced by the British delegation that they could not support the proposal made by the French. The United Nations representatives had looked astounded and the Kurds had been livid. The KRG ministers had risen from their seats and had broken from the English language to castigate the British and shout that this would be the last time they would allow the British to simply say something and then decide upon the complete opposite.

He had felt the eyes of General Murdoch flitting over him but he had kept his cool. His unrelenting stare into the faces of General Douglas and the two Secretaries had a look of revengeful hatred. He wondered if General Murdoch had felt that hatred transmitting through the caustic atmosphere of the conference room.

He had thought to himself, 'There will be retribution for this foul deed. I will make sure of it.'

Early the next morning the executive jets had left Erbil Airport and the Kurdish Regional Government Ministers had retreated to their nice homes in the suburbs of Erbil. Ardavan Kamandi had returned to his room after breakfast, gathered up his belongings and sent coded messages to his closest staff. He left, in a hire car arranged by the concierge some minutes later, to his house beside the Grand Mosque in the little town of Haji Omeran, in the north- eastern corner of Iraq, close to the Iranian border. His anger had boiled up inside him as he drove along the damp road to the east.

Within the confines of their comfortable blue leather armchairs in their homeward bound executive jet, as it travelled swiftly westwards the two British politicians were in animated discussion. 'Well if we let everyone who wanted independence get their own way, we'd be up the creek without a paddle. Look at the trouble we have with the Scottish Nationalists, for goodness sake.' 'Yes, just look at what the Kurds have got now, a Regional devolved government, stakes in both Iraqi and Iranian parliaments, a growing autonomy in Turkey, representation in 14 foreign states and even Consulate Generals from France, Italy and Germany in Erbil, with equal representatives in Paris, Berlin and Rome. With us, as you know, it's the same.'

General Douglas chipped in with 'I had a word with Murdoch. He was very good. I'd like him as my right hand man as Chief of General Staff, when I step up to Chief of Defence Staff in the new year. On the weapons front we should let the Albanians, Cypriots and Estonians keep on supplying them with the inferior weaponry, which they have been sending over the last couple of years. That'll keep the squaddies happy and maybe their politicos away from us for a spell. What do you think about the Kamandi fellow? A right bag of vipers hidden inside him, I would say. Can we get the Firm to keep an eye on him?'

'That's one I need to discuss with the PM and the Home Secretary when we get back, Patrick.' said the Defence Secretary. 'I'll put forward Murdoch for you.'

2 Promotions of Generals

By the end of the following January, General Douglas had been promoted to Chief of Defence Staff and he in turn had General Murdoch as Chief of General Staff, alongside Admiral Robert Anthony, First Sea Lord and Alan McIntosh, Air Chief Marshall. All of them were highly decorated, had seen active service around the globe and had not spent their whole lives pushing pens across a desk.

Around the same time Ardavan Kamardi's group, messaged after the debacle in Erbil in December, got together in a villa on the shores of Lake Bled, just below Straza Bled, the toboggan run. From the dining room in the villa, the view across the frost encrusted lawn took in the castle on the hilltop across the lake and the postcard pretty church standing on the island. There were just the three of them. Ardavan liked to keep the group small, as there was less chance of leaks getting out. It was also easier to find the source of any leak – it had to be one of only two. He had found out that to his cost on one previous occasion.

He handed out four photographs, head and shoulders shots of the British Secretaries of State, for Foreign Affairs and Defence and the two Generals who were in attendance at the fated conference. He also distributed four full body shots on a scaled background of ten centimetres by ten centimetres, showing each of the four in height and width and head shape. The colour of hair, eyes and complexion was also noted. Ardavan spoke for the first time.

'After the betrayal of the British at Erbil last month I have been incessantly thinking how to get back at these traitorous swine. These are the four men who let our nation down so badly, who took everything we had to give in the fight, quite regularly alongside their own soldiers, against numerous foes, for decades. They let us down after the First World War, after the Second World War, The Gulf War and against Daesh and its forebears. We honestly thought that the time had come to count on their support but it was not to be. We have to take revenge, in any way we can. I have come up with a plan. It is both daring and difficult. It might even be impossible but we will try, for the good of our nation.'

He jutted his chin forward, his beak of a nose more prominent, and continued, 'Rohat Dilhan – you are tasked with working out the best way to attack and the weapon of choice. Fatima Ardalan – you are tasked with the transport of the weapon of choice to the point of use. This should be a very simple operation. We can use others in our quest, from the Kurdish communities at home and around the world. Some of them have been sent out as sleepers, awaiting instruction when the time comes. I will give you names and contact details when needed. Only three of us will know the full extent of this mission. I will trust nobody so give me your sworn allegiance or I will know. Any questions?'

Fatima asked 'Do we have a particular date for this action to be carried out, or at least a timescale to completion?'

'I do not have an exact timescale. This will depend on the weapon and the delivery, but certainly both within a year,' said Ardavan.
Rohat made small nods with his head and she said, 'Good. This will get my unbridled attention with immediate effect.'

Ardavan told them that he would meet with them again on the following Friday. He told them to stay in the villa and work out the details of their respective actions. They were forbidden to go out of the villa, except to be in the garden. He told them that everything they might need was in the villa. 'Go to your tasks!' he commanded.

He raised himself from the chair and left the room and Rohat and Fatima were left to ponder on their immediate tasks.

Rohat excused himself and went to the bedroom allocated to him, while she stayed at the table, cogs whirring.

By the end of the first day Rohat had made up a list of weaponry, how it could be deployed, where it could be deployed, when it could be deployed and comment as to the effectiveness of each selection and outcome. The list ranged through poison, knives, pistols, rifles, grenades, sniper fire, pipe bombs, rocket attacks and even martyrdom. The list was extensive, and included their use in daylight or darkness, how many operatives would be needed, countermeasures that could be employed against them, camera and visual surveillance aspects and even some technological wizardry.

He sat down with Fatima and presented her with his findings. It was now up to her to work out the logistics of getting each option to its final target. Each of the two politicians was high profile, with secure transport, maybe with police outriders, in car or motorcycle form. Their movements were not scheduled very far in advance, but they did like a photographic opportunity, so they could be targeted out in the open. But this was usually in a secure environment, with a liberal dose of police around, no doubt some in plain clothes. In cold weather they could very well conceal body armour below their outer layers. A shot to the head would be more difficult. Armour would deflect knives. The opportunity to get close enough for poison would be rare, but if a kitchen dish was spiked then there may be a way around that problem.

She prevaricated over all of the options that he had listed. She concluded that they had to collectively gather the four of the targets together, or find an occasion when the four of them would automatically be together. If not, then one would be forewarned, maybe even two. Would Ardavan be satisfied with a 25% success rate? She would have to ask.

No matter which method was employed she reckoned that it would have to be done in their back yard, in England, and most likely in London.

Ardavan came back to the villa on the Friday and they went right to work. 'What have you concluded?' He said, to open the meeting.

Rohat laid out his findings, which Ardavan studied intensely, stopping briefly to ask a question now and again, then sat back in his chair and asked Fatima to give him her update.

She started with her conclusion 'It is my opinion that there is only one way to get to all four. We have to find a mutual meeting place for all of them and hit them with a rocket attack. This will have to happen in the greatly defended capital city of London, where camera surveillance is likely as concentrated as in Moscow. Any other form will either give warning, could be intercepted or could lead to martyrdom.'

She had Ardavan's attention. 'Tell me more, Fatima. Well done, Rohat. Your further input will be necessary I think.' Ardavan gave a grimace of a smile, his eyes stayed still, like two black glistening bullet holes in his head.

By the end of the day Ardavan had decided upon the weapon of choice and that they, as a group, would need to set the attack for a certain day, when it was expected that all four would be together, in the open, or in an enclosed space. This would be the solution. The plan would likely lead to martyrdom for one of the Kurdish nation.

His thoughts turned to the procurement of the weapons. The Kurds had been supplied by the Armenians, Cypriots and Estonians before, but getting military equipment from Northern Iraq, Syria, Iran or any of the supplying countries could be problematic. He ruled out parachute drops from an aircraft. He thought that ferry travel with weaponry into the busy ports in Southern England could be fraught with difficulties, as there was also drug running and people trafficking to counter at ferry ports. Checks might be too severe.

He decided to make calls to some of his agents scattered throughout the world. He discounted all continents barring Europe and western Asia. His weaponry and travel must be concentrated within these zones. Three agents stood out in their discussions, a shipyard worker in Bulgaria, a freelance photographer in Hamburg and a musician in London.

After Ardavan had mulled things over for a few days he called each one in turn. Each time he used a different pay phone, once from Klagenfurt in Austria, once from Tarvisio in Italy and the third from Pula in Croatia. From Klagenfurt he telephoned a man in Bulgaria, from Tarvisio to a man in London and to Hamburg, from Pula, to a woman. The calls were short and all asked the caller to call another number at hourly intervals that evening.

The first caller was answered by the name he had been given and asked about his uncle. Both Ardavan and the caller knew that it was safe to talk. The caller was asked if he could take delivery of a package at the shipyard where he worked, secrete it for a while and then pass it on when needed. The caller in turn asked about the package, its size and weight, and was answered, with the addition of, 'There will be two packages, both will arrive to you and depart from you together. Understood?' The caller confirmed and the call was broken.

The second caller was greeted in a similar fashion and answered accordingly. Ardavan said this time 'Are there any ferries running from Northern Germany to England? Can you arrange to meet a delivery at a safe place in Northern Germany and pass the driver some further instructions?' She answered that she could meet a delivery and as far as she was aware there were no ferries, as the crossing time would be too long. 'There used to be connections between the Scandinavian countries and northern England and maybe between Holland and Scotland but I don't think they run any more either. There was a summer service that ran between Norway and Scotland, but I would have to check to see if that is still operational. Can you give me some time to check them all out?' Ardavan replied that she could have four days. He told her to phone the same number, to enquire about her relation, at the same time in the evening, after she had finished work and hung up.

The third caller waited for four rings, as suggested, and enquired about his aunt. Ardavan answered and asked him if he could make himself available at short notice, to carry out a collection of a package. If he was committed to concerts already diaried, he would have to make an excuse and call off. He would be recompensed accordingly. The caller agreed and the call was cut.

Now Ardavan had his mission worked out in principle. He still had to procure the armaments, arrange the drop off in Romania, transport them across the open borders of Europe and deliver them to London, without using the normal ferry ports to England from the continent. Any loose ends would have to be formulated before the hit could be arranged. But time was not against him. He could wait for the right opportunity.

Four days later the phone rang. It was the woman. She told him that there were no ferries north of The Netherlands and that security at the Dutch end as well as the English end was very strict. She went on to say that the summer service between Norway and Lerwick, the farthest north archipelago of Scotland, had been cancelled due to lack of passengers. That route had been originally to Iceland and now just went there, missing out the Scottish connection. She did however suggest that a fishing boat or a leisure yacht might be an option. That was another problem for Ardavan to solve. He thanked her, told her that her relation was much improved but still in care and replaced the receiver.

He mulled over the information that he had received and made a call to Fatima. She was ordered to go to Norway and search out a suitable fishing boat or yacht that could take the packages to England or at the very least to Scotland. They were after all one country and security could not be as onerous between the two locations.

Fatima arranged to travel to Norway, to its capital Oslo, and set to work, in one of the severest winters Norway had seen in a long time. It was not a great time to check out sea going small vessels, especially not yachts. She would concentrate on the fishing boats.

....

Little did Lorenzo Russo know, when he left for the marina in Carrick-on-Shannon, in Ireland, on that fateful Monday in the first week of February that his world would be turned upside down and that fate would become a yoke for him to carry and that he would turn into a completely different person.

The news bulletin had screened the headline of some problem in China with animal scales and bats, but that was away on the other side of the world, not by the swirling waters of The Shannon.

His wife Lucy was working nights as a theatre nurse at the hospital and he saw little of her, what with shift rotas and different sleep patterns. Even the weekends were different. Michael, his first son, was always out on the building sites, trying to keep up, pulling wires and fitting sockets and whatever else he did in the electrical engineering business. And at the same time, second son Pietro, the coach driver, had just invested all his cash in Carrick Coaches, when he bought out old Seamus.

Things had been tough through the Irish recession but they had all come through it with the family intact. Linda, his daughter, had even met the man of her dreams and had moved away to be with him in Birmingham, where he worked on the High Speed Rail System. The baby was due in the next six weeks and so she had moved back to Carrick for family support, to once again be one big happy family.

Pat O'Mahony, Lorenzo's boss at Shannon Cruise Line was in the office early that day and was looking pretty agitated, shuffling paperwork and scrolling through files. His mood didn't change when Lorenzo stuck his head inside the office, as he did every day. There was a polite 'Morning' from Lorenzo. 'What the feck is he so happy about?' thought Pat, but never lifted his head to reply. Lorenzo thought that a bit unusual, but hey ho, another day another dollar, or euro to be precise. He headed to his workbench, switched on his computer and screen and turned to the paperwork and work schedule he had for the day. The project noted at the top of the schedule was to be resolving the bent safety handrail on Number 3 Broom, a six berth cruiser. The damage was up at the front, by the anchor locker, on the starboard side. Bookings were picking up in the cruise business with the new season in the offing, and in general business seemed to be picking up in the new booming economy in Carrick and surroundings. Pat had said only the week before that he might have to take on another engineer to assist Lorenzo and he would get a step up to Lead Engineer. He might get a bit more money, maybe a better car. Maybe the new guy, or gal, would get his old stuff and he would get brand spanking new kit.

Pat finally pulled himself away from his searching and wandered out into the workshop with a, 'This fecking virus thing is going to play havoc with our lives again you know. The Chief Medical Officer is saying that it will be here in no time and we will have to deal with it like the Chinese. They've put a whole million plus city in lockdown and nobody can go out or go to work. If they don't do it they're all going to die. Apparently the Chinese gave it to the Italians and some fellas up Dublin way took it back with them after a ski-ing holiday in the Alps. If a lockdown happens here this will crucify the business once again and it'll be worse that the last recession, which is not that many years back. Look how long we took to get over that one. I've just got back on my feet, as you well know.'

Lorenzo looked up from his project work. 'Don't worry yourself Pat. We can't do anything about it. It's like flu, we all go down for a few days and then get right back in again thereafter. What else can we do for now? Stop?'

His thoughts immediately sprang to the money side and what would happen to the family earnings if everything came to a grinding halt. Under one roof, with four out of the five of them breadwinners, there would be no more building work, no more transporting and nobody wanting to hire a river cruise boat. At least Lucy would have the earnings off nursing, but that wouldn't be enough to go around.

He thought to himself, 'Why me? Why does everything happen to me? I'm not a bad person. Okay I used to be a bit of a lad when I was in my teenage years, running with the gang. But that's history. If the engineer's job in the cruise line goes, then I will find something else. I always do. I'm a grafter. I've been that ever since the day I left Nola, my home town, on the outskirts of Napoli, Italy. And Lucy was good for me. We're a dream team these days.'

Back in Italy in those days it was the system of a different kind, where every boy had his Don and 'work' had a different connotation to it. The rules were followed and if not, then at the least there was a kicking and at the worst you ended up on a bit of wasteland as another statistic. The police were not in the slightest bit interested, as long as Captain Alfonso got his slice.

3 North Sea quest

It was the middle of February when Fatima's quest took her from the city life of Oslo and down the coast to Kristiansand, then up again to Stavanger, Haugesund and Bergen. Her first few days were spent in Stavanger, listening mostly to tales of oil and gas exploration and food factories. There was a NATO Joint Warfare Centre located there, with quite a few military types to be found in restaurants and bars, so she quickly discounted the city as one to ship the packages from.

Further up the North Sea coast was Haugesund, a city of 100,000 residents, with a large herring processing facility. 'An ideal opportunity, perhaps, for a fishing boat charter,' she thought. Her journey took her across bridges and by ferry until she arrived in the city. She delved further, in and around the quayside bars and cafes, and found that the local fishing boats did not charter, but were fully crewed vessels with journeys close to shore. They came and went quite regularly, but not from one side of the North Sea to the other. There were a good few yachts in the harbour and some pulled out of the water on slipways and docksides, over wintering.

She was left pondering about the use of a yacht, or a charter and would compare Haugesund with further north, at Bergen. She had learned from a talkative bar owner in Haugesund that Bergen had a burgeoning yachting marina. She packed her bags once more and set off in her hire car.

It took a full day to drive between the two, what with twisty coastal roads, bridges between land masses and ferries. She arrived just as the early dusk was falling, the sun already a half globe squeezing between the grey clouds and the sea, casting a warm glow on to the clouds. She had decided on a central hotel and had pre-booked a standard room with a harbour view, The Clarion, on C. Sunds Gate, with old Bergen on the opposite side of the harbour.

She spent a few more days, scouting out possible transport links and it was a chance visit to the museum that she got the idea into her mind. There was a piece, with quite a few photographs of a cross North Sea yacht race, the Pantaenius Shetland Race, which starts at Marstein Lighthouse at Bergen and finishes at The Sound of Bressay, in Lerwick, Shetland Islands. The race was always held on the last weekend of June. Fatima headed back to the hotel and made some further investigation into the routing and logistics.

Later that evening Fatima made a call to Ardavan, explained what she had found and asked if the rest of the timing could be worked around to make this the date for the crossing, surreptitiously and well away from ferry routes and invasive customs checks. She went on to say that there was a regular ferry from Lerwick to Aberdeen. The links from there to London could be by a variety of transport types. All they needed was a suitable yacht and skipper.

Ardavan said, 'I have some reservations about the timing. The race might come too soon. We still need to decide upon the contact point, but stick with it for the moment. I will be speaking to my contact regarding the material of choice tomorrow.' Fatima cradled the receiver and helped herself to a coffee from the machine in her room. 'He seemed pleased again. I wonder how Rohat is getting on,' she breathed to herself.

The weekend came around and still the rain and snow fell from the dark skies. Snowflakes and slashes of sleet blew around her in the north west wind, as she hurriedly made her way out of the hotel to the Thai restaurant on Ovregaten. She was looking forward to a nice bit of spicy food, to remind her of home. She was warmly greeted and ushered to a table for two to the edge of the room, away from the door.

In time, two men walked in, smart looking and speaking English, one with the unmistakable accent of a Scandinavian, well educated but not strongly accentuated, like some she had heard on her travels through Norway. As she began to eat her starter of Moo Sam Cha Tod, she eavesdropped on the conversation and discovered that one was called Richard, a lecturer at a college in Hertfordshire in England and the other was a retired professor from Bergen, name of Kjell.

As she supped on her starter she strained her ears at the mention of a yacht, which Kjell owned. After his wife had fallen ill and especially since his wife's death in the autumn, he'd not been out in the boat much and he'd had the yacht lifted out of the water and stored in the Marina boatshed. 'However, Richard, I've decided to refit her and will get started on that at the end of this month. I reckon with equipment deliveries and the actual work I'll have her ready by about mid May or the beginning of June.'

'That's great Kjell, I'm pleased to hear that. It's time you released yourself from the grieving process. What are you going to do to her?' asked Richard.

'Well the usual annual scrape of hull and keel, rub down and re-coating. There are still memories of my wife every time I step aboard, down to the colour of the upholstery that was foisted upon me, so I'm going to fully re-upholster her, spruce up all the teak gangways and decks and fit some new equipment in her, ready for the North Sea again. I might even go for the Pantaenius this year, but I think I'll have to brush up on my skills and six weeks to do that would be a bit tight. I know that grandfather would be looking down on me thinking – what an idiot.'

Richard replied, 'Yes, he might at that, but see how it goes. Maybe you can still head for Lerwick again, but at a more leisurely pace and loaded with some nice treats and home comforts, not stripped back to the bare.'

As Fatima welcomed her second course of Khao Soi, she reflected on what she had just heard – a yacht whose next journey could be from Bergen to Lerwick, maybe by late June, but then again maybe later. She needed to find where the boat lay and how she could get material aboard her, without the boat owner's knowledge.

She noticed that they were half way through their main course and although she was quite full, she decided to stay around for coffee and see if she could glean more. She was out of their direct line of sight and they were not paying particular attention to her.

As the evening wore on Richard and Kjell finished up, paid their bill and left, followed closely by Fatima, who wanted to find out where their travels would take them. Their next stop was to a cocktail bar just a stone's throw away from the main harbour pier. She walked around for a few minutes until she felt chilled to the bones and then waltzed in to the bar and took a stool at the corner, but, again, within earshot again of the two men. She ordered a pink gin and then had an, 'Oh no!' moment as the music on the speakers increased in volume. Her night was over. She could not take a chance on another surveillance of the two men, so she finished her drink and called it a night. She had three things on her mind – where was the yacht, where did the owner stay and how many crew would there be on it.

To stay in a hotel in Bergen, without access to skis or proper winter clothing was tantamount to standing on top of the lighthouse in a fluorescent jacket and she made a mental note to change her clothing.

....

Ardavan made a call to the KRG representative in Rome. It was the first week in March. His call was answered and listened to intently. The person on the other end of the line vowed to return the call to Ardavan, on the number given, later that night and to ask the relevant question. At seven in the evening Ardavan answered the telephone set in his room, exchanged the coded message and continued.

‘I have a need for assistance, that which will greatly bolster our nation’s long held wishes for autonomy in the world. I will get straight to the point. I need weapons, ones that cannot be traced back to us, ones from a black market source, where the seller will be paid above the market value for their trouble. Is there anybody in Rome, or in your contact list, who could do this for you?’

‘I can indeed think of one such person. I did him a great favour some time ago and I could call it in. The man is not a citizen of Rome, but a citizen of Napoli, that den of iniquity to the south. He has fingers in so many pies and his life is otherwise a secret. He lives in a villa on Capri. I can contact him there. He is old school. He doesn’t trust telephones, never mind mobiles and laptops. In my opinion he could be trusted. Weaponry is not his usual thing though, so he might baulk, but I will just have to apply a little pressure. I will contact him directly and then you can have a discussion face to face or by carrier pigeon if you so wish.'

Ardavan dismissed the sarcasm and agreed to the scenario outlined. The caller agreed to call back at the same time, using a new code exchanged between them, in two days' time.

Forty-eight hours later Ardavan answered the call and was left with a date, time and place for a meeting. Later that evening he made two calls, to Rohat and to Fatima. He told Rohat that there would be a meeting to discuss weaponry and that he was still of the opinion that a surface to surface rocket propelled grenade attack would be the one of choice, but that the heads would have to be made not just as an anti personnel type or a standard anti tank type, but a time fused fragmentation grenade. They could then determine a fixed distance and maximum casualties within a radius of five metres, heavily wounded within a radius of fifteen metres and a final shrapnel spread radius of over two hundred metres. Rohat was to arrange the expertise to make the alterations to standard munitions accordingly. He would be called on this further.

Fatima was next. She updated Ardavan on her intelligence findings to date, her preferred route, a timing for a window of six weeks between end of

June and end of August, if that was suitable. He confirmed that it was and that an attack profile had not yet been finalised but the method would be. He also reminded her of their contact in London, a musician by occupation, who could be trusted to travel to Lerwick and carry the packages onward to London.

The following week Ardavan was contacted by the Neapolitan and a meeting place and time was set for the coming Friday.

....

In Aberdeen it was cold and grey and the grey granite buildings added to the feeling of a miserable day. Fatima had stood in a queue outside the airport terminal building, waiting for a taxi which would take her into the city centre and Jury's Hotel, which was perfectly placed for both train station to London and ferry terminal to Lerwick. The hotel desk clerk gave her a local map and some basic directions and she set off on foot, firstly to the train station through the enclosed shopping mall. From there the woman in the ticket office explained that there were regular trains to London and the best would be the LNER express train, which left every two hours or so. It would take around seven hours for the journey. First class seats were limited, but usually available if there was only a single passenger, or second class would still be comfortable. There would be Quiet Coaches available too.

She thanked the girl behind the screen and then headed out into the occasional showers for the Ferry Terminal, as seagulls swooped and squawked overhead. Oil production platform supply vessels sat at the quays, loading piping and other hardware aboard. A short walk later she found the ticket office and was informed that there was a daily ferry, which left in early evening and was scheduled to arrive in Lerwick in the early morning of next day. Various ticket types were available, from reclining seats in the main area, through multiple bunk cabins to single cabins with full facilities. She would find a café, restaurant and bar aboard. She arranged for a single cabin, the first one available, in two days time. She would need a return in about a week but the clerk stated that she would have to arrange that at the Lerwick Terminal, to suit her timing.

Later in the week, when she arrived in Lerwick, a taxi picked her up from the Holmsgarth Ferry Terminal and drove her the short distance to the Kveldsro House Hotel overlooking Bressay Sound and the island of Bressay. This would be her base for the next few days as she scouted out the next piece of the travel puzzle for the package. The transfer had to be safe and understated.

Reception offered her some information packs about places in and around Lerwick to investigate and passed her a street plan of the town. She decided to walk around town that day and perhaps hire a car if she needed to check out any of the more outlying sites. She learned of the archipelago's Norwegian roots and the days of the Vikings, with an archaeological dig at Sumburgh airport to the extreme south of what Shetlanders called the mainland and the Up Helly A. This turned out to be a festival which parades a replica Viking longboat alongside armour clad warriors with winged helmets, wielding blazing torches, through the streets of the town, before throwing the torches into the galley and setting it afire.

She wandered down to the flagstoned Commercial Street and the Victoria Pier at the harbour, where she decided to book a trip out to sea at Shetland Seabird Tours, to get a feel of the Sound of Bressay, where the Bergen to Lerwick race would finish.

She enjoyed the voyage, in the small swells of the bright day, as the skipper pointed out Gannets diving through the cold grey blue sea, Dunlin and Eider, Cormorants and the cute little Puffins, Arctic Terns with their streaming tail feathers twitching behind them and the ever present Fulmars, soaring on the light breeze. The nesting cliffs were full of Gulls and the guano was clinging to the rock faces, like the ivory keys of a piano. There were no ocean going yachts at sea, only supply boats, small tankers and fishing vessels coming and going and the Bressay Ferry going to and fro to the mainland.

When she returned later in the afternoon there was a small flotilla of sailing dinghies with school age children pushing off from shore below the sailing

Club and Fatima wondered about the crossing from Bergen once more.

That evening she wandered the mostly deserted streets of the town, climbing up to the old military Fort Charlotte, returning back past the Town Hall and the Islesburgh Complex before turning down one of the narrow pedestrianized lanes to Captain Flint's Bar, to see if she could pick up some local gossip. She sat alone for one drink and left, at the barmaid's suggestion, for a bar not far away, called The Lounge. The Lounge was up a narrow stairs and as she walked into the bar, with its wood panelled walls, a few faces turned to greet her. In the corner were a group of musicians, playing violins, accompanied by an accordion player.

She ordered a drink from the small bar and sat down on a stool, fascinated by the array of banknotes from all around the world, pinned to the ceiling. She wondered when there would be a Kurdish one up there with the rest of them. She soon struck up a conversation with the barman and found that the band were not really a band, but a bunch of locals having a get together over a drink or two, to play a variety of Shetland Reels on their fiddles, as they preferred to call their instruments. As she listened to the reels she formulated a plan in her head to use Kjell's yacht in the process of crossing the North sea. She would need to enlist the help of the musical friend of the Nation. She would take the plan to Ardavan.

She found the next couple of days to be interesting but not very fruitful, yet she had to play the tourist for a bit, before booking her return ferry to Aberdeen and the train connection to London. She left Lerwick on a very blustery evening on the sail back to the real mainland of Scotland. She felt a bit queasy in the first few hours, until the boat was south of Sumburgh Head where the rough seas abated and she slept the night away in her bunk.

Disembarkation at Aberdeen next morning was into a beautiful sunny day. The rays glinted on the quartz elements of the granite and the whole dock front across the harbour seemed to sparkle like a night sky. She reckoned that she had enough time for a leisurely coffee and a meander within the Union Square shopping mall before she took her seat in First class at the front of the train to London at 09:47. She would be in London before dinner, but the expected snacks and drinks in the carriage would suffice until then. She would speak to Ardavan when she reached her hotel at St Pancras, but firstly she must alight at Kings Cross.

....

Two years earlier Michael had been admitted for his COPD and had been put on a ventilator for three days. This time was worse. He died in the early hours of the morning in the Intensive Care Unit, with five medical staff in full protective gear around his bed. Nothing more could be done.

There was no funeral.

The Prime Minister of Ireland introduced drastic laws. He ordered a full lock down of the country in mid March and the 'Two Metre Distance Apart' rule had been applied.

Funeral homes, churches and graveyards were out of bounds. Pubs were closed and St. Patrick's Day was cancelled. Schools and Universities were closed and all but essential work was done from the homes of the citizens.

Michael's body was put in a coffin and stored in one of the bank of refrigerated freight containers, which stood as sentinels in the car park at the marina, on the bank of the River Shannon

Lorenzo, Lucy, Linda and Pietro were devastated. It was bad enough losing a loved one but they were without finality. Michael was still there, locked up in the big white refrigerated box, like a carcass of meat from the slaughterhouse.

Lucy was the next to catch the spread. The hospital was like a battlefield. Five elderly residents in a palliative ward had died, a painful and terrifying death, without ventilators and very little oxygen. The ICU had all the masks, coveralls and gloves for personal protection. Under normal circumstances Lucy could go through thirty pairs of disposable gloves and half of that again in disposable aprons. Somehow the virus had got in around the protection and invaded her. Lucy was a fit woman, she went to the gym on her days off and found time to walk or cycle between shifts. No wonder Lorenzo and

Lucy found so little time for each other. She had called in sick, planning to self-isolate and then return to assist within a fortnight. The virus took a hold. She worsened considerably, phoned the hot line and was whisked away in an ambulance the following day. It was eleven days before she died, another lonely and horrible death.

Lorenzo was left numb. Once again he could not hold his loved one in his arms. He could not tell her he loved her and he so wanted to hold her and help her through the storm. It was only the ICU staff who could do that. The tears drained from him. It was worse than a car crash. At least then there would have been some hope.

Another statistic for the Health Service, unlike the elderly folk dying in the Woodend Care Home down the road, who were not recorded.

Yet more cadavers for the refrigerated container.

4 Mafia connection

Ardavan drove up to the entrance and headed for the car park at the ruins of Pompeii. It was quiet at this time of year and the pale sun was low in the sky. It was cold enough for an overcoat and he stretched back and took the camel coloured long woollen coat with the black buttons from the back seat and donned it. Next was the black 1930's style woollen cap and he fitted it snugly on his head. The final part of his attire were the black leather gloves, Sony camera in its black leather case and the gold rimmed sunglasses, which for the moment he held in his hand as he ambled to the cash desk.

He bought his ticket, took the site plan which was offered and moved through the building and back into the sunshine, where he slowly pulled his gloves on. The camera was swung over his shoulder and, lastly, the sunglasses on his beaky nose. Ardavan checked the time on his watch, thirty minutes to go, and located the Roman bath house on the site plan.

He strolled along, pausing to look in more detail at relics from days long gone, following the lines of the rutted cobblestoned roadways, passed mosaic murals and painted walls, taking pictures at obvious places, until he reached the Roman baths, where he removed his sunglasses and dropped down inside. The building was empty, except for one well kept frame, in a blue puffer jacket and jeans, with a red cap in his hand, the attire he was expecting to see. Ardavan opened in English with 'Hello, we've got the place to ourselves today. It's a good job that it isn't mid July,' to which the reply was, 'Yes, it is and I'm just leaving, so you can bathe for as long as you like,' and with that the man with the red cap rose up from where he was sitting and left for the bright light above. Ardavan sat, as agreed, and the man in the red cap was replaced by an older gentleman, obviously of some wealth by the way he was dressed and his smaller stature was topped off by a tanned, shiny bald head.

The replacement immediately spoke, 'I do not need to know your name, nor do I need to know exactly why you want the things that you want. I was told that a favour had been called in, but I cannot just do anything. This has to be something that I can do as part of my normal activities. Maybe stretching it a little.' He shrugged and opened his hands. 'Proceed,' he said.

Ardavan knew that this was the Andrea Cicciano that had been described to him by his compatriot in Rome. He outlined what he wanted, restating the case most forcibly, when he saw the downturned facial features of the Neapolitan and said, 'This has to be done. The favour will be removed and you will no doubt need us to help you again in the future, to your benefit. It's a win win for you.'

Andrea thought for a minute, mulling over what had been asked of him and finally came out with, 'It's too dangerous. I cannot do this thing that you ask of me.' With that he turned and climbed the stairs to the safety of his waiting colleague. One quick word to his henchman and they were on their way. He was a worried man.

Ardavan waited five minutes and made his own way up into the warming day and replaced his sunglasses. The meeting didn't go according to plan. He would have to get Rome to apply more pressure on this Cicciano, otherwise he's not worth having as a contact and he now knows too much and would have to disappear.

On the following Monday he made another call to Rome and arranged to meet the Kurd from the city, in a café bar, just around the corner from the Trevi Fountain. He explained in quiet tones what had occurred at Pompeii. They agreed that some form of pressure had to be exerted on the Neapolitan to get him to dance to their tune. This could be in monetary terms, goods or activities conducive to his needs, or if all else failed, a physical threat.

After a few messages had been passed and eventually threats had been given Andrea Cicciano arranged with his fixer, Paulo, to set up a meeting in the usual place with three guests. He set out the date, time, and the guest names.

....

It was early morning but the sun was still burning the back of the neck of Felice Capasso, as he made the final adjustments to his P&M Aviation QuikR 912S Microlight. He would be flying the tandem machine solo today, up in the cool of the airflow around the shell of the aircraft.

His friend Paulo Esposito had called off at the last minute due to some business issues in Sorrento. There was always something happening with Paulo, so it wasn't unexpected. His boss seemed to call on him day and night, but he was like a faithful little puppy as far as his boss was concerned. In the few years since he had first met him at Salerno Flying Club, Paulo had never exactly stated what he did for a living. It was always 'a little bit of this, a little bit of that', but he was a genial guy and always generous with his time and his money. Paulo had always been interested in flying, but never seemed to have the time to put in the thirty hours or so needed to obtain his microlight licence. He was always first choice for the rear seat passenger though.

Today Felice would take a slightly different route, taking the north west takeoff route, rising from the airfield before turning north, over flying the E45 auto route in a north westerly direction to San Mango Piemonte, then heeling ninety degrees left on a south westerly course towards the harbour at Salerno. The flight might be bumpy at low level as the cliffs of the Amalfi coast loomed up, so he would take the microlight out over the sea with the landward view on the right until Erchie. Then another heel, at ninety degrees to the right and head for Maiori. With enough loft on the seaward leg the QuikR will get up to three hundred metres and over Scala and towards Castellammare.

The view towards Vesuvius and the conurbation of Napoli would be in the distance, but too far to see what Paulo was up to. Another right turn at Castellammare, then head for the bend in the E45 at Nocera Inferiore, with a final right and the glide down to the airfield about thirty kilometres away.

Felice made his final checks on his payload. The aircraft would easily exceed the minimum weight of 270 kg stipulated for takeoff. He would have his suited up body weight of 85 kg and a sixty litre fuel load of 60 kg to add to the empty weight of 205 kg, so 350 kg would be his mark. Wind was light, at just over 10 kph from the north.

He donned his flying suit over his day clothes and slipped into his trainers, gave his long fair hair a swish back, then pulled on his helmet and stuffed his gloves into the pockets. He lifted his tall, lean but athletic frame up and into the cockpit, and muttered, 'Ready for the off!'

The QuikR had been pulled out of the trailer by his Hilux truck one hour before and the wing had been unfolded and aligned and the whole contraption checked for structural integrity. Now he was ready to go and ambled over to the Control Building to lodge his flight plan. He obtained his clearance, returned to the aircraft, turned over the engine for a couple of bursts of five seconds to get the oil flowing, slipped on his gloves, checked the wing for movement and radioed the Control Tower for permission to take off.

He took it easy down the runway and two hundred metres later Felice was airborne.

Paulo Esposito had left the family apartment on Via A. Ciccone as soon as the pasticceria directly below had opened that morning. The girl at the counter thought Paulo to be the most handsome man in all Italy, and Paulo thought that she was right. As he sat on the top floor balcony, sipping his espresso and munching at his sfogliatella, he mused about what was to become of him that day.

The meeting would be in Bar Nico, which was a bit ironic, as it was located right next to the Cattedrale di Santa Maria Assunta. He had to pick up Andrea Cicciano at the usual spot in the marina in Napoli at 10:00, but he needed to ensure that all the others on the guest list were already at the bar.

Erica would be washing down the pavement outside Bar Nico, sweeping the entrance door mats and making the place look spick and span. Roberto would carry out the tables and chairs and carefully place them in exactly the same spots as he always did. It was nice to sit outside the bar in the morning, in the shade of the cathedral, waiting for the sun to rise, bathing the whole of Piazza Duomo's cobbles in toasty sunshine. It had been this way for centuries now. Everything in this world had some logic and a path to follow. What was to be the path today?

His contacts had not heard of anything amiss and there were no apparent signs on the streets of any malice being created by any neighbouring organisations, so what was the meeting about?

There would be five of them, including himself and Andrea. He would need an hour and a bit to drive to the pick up point behind the fifteenth century fountain, the Fontana del Gigante, which overlooks the marina entrance. He would see the liveried launch coming from Capri and make himself ready from the vantage point.

In Capri, Andrea Cicciano was sitting below the sun canopy, on the blue and white terrazzo terrace, in the shade of his villa eating his muesli and fruit and drinking his large cup of breakfast coffee. Ever since he'd had his operation he'd had to curtail his preferred Italian breakfast and espresso, for a more French Swiss diet. He'd lost a bit of weight but was still rounded. He rubbed his hand over his shiny, bald, head and considered once again if he should carry out the task he'd been asked to do. It really all boiled down to a favour and he was due his business acquaintance a quite large one, considering what had happened the year before.

The cryptic message had been delivered to Andrea, at his home in Capri, to make him acutely aware of the calling in of the favour. He had read it intently. They knew where he stayed! He considered the consequences and then decided that the meeting must be called, to action what was required. He let them know that he would carry out the favour under duress, but after this his slate would be clear.

‘I have to arrange a meeting. It is not good news!’

His wife Gianetta could see the worry on his face, but she knew that worries came and went like snow on a fence in the Dolomites. She knew that he himself would not be in any harm. He had plenty of people to do things for him. She sallied over to him, put an arm around his shoulder and said, ‘Everything will be fine Andrea. Go to your meeting. Discuss what you have to and I will see you back here for lunch. ‘Ti amo, Ciao.’

Andrea rose from his chair and left the house with his cap and sunglasses perched on his head. He threw over his shoulder a quick, ‘Ciao Gianetta,’ and pulled down his glasses as he felt the full heat of the morning sun on his face. He headed down to the marina in his electric golf cart and was glad of the shade as he sat below the cart canopy. It was going to be hot today. It was nine o’clock. Forty-five minutes later he was down to slow knots and entering the marina on the opposite side of the Gulf of Naples, heading towards his private berth. He’d noticed Paulo up by the fountain. Every time he passed that spot pride rose in his chest as he thought about his ancestors being a big piece of the city fathers five hundred years ago. He made a point of reminding people at every opportunity of his family’s dealings and importance in the city since that time in history.

Paulo was waiting with the Maserati as he slowly climbed up the ramp from the marina. Andrea had to walk some of the day, another part of the doctor's orders. This was the easiest piece as the Capri side was much steeper and he needed the cart.

Thirty minutes later they arrived at Piazza Duomo. In the car Paulo had gone through who was at the bar and at what time each had arrived. He had ushered each inside and closed the door to customers until business was done. Andrea asked all the usual questions regarding the business, down to fine details. Paulo never had to check later. He had it all in his head, just like a computer.

Roberto was standing outside the door and the tables and chairs were all dressed with tablecloths, held down at the corners with stainless steel clips. A posy of fresh flowers in a small vase adorned each, alongside a stainless steel ashtray. As the car drew up Roberto glanced around and opened the door for Andrea, before shepherding him in to the bar. Paulo closed and locked the Maserati and followed him in. Roberto stayed outside.

The cool air in the bar was nice, naturally nice, not due to windy air conditioners, but due to shade at that time in the morning. The emotive music of Andrea Boccelli was playing softly in the background, as it would always be when the other Andrea, the boss, came to call. The three guests rose from their chairs around the circular table in unison and gave short bows of the head in recognition. No names were spoken, nor were they needed. The Italian hugs and cheek kissing were dispensed with for the moment, with everyone at arms length. There was business to get on with, despite COVID 19.

Erica came over with the espressos and a plate of crunchy almond biscuits, Andrea's favourite kind, in the shape of orange segments. She laid a half corona, gas lighter and ashtray at Andrea's place and padded off into the back room. He lit his cigar and sat back in the wooden chair, looking at each pair of eyes intently as he did so. He would enjoy his sneaky little espresso and let the wafts of smoke curl around him, disobeying all the doctor's rules. If Gianetta smelt the smoke on his clothes she never said anything to him about it.

Paulo thought, without blinking, 'This is going to be serious.'

Andrea started in a hushed voice and all the guests crowded around, leaning in on their elbows - 'I have been asked by a business associate to obtain and prepare something that we do not usually get involved in. We will be handsomely paid for our work and the work will not and cannot be known to anybody who is not at this table. Do I have your word on this?'

He looked at each one in turn and got a brief nod from each.

'Okay, then this is what I have been asked to do. I must purchase, from a reputable source on the black market, the following items. They have asked for two sets of identical weaponry. Each of the sets will comprise a pair of RPG7D, the rocket propelled grenade, mark 7, the version which can be broken down into smaller parts, the one used by Russian paratroopers, should there be any questions over this description. Each RPG7D will have two OG7 fragmentation grenades, NOT the TGB-7V thermobaric warheads, to be known as missiles. We will need the three sections – Booster, Sustainer Motor and Warhead, again for each missile. Each missile will be adapted, somehow, and we are to figure this one out, into a timed fragmentation device that will explode after a short time cycle and break apart, showering anybody and anything around the scene of the detonation with a mass of ball bearings. Each missile must weigh no more than three and a half kilograms. Needless to say we will need spare missiles for testing and I must stress that nobody else must detect the test firing. I do not want ANY leak on this as it will come back to haunt us in a most horrendous way. We have a limited period of six weeks, commencing today, to find the ballistics, adapt them, test them and deliver two sets of launcher and missile packages to a shipyard in Europe. Each finished package will comprise two adapted missiles and two launchers, in their broken down state. Each set will be bubble wrapped independently and covered in opaque white pvc wrap. Any questions? Before I leave I need to know who is tasked with which part of the business? Needless to say I will not be involved, nor will I be available for contact on this issue from the moment I leave the bar. All communication will be held through Paulo. Understood?'

There were four nods of agreement.

Paulo looked directly across the table at Guest One. 'Can you root out the basic machinery within a two week time frame?'

A nod of the head.

He looked to Guest Two. 'Can you make the alterations and carry out the tests within weeks two to four?'

A slight wave of the head, a shrug of the shoulders and he replied 'Have these RPG's been previously altered into what they want? Is there a precedent?'

Andrea looked wickedly at Guest Two and butted in with a sharp retort. 'I don't know, nor do I care. Answer Paulo's question!'

Guest Two said, very quickly, 'I can make my enquiries in the initial two weeks and then I can manage the alterations in weeks two to four, Paulo.'

Paulo turned to Guest Three and asked, 'Can you effect delivery in the way the package has been described in week six?'

A nod of the head again.

Andrea turned to Paulo. 'I assume that week five is for any contingency, Paulo?' Paulo nodded and smiled.

‘Good, people. Let the project commence. Come Paulo, take me back to the marina.’ Once they were in the Maserati, Andrea said, ‘I want to go first to Sorrento, to check on a couple of things. You can drop me off at the entrance to Parco Lauro and I will meet you for lunch later at Carouso’s at 12:30. You must keep an eye on this one. It is a big favour that has been called in and nothing, not even the slightest thing, must go wrong. Understood?’

‘Yes Andrea, your instructions were abundantly clear to me and all the others around the table. I will oversee every part of the procedure, stage by stage, leaving nothing to chance. I think that the first port of call will be our Albanian friends. We will use them for procurement and testing, both within their domain. The issue of delivery will cause us no problems realistically, as we will have no border crossings within the free movement zone, apart from the Albania to Italy leg, which will, I think, be best done by fast rigid inflatable boat across the eighty kilometres between the south and Albania. If you remember we have used that before. We took the RIB over and back the same night, from Otranto to Zvernec, beside the Narta Lagoon, you know the place just north of Vlore.’

‘Yes,’ Andrea mused, ‘That would certainly get over one of my worries. I didn’t want to think about any actions that would draw attention to our neck of the woods. Best to keep that at arms length, but it has to be our people. We can’t involve anybody else in the alterations, unless we really have to. We really don’t want any deeper involvement in this venture.’

‘What will be our further involvement, Andrea?’

‘Paulo, I can’t get into that now, as even I do not know the full story. Suffice to say that, when I know you will know very soon after.’

‘Yes I guess so Andrea.’

Paulo concentrated on the traffic as he drove through Castellammare, passing the journey talking about the weather, the new Captain of the local Caribinieri, how Gianetta was keeping and life in general.

‘Andrea, do you have a fixed timescale for this? We talked about six weeks, but if we are ready, do we go earlier? I reckon we can’t be late, but it might suit us to go earlier if we can and move the heat, if there is going to be any, well clear of our domain?’

‘Hey, that’s good thinking. I thought that we’d need all the time when I first agreed to do this, but it would be good to get it over with early and allow us to concentrate on what we do best. Anyway, here we are. Just let me off here.’ He picked up his cap, slapped it on his smooth skull, adjusted his sunglasses and stepped out into the sunshine.

‘An hour to kill,’ thought Paulo, ‘then a nice leisurely lunch in Carouso’s, back to the marina with The Boss and then arrange another meet with the other three to discuss the details of the project. But it could not be in Bar Nico.’ That location was reserved for meetings with Andrea.

5 Assassin

Linda Russo left her family in Ireland, after she had grieved for her mother in the only way she knew, but without friends and relations to help with the comforting process. Again, there was no wake and no funeral. She headed for home in Birmingham later that week on the last flight to leave Dublin for Heathrow. She was deeply concerned for herself and more especially for her unborn baby. Dublin airport terminal was very quiet, with a most sombre feel. The journey, in the congested confines of the aircraft, Heathrow Airport, the Heathrow Express and the final leg of her trip back to Birmingham on the train was a nightmare. Jack picked her up from the station. She was a bit peeky even then, he had said later.

....

The Guests met Paulo the next day in Il Lazzaretto, on the causeway to Nisida, overlooking the marina. He had chosen a shaded table and asked the owner for a bit of privacy as usual, while he conducted some business. The owner knew then to place reserved signs on a few of the empty tables around Paulo's chosen one, to prevent any eavesdropping. The conversation was conducted over their bresaola, olives and bread, their main course of veal saltimbocca and a few glasses of Chianti.

Their conversation steered towards the Albanian connection. The weaponry would have to be sourced, altered and packaged in the country and the Adriatic crossing positions were fixed, together with the vessel type. The crossing would be in a darkened boat and would pass between Albania and Italy during the hours of darkness, without any lighting, so the risks had to be weighed up and ironed out.

When asked by Paulo, Guest One said, 'I have had a tentative conversation with my contact in Albania. He says that he can obtain the hardware that we want. It will come out of the Albanian Army arsenal, from their testing ranges, to the east of Vlore. He can arrange for the shipment of the base weapons and the grenades very quickly and has even identified a suitable site, only a few kilometres away from their test ranges. That way there will be no questions asked if a test was to be carried out in such close proximity to their ranges. Any noise and resultant explosions will not be singled out as the local population is used to hearing war games going on in their backyard.'

Paulo said, 'There will be no change to the end date. The boss has already committed this project to the buyer and we cannot fail him. Keep on it. Everything hinges around your scope of work in the first instance. Without the weaponry we are nowhere and it will be frowned upon by our client, and may indeed have far reaching consequences.'

Paulo received a call from Guest One the following week. 'The machinery has been purchased in its entirety and is on its way for adaptation and testing. The adaptation, I am told, is quite tricky, as these units were never designed to be used in this way. We will advise further.' The call was cut with a curt, 'Thanks' from Paulo.

....

A couple of weeks passed by. Everything comes in threes, thought Lorenzo at the time. He was told, in a very emotional call from Jack, that Linda had miscarried and ended up contracting the virus in the maternity unit. She had died three days later. By this time Great Britain was following Ireland's lead and yet again no funerals were allowed.

Lorenzo had screamed from within. He'd lost his wife, two of his children, the baby, who would have been his first grandchild, and his livelihood. He still had a sizeable chunk of a mortgage to pay, as Lucy and him had extended the term during the Irish recession. He was still grieving and he was feeling as down as he could possibly be. What he didn't know was that Pietro was in a deeper depression than his Dad was. He'd lost family too, his rip roaring business, Carrick Coaches, was heavily mortgaged and he knew that it would go under. Lorenzo found him hanging from the loft hatch two days after Linda's death.

The date was April 18th. Britain and Ireland were in full lock down His entire family was gone. Lorenzo had no brothers or sisters and his parents had died of natural causes some years previously. It was only by talking to Euan Hall, his brother-in-law, back in Aberdeen in North East Scotland, which kept him sane in the lonely and angry place he was in.

Euan was married to Lucy's sister and they had met in Cork a long time ago, at the annual Jazz festival. He could talk easily to him about anything and everything. Euan had suggested that he get away from Carrick, whenever he could, once restrictions had been lifted, and stay in Aberdeen for a while. He could have the spare room, with its own en suite, so he would have his space, yet still be with friends and family, while the healing took its course, however long that would take.

Lorenzo took the next few months to settle all the family affairs, pay whoever was due what and sold the house to pay off the mortgage. Lucy's life insurance policy had been paid out. He was debt free and had a good few thousand euros in his AIB account to see off the immediate future. He was exceedingly angry in his loneliness and grief and still wondered on a daily basis – 'Why me?'

....

Fatima Ardalan, on the instructions of Ardavan Kamandi, Brigade Commander of the KRG Intelligence Unit, made the phone call to England. It was to Felek (Lucky) Kinar, a musician based in London. His occupation, on a self-employed basis, was that of a violin maestro. He was also a fiercely partisan Kurd, having been brought up in the Northern Iraqi city of Sulaimaniyah, the son of a college lecturer. He had been taught to play the violin, an instrument fairly new to Kurdish music, under the tutelage of the great Didier Hussein. Kurdish music had incorporated the violin in the early part of the twentieth century as an accompaniment to other Kurdish stringed instruments.

'Hello, my name is Fatima. I work for a person very dear to you and the Kurdish cause. Our nation needs you to carry out a task. It is dangerous, but does not involve the handling of drugs, as you – and we - abhor the use of drugs in any shape or form. The call will be short. May I continue?'

'Yes, I believe I know who you are talking about. Carry on.'

'We need you to collect two packages and transport them back to London. Both packages will be in the same location. You cannot use any flights on your journey, either there or back. We will call you to deliver more information, on a weekly basis, on this day of the week, at the same hour. Do you understand?'

'Yes I do,' said Felek, and the call was ended.

Fatima glanced at Ardavan, who had been listening on speaker and asked 'Did that go all right? Will he do it? Was the call short enough?'

Ardavan replied, 'Everything went fine. Another box half ticked.'

....

Back in Bursa, in Turkey, Ardavan had decided upon a date and time for a strike, together with a location. He mentally noted to speak again with Rohat and Fatima. The following day he made his two calls and sent the two operatives off on a mission in the name of the cause. The target would be General Sir Patrick Walsh Douglas, who would be speaking at a dinner.

General Russell Murdoch had taken over at the last minute from his superior officer to speak at the Royal United Services Institute dinner.

He'd talked about Russian activity in the North Atlantic, the continuing war in Syria and the involvement of Russia, Turkey and the Kurds. Iraq was in public disorder and there was disquiet in Lebanon. There were challenges ahead in the Persian Gulf in connection with freedom of movement, changes within the oil rich Arab states and their new wealth shifting regimes. On top of that there was civil war in Yemen and the likelihood of a similar occurrence in Libya. The Kashmir region held underlying tensions and, all in all, there were armed conflicts around the globe in seventy countries. This was not a time for complacency.

He had gone on to speak at length about the instability of the oil prices, with some changing to negative costing. There was a burgeoning population in Sub Saharan Africa, which may cause issues going forward.

British forces had presently naval exercises in The Baltic, land forces in Estonia and a withdrawal from Germany after seventy-five years. Forces were deployed in one form or another, sometimes in a performance role, some on peace-keeping duties or training of other nations' forces. The Poseidon P8 maritime patrol aircraft had been fully deployed and there was a more concentrated effort into technical and political warfare, which was on the rise.

Russell Murdoch went on to state that Britain needed to get away from a 'Reservist Force Policy' and 'Just In Time Logistics'. The forces of the nation must be better armed and better prepared for the events ahead. Strategic battles were moving away from normal activity into 'Out of Line of Sight' technological capability. There should be the creation of a Strategic Sentinel, which will need to hold the locus of all information. Modern warfare needed to get away from the 'need to know' and into an 'all must know' scenario. In that way everyone across the British army, navy and air forces, together with GCHQ, MI5, MI6 and Speciality Armed Police Forces would, going forward, have a common comprehension, credibility and communication. The common bond would give the best force that in turn will give us the best ability.

He finished by saying, 'We will then ensure domestic security and maintain our leading position in the world. Be vigilant at all times and do not drop your guard. Thank you.'

Russell Murdoch sat down to a standing ovation, with handshakes from his nearest top table guests. He had earlier enjoyed the food and the small glass of wine and now declined the offer of port or a digestif with his coffee.

He pulled out on to Whitehall from the car park at RUSI and headed along Whitehall, thinking that Paddy Douglas should be pleased. The speech that his superior, the Chief of Defence Staff, had written had been well received. General Russell Murdoch had received the standing ovation, but all credit would be going to the top of the tree.

Russell Murdoch continually scanned his mirrors and the sides of the road as he drove towards his London flat. A black clad motorcyclist on a Triumph Tiger pulled in behind him from the direction of Westminster Bridge, followed by a small hatchback car. As he carried on along Abingdon Street and Millbank he noticed the big motorcycle fall back and the hatchback was now leading. 'That's unusual,' he said aloud. 'Usually it's the bike that overtakes the car in my experience.' He became more watchful.

He decided to miss out Grosvenor Road and took a detour over Vauxhall Bridge, turned again parallel with the Thames, past New Covent Garden Market and Battersea Dogs Home, before crossing The Thames again over Chelsea Bridge. The motorbike was still behind him but the car was not following. He took a left, heading for the National Army Museum, down West Road, looped around and headed back to the back of the Museum. The Triumph was waiting on the corner.

Without pausing he swiftly turned the wheel and drove into the stationary motorcycle, flipping the rider off. He grabbed his service automatic from the seat pocket and was on the rider before he could get up. He saw the pistol in his hand and shot him in the head and the heart, without even the blink of an eye. He got out his mobile and made two calls, one to general command and one to Special Branch.

The whole thing was hushed up and the media were never to know. Special Branch would investigate and let General Murdoch, one-time SAS Squadron Commander in Bosnia, know in good time.

....

In Lyon, Bernadette Bucheron took a call from Chief Inspector Victoria Douglas. Vicky was British Special Branch in London, responsible for disseminating information arising from attempts on life, but not of a domestic nature. Her world was that of international criminals, religious killings, crime within British Borders carried out by foreign criminals and homeland security. She had been in the police force for twenty-two years, but the worries of her position did not show on her face. She was still a beautiful woman, but filling and drooping just a little bit. Her short, fair hair was of the manageable, not decorative type and her fingernails were short and coated with clear lacquer. Not the type to stand out in a room full of people, but worth a second glance nevertheless. Everybody took notice when she spoke.

She had a photograph, DNA sample and prints that she would like Interpol to check out and a description of a middle eastern looking male, dark hair, swarthy features, athletic build, good eyesight and no tattoos. Only a few scars, which could have been made by conflict contact or underworld exposure. She'd send over the details to Bernadette, to take a look at. It was in connection with a killing. Vicky had said to her superiors that murder always took higher priority within Interpol than other more mundane matters, such as international theft, and that Bucheron would work on it very quickly, if her past work record was to be measured.

Vicky Douglas went home that night and spent a lovely, if not very regular, evening dinner with her husband, General Patrick Douglas. The events of the previous night were not discussed, but both tossed the event about in their minds as they ate.

....

Ardavan never received the pre-arranged call from Rohat. Was he taken? Was the plan in tatters? Fatima had returned with no further knowledge as to his fate.

6 Killing machines

Guest One had been kept up to date by his Albanian contact. After the rocket launchers, rocket propulsion units and the grenades had been sourced, the Albanian had demanded immediate payment, at the agreed figure and Guest One had to open a Swiss bank account in a fictitious name for the Albanian to access, but only after the weapons had been altered and delivered to him. This was quite a normal occurrence and the manager at the Organisation's chosen bank in Geneva had arranged the details without question, at the usual extortionate fee. Transactions would be credited and debited in United States dollars.

The Albanian told Guest One that the test would take place in a dense forest, away from prying ears and eyes, with a dead ground radius of one kilometre. This would be well outside of the two hundred metres strike distance from weapon to target that had been stipulated.

The Albanian had to employ the services of a Bosnian munitions expert, as the change to the warhead required knowledge that the Albanian simply did not have. Additional monies were deposited in Geneva. Once the altered munitions were ready, the Albanian told the Bosnian the grid reference in the forest for delivery and the two met and discussed their work.

....

Four weeks after the weapons had been sourced, they had, by careful calculation and clever design one explosive warhead which had been adjusted to give a fragmentation with a twenty metre radius and the firing mechanism had been fitted within each, capable of being adjusted from 0.1 to 1.0 second.

The standard grenade would normally self-destruct in five seconds at a distance of around nine hundred metres. After the second alteration and test it had been decided that the target would have to be within two hundred metres or less, to be zone effective. The explosive would travel at nearly three hundred metres in a second after the initial ignition launch phase, which would take the grenade the first eleven metres, thereafter the rocket propulsion would take over its momentum.

The lowest timer setting would be therefore forty-one metres distance at detonation, one hundred and sixty-one metres at 0.5 second timer setting and so forth. Two more of the spare altered RPGs were tested at the woodland site they had chosen in Albania, one set at 0.6 seconds and one set at 0.3 seconds.

The munitions expert handed the RPG to the Albanian and he slid it into the launcher. He checked to see that the blast area behind was clear and aimed for the tree marked with the orange paint at the 0.6 second delay fuse. The result was a catastrophic blast immediately in front of the tree, which sent shards of metal in the twenty metre blast radius and totally demolished the base of the tree and riddled quite a few nearby.

The second RPG was loaded and the Albanian aimed at the other, closer, marked tree and the results were identical.

When they walked up to the sites of the two impacts they could plainly see the close at hand major damage, but as they expanded their investigation, they could see the shard damage over the much wider area, again as predicted.

The epicentre of the explosion was measured and both results proved to be within the tolerance set by Guest One.

....

The next phone call received by Paulo confirmed that alterations to the machinery had been completed and that the order was ready for dispatch, or collection if the customer preferred. Paulo agreed to collect 'at the factory gate' which meant the shoreline pick up point they had chosen in Albania. 'Meet me tomorrow at the restaurant. Release the funds,' Paulo said, and cut the call.

....

Fatima went about her new task set by Ardavan, to check on the health of General Douglas and found that he was alive and well and still at work in his office at the Ministry of Defence. She relayed this to

Ardavan. She felt the anger and frustrated tension in his voice. They had to carry out a single action, otherwise the security services of Great Britain would be down on them like a ton of bricks. The RPG attack just had to work!

....

Guests Two and Three met Paulo again at the restaurant on the causeway and went through the details of transportation of the packages from Albania to Italy. Each of the four launchers and each of the four rocket propelled grenades would be wrapped in oil impregnated tape, covered with plastic sheeting, sealed with duct tape and then placed individually into wet bags, the kind canoeists and yachters use. Each of the wet bags would be secured to the rigid inflatable boat, which would uplift them off the beach, with lanyards to the RIB grab ropes around the top inflatable tubes.

Paulo finished by saying, 'The date will be Monday 11th May, at 23:00 hours. The packages will be available at that time and date and the pick up location will be in Albania. There is a place named Vlore, on the Adriatic Coast. To the north of the place is a lagoon, separated from the sea by a narrow necklace of land. The lagoon is called Narta Lagoon. To the north again of the lagoon there is a beach. At the beach there are three bars, Bar Xamo, Bar Dolphin and Cela Beach Bar. About two kilometres south along the curve of the beach there is an outlet of a drainage channel into the sea. Beyond the channel about two hundred metres further on is a headland, with no access to the beach. It's a very quiet spot and the beach is a shallow rise from the sea, ideal for the RIB to get in to pick up the packages. I will be in the fast RIB myself and you two will take a vehicle to the café area and under cover of darkness you will make your way to the north side of the drainage channel. I will signal with two bursts of a white torch and then a two second red. You will signal back in the same manner and I will come to the beach. If anybody sees the lights it will be mine, from the RIB, not yours. Before they can react the kit will be loaded and tied down. I'll expect to be on my way within two minutes. You will return to the vehicle and get back to Napoli whenever you can, by whatever means. Understood?'

'Understood.' replied the Guests.

Paulo received a call the following day stating that the wrapped machinery was placed in a car at Bar Xamo. The Guests would walk along the beach at dusk and if anyone questioned them, like the beach bar people, as to what they were doing, they would say that they were going to have a barbeque on the sand with a few beers. The wet bags would cover their real meaning and their car would not be out of place, even if the beach bar staff and customers had left for the night.

Paulo headed for Otranto, at Italy's closest point to Albania and headed to the marina. He'd already headed down from Napoli towing the RIB behind him on a trailer and had launched her from the public slipway off Via Del Porto. With a bit of bartering he'd managed to fix himself up with a temporary berth in the last bay before the open sea, which would perfectly suit his needs.

He had made a show of transporting some heavy wet bags down to the RIB from his SUV, the same kind and colour as the Guests would be using. He had fully filled the long-range tanks that were fitted to the RIB and trolleyed down a couple of extra filled fuel canisters as well. He would have a round trip of nearly one hundred and sixty kilometres ahead, across some major shipping lane routes in the Adriatic and might have to make a few detours along the way, from his chosen course.

Paulo took advantage of the daylight hours to plot a course that would initially take him northwards to the long beach, so as not to arouse the suspicion of the Coast Guards, before setting his course east and out to sea. The sea was calm and the night was clear. The moon would be in its first quarter and light would be very limited, so he'd decided to don the night vision goggles once he was over the horizon from Italy.

His crossing went well and he only had to move around a tanker and a ferry in the Italian waters and the rest of the run was smooth and uneventful. The seven metre RIB was covering the distance at below its maximum speed of 100 kms/hr and he headed across the tip of Sazen Island with the beach rendezvous directly ahead. He killed the speed to reduce noise and gently motored to shore for the last eight kilometres. The twinkling lights of Vlore were just visible on his starboard side, but the way ahead and to his port side was dark, with only a slight sheen from the moon casting on the slight swell.

The engines mounted on the dark RIB were set to tick-over revs as he estimated his distance from shore opposite the beaching point. He took his two torches out of the locker and gave the signal. Two answering whites and a two second pulse of red signalled back and he pushed the throttle lever forward and was coming in to the shallows in no time. The Guests were waiting, and they waded in to the gentle surf and placed the wet bags two by two inside the RIB. While the gentle throb of the engines held the RIB against the beach, Paulo tied off the wet bags to the grab ropes. He passed over the replacement dry bags and with a sardonic 'Enjoy your barbeque, lads,' he was already reversing. Once he'd checked the fuel gauge and other instruments, he reset his plotter and was clear of the shelving beach. Paulo swung the boat around and headed back to Otranto.

The RIB rose up through the glistening sea and left a foamy phosphorescent wake behind. He was well clear of the Albanian coastal waters and decided that he would be better to take a fill from the spare fuel dump he had aboard. He killed the engine and by the light of his head torch pumped through the siphon hose into the main tank using the hand crank pump. Swiftly the level rose and he closed down the system, secured all the kit and started up the big motors. He thought to himself that with a full fuel load he would be able to hit full revs across the remainder of the Adriatic.

……….

Paulo arrived at the Italian coast in the early hours, at his selected spot. He didn't want to arrive back at Otranto in the middle of the night, so he headed for the small pier in front of Casino Cannime, the lookout tower south of Otranto. He arrived at the pier, but decided to anchor a little bit further out in the bay and ride out the rest of darkness without fear of random prying eyes, or worse still, sticky fingers, getting near to the craft. The gentle lapping of the wavelets as they broke on the rocky shore were soporific and soon he was fast asleep.

He woke with the sun rising from the Adriatic and decided it was safe enough to set out for the marina at Otranto. He covered the six kilometres at a steady, but not raucous pace and was soon tied up in the marina. He fetched the SUV and trailer from the car park and reversed down the slipway into the water. The berth was a short stroll away and there were only one or two sailors up in the early morning tending to their lines, checking their fenders and starting up their kettles for their early morning coffee. As he undid his moorings and moved away from the berth a few more heads appeared at cockpits and on stairs to fly bridges.

He drove straight on to the rollers on the trailer and sat astride the prow, grabbed the winch clip and attached it to the D clip. He made his way along the frame of the trailer, the water cold around his ankles, released the winch brake and winched the RIB fully on to the trailer, up to the rubber vee stop, braked it again and shoved through the safety pin. Once he had towed the trailer out of the water he affixed the tie down straps and secured the RIB to the trailer. The wet bags were offloaded into the SUV, together with all the loose kit remaining in the RIB and off he set back to Napoli and the car repair workshop, which was to be the store until Andrea advised him further.

Later that morning, at a time when he knew Andrea would have breakfasted, he made a call to the villa on Capri. 'Pronto.' said the female voice. 'Buongiorno Gianetta, may I speak to your husband please? It's Paulo.'

'Yes Paulo, I will get him for you. He's on the terrace.'

A few seconds of quietness ensued then Andrea came on. 'Paulo, how are things? Good I hope.'

'Yes, everything went according to plan and the machinery has been delivered as discussed. Just advise me when the order should be dispatched.'

Within a short time Andrea had made a call from his home to a number in Turkey. Ardavan picked up at the fourth ring. Andrea made a play about asking about the health of his uncle and asked Ardavan where he should send his gift.

Ardavan spoke quickly and told Andrea to meet him in three days' time. 'Meet me inside the Bar di Trevi, just on the corner of Piazza di Trevi in Rome. Take the train and walk to the bar. It will take you about half an hour. The time will be 14:00. Come alone. I will be wearing a white Ferrari cap. I take it that you will recognize me again?' Andrea called his wife in from the kitchen. 'Gianetta, find out the times of trains to Roma from Napoli. I need to be there – at the station – by one o'clock, three days from now, but I must be prepared.' Without a word, Gianetta gave a quizzical look at her husband, then a nod, and scurried off to attend to the task he had given her.

Andrea phoned Paulo. He said, 'Paulo I have to go to Rome in three days. I must go alone and meet our customer, but I want you on that train and following at a discreet distance. I have to be at Bar Trevi, you know the place, really touristy, just beside the fountain. I'll let you know the train time, once Gianetta has done her homework.'

Andrea was hardly off the phone to Paulo when Gianetta came in and said, '11:14 from Napoli, 13:08 at Roma. I've booked a first class open return for you and I've printed off the electronic ticket for you. All you will have to do is stamp it at the machine at the end of the platform, both there and coming back. Hopefully you'll be back home in time for dinner, Andrea.'

Andrea phoned Paulo again and relayed the details.

There were three people of note on that train that day, Andrea, Paulo and a rather attractive Fatima, who had a description of Andrea in her mind. She sent a message to Ardavan. 'Watch him, he's not alone.' Even though Paulo and Andrea were in separate areas of the train, Fatima had been waiting at Napoli. In her eyes Paulo stood out like a sore thumb.

As Andrea arrived at the designated bar, a bare headed Ardavan came up behind him and whisked him away round the corner, out of sight of the shadowing Paulo, and into a restaurant a few doors further up on the other side of the street. As he did so he whispered in his ear, 'I told you to come alone. You are not to be trusted Andrea. Do you know that you are being followed?'

'If you mean Paulo, he always comes with me. We are like twins, joined at the hip. He watches my back.'

'Well he obviously does not watch it enough. I knew he was coming and I've been in Rome all morning,' said Ardavan.

At that precise moment a very disgruntled Paulo was ushered in to the restaurant by the inimitable Fatima and they sat down at the table. The foursome ordered food and wine before the conversation began in earnest.

Ardavan told Andrea. 'Your drop off location will be in Burgas, in Bulgaria, on the Black Sea. There is a narrow neck of land between Burgas Bay and Lake Burgas. Your destination in Burgas will be a shipyard, in the Southern Industrial Area, called Burgaski Korabostroitelnitsi. The name is long and you cannot miss it. Access to the industrial zone is from the roundabout at routes 9 and 79. You will make two packages for insertion in each of two polyethylene tanks and they will be wrapped by you in oil impregnated cloth, bubble wrap and white plastic sheeting, so that they do not show through the walls of the tanks, nor damage them. Ask for Aleksandar Chavdarov, who will take delivery of the packages. All the unloading – from a small white Fiat delivery van - is to be done under cover in the confines of the shipyard within the screens of a welding booth. You will ask for Alexsander by name at the facility security guard house and then drive in directly to the booth under his direction. Once you are fully unloaded you will immediately leave Burgas and return to your home location within forty-eight hours. Call this number again when you return with the empty van.' He handed Andrea an envelope and said, 'It's all detailed here. Open this when you get home and not before.'

'When do I do this?' said Andrea.

'I will contact you again when we are ready to receive.' The conversation was ended.

As he closed the door of his villa behind him he tore open the note, handed the envelope to Gianetta and said, 'Burn this right away, rake the ashes and put them in the flower pots. Cover them with earth. I'll be back for a late light dinner. Ciao Bella.'

The golf cart ride to the marina was swift. He clambered aboard the power boat, started up the engine, checked the gauges and cast off. His speed leaving the marina was likely a tad over the limit, but he had to impart this vital piece of information as quickly as possible. It was the only copy and he did not want it to be in his possession for a moment more than was necessary.

Paulo saw the craft pull in to the marina as he stood below the fountain. He drove down in the Maserati, picked up Andrea and headed for Nola, to Bar Nico.

Andrea sat in the cool of the air conditioned car, while Paulo went inside and sorted things out with Roberto. Shortly thereafter a few wizened locals left the bar and sat at the outdoor tables. Paulo opened the car door and Andrea stepped quickly in to the cool of the bar.

They crossed to their selected table and sat down. Erica wandered over and placed two espressos, two waters and two pastries down on the table, followed by a clean ashtray, a small cigar, lighter and a couple of small napkins. When she was out of earshot Andrea lit up and leaned in to the centre of the table, with Paulo closing in to follow.

'Paulo, this is the only copy of the instructions for delivery. The date and time are as yet unknown.

Memorise the information and take care to burn and crush the paper. Do it quickly, but not here. Do it at home, where you know it is safe.'

'Understood Andrea.' was the reply.

....

In distant Bulgaria that same nugget of information was being made known to a shipyard worker and the same order was given to commit to memory.

....

In a couple of days Paulo had worked out the route. From Napoli they would drive a white Fiat hire van to the shipyard. The journey would not be subject to tachograph checks. Guests Two and Three could share the driving and they could be at the destination within forty eight hours, with an overnight stop along the way. This would mean that they stuck to road travel only and avoided the shorter but more perilous and customs controlled ferry crossing between Bari and Albania. They would have to pass through Italy, Slovenia, Croatia and Serbia before arriving in Bulgaria. All Paulo needed was a date for delivery and the sooner the better. Andrea would be more than anxious until the packages had left their hands.

7 Readying Naaskel

It was funny how things turned out for Kjell. After losing his wife he had become very despondent. He reflected on their life together and would always treasure the memories. Their time spent aboard Naaskel had been very precious, so he vowed that he would take the yacht out of the water, but scrub every vestige of the pretty colour and finish that Bente had insisted upon, when they first saw the vessel in Cartenega. Then he would put everything back in the style and colours of a man, with a liberal show of her photographs around the saloon and the master cabin. This would be his headstone to the lovely creature. Her memory would always greet him as he stepped aboard. He wouldn't have to walk to a dreary graveyard at the edge of town. She loved sailing in her, letting the full power of the sea wash over her. He would entirely refit Naaskel and to hell with the expense.

Now, as he ticked through all of the checklist for her final inspection, his thoughts turned to where he would sail to, and it was at that moment that Egil Hansen had appeared by the slipway, ready to carry out a training rescue with the Lifeboats. The ever ready banter from Egil was well received and the gloom lifted from Kjell's features. His hunch was gone, his back was straight and a big grin split his features.

'Kjell, you old bastard, how are you doing. It seems like weeks since I've seen you! How's it going with

Naaskel? She's certainly looking swell from the outside. How's below decks doing?'

'Hi, Egil, I've entirely refitted her and she's just about ready to sail. I'm waiting on new sheets, some safety netting and some cushioning from the upholsterers, but other than that she's ready for the North Sea again. I'll do some inshore stuff, just to check everything out. Do you fancy joining me? I can work round your guiding or Lifeboat training!'

'That would be great. She's a great yacht and to get aboard her again and feel the pull on the sails would be exciting. I'll call you later, when training's over and we can meet at the marina clubhouse for a beer and a chat. How does that sound?'

'Perfect! See you in a couple of hours. Have fun in the RIB.'

....

Kjell Nilsen and Egil Hansen stepped aboard Kjell's ocean going yacht, Naaksel, at Marineholmen Gjestebrygge in Bergen. It was early evening and they had enjoyed a nice supper of pickled herring and beetroot salad, washed down with a couple of beers at the marina clubhouse.

They had been friends for the past 28 years, after meeting at school. Kjell was the intellectual one of the pair and Egil had slaved away at menial jobs, switching every so often on a whim. They talked about what had kept them together as buddies for so long but it was the camaraderie and laughter that was their common bond.

Egil was always up to mischief. He had not really grown up. There had been lots of misadventures to list but too many to fully remember, usually down to alcohol. But today he remembered being pulled over by the Marine patrol in Bergen. He was seventeen and had taken, some say borrowed, his father's rigid inflatable, the one with the twin 200hp outboards, on a social trip. It was the May Day holiday and everybody met at Zachariasbryggen for some food before heading back to the flotilla of small boats and the cases of beer.

As usual he had opened a few more cans than he should have, thoroughly enjoyed himself and set a wavy course for home. His concentration levels were low so he did not notice the craft's speed increasing way above the permitted harbour speed limit for nautical traffic. The Kystvaketen, the Norwegian Coast Guards were sitting in their fast launch, in its dark grey painted hull, in the shadow of the Clarion Hotel Admiral, and Egil never stood a chance. His father was almost as disgusted as the court, when he was summoned in front of the magistrate, but he still saw the funny side of it and did wonder if his son would have found his way home without the assistance provided to him by the state.

Kjell had, for a number of years, taken part in the Bergen to Lerwick Pantaenius boat race, in memory of his grandfather, who perished on 8th

December 1942, while sailing the original Aksel north of Shetland in a storm. He had been spotted in the raging seas in their lifeboat, with his crew and some refugees escaping the occupation, but the Catalina flying boat, which answered the Mayday call, could not land and recover them due to the breaking waves. They had all perished that day.

This time it would be just for pleasure and the reward would be meeting up with his friends at Shetland Boat Club in Lerwick. Earlier in the month he'd spoken with John Stevenson, his old friend from the race days.

It was Katie who'd answered and he'd thought what a lucky lad John was to have such a lovely woman in his life, who shared his love of sailing. Bente had died from cancer seventeen months before and his life was a pale shadow of what it had been.

'Hello Katie, how are you faring these days? I kind of lost contact with you after Bente passed away.'

'Hi Kjell, it's really nice to hear that Norwegian accent again. You must miss her dearly, but none of us are immortal and I guess we all have to move on in some way or another. But hey, I know you don't want to pass the time of day with me, so I'll go and get John. He's tinkering with the yacht's dinghy on the lawn. It's a lovely day looking over to Bressay. Goodness, it does not seem like eight years since you first sailed into the Sound. Hardly a breath of wind that day and you had to tack I don't know how many times until you crossed the finishing line. Third place was good, even though there were only six yachts back then.'

'John, a blast from the past on the phone.' Shouted Katie across the lawn.

'Who the hell is that,' John wondered, set off across the grass and took the handset from Katie with a, 'Thanks love.'

'Hey John, I heard you were out there sabotaging good marine hardware.'

'Kjell? You rascal, what the hell are you doing with yourself? We haven't had a blether in ages.'

'Well John, I've had a lot of time on my hands recently. I've done all of the house and garage clearing out and now I fancy doing some long distance sailing with Naaskel. I've still got her and she's looking better than ever. She's been out of the water over winter and I decided to take her inside out of the weather and so, for the last several weeks I've titivated and preened her and I re-launched her just last Thursday. So I was thinking that I would like to come and visit you six weeks from now. I spoke yesterday with my old friend Egil and he has agreed to crew for me, so there will just be the two of us coming this time.'

Kjell's boat was a Bavaria 44, launched in 1996 and he'd bought it in 2003 from a Broker in Cartegna, Spain. It was Bermudan Sloop rigged, 13.6 metres overall length, a beam of 4.2 metres and a draught of 1.9 metres. The single Volvo Perkins diesel engine was good for 6.5 knots at cruise and a range of 210 nautical miles. While the yacht, Naaskel, had been out of the water he'd re-upholstered her, stripped the hull and keel back and primed and anti-fouled her. He'd also replaced the engine start and house batteries and fully serviced the engine, the water and bilge pumps. The Avon Rover 311 dinghy and its Yamaha 4hp outboard had been given the once over and the navigation aids, ground tackle, general equipment and safety equipment had all been checked and replaced where necessary. 'A job well done,' he had said, and he was proud that the full extent of the work had been carried out entirely by just himself and the marina engineer.

'Well Kjell, It would be great to see you again, but Katie and I will be heading off for our own trip down to the west coast of Scotland around that time. You know how it is when the weather is fine – we've got to set sail and just go. That's what retirement is all about for us these days. I'll need to check the diary with Katie. There's still none of this electronic scheduling for me. I've always been a paper man. Which dates were you thinking about? If we are here we could certainly accommodate you, providing that you don't mind sharing in the twin. But then again you'll have shared the confines of Naaskel for a few days before you arrive, so you might fancy a bit of time apart by then!'

'Hmmm, that's a thought John, Egil is a great hand to have aboard, but he still has a penchant for a can or two. Is there still an apartment at the back of The Lounge bar? That would likely do us, as it has two bedrooms and he won't have far to stagger back at the end of the night. I'm sure that he'll enjoy the fiddles and the songs, if the tradition has been kept alive in there.'

'Oh yes indeed, they're still doing some Shetland Reels in there. They're all amateurs of course, getting together for a soiree. I'll check with Michael Lawson if the flat is available, so we're covered both ways and I'll get back to you. Is your number still the same? What are your dates?'

'We intend to set sail from Bergen on the 1st July and we've allowed three days, so we expect to sail into Lerwick on the 4th, weather permitting. Remember that I've done the trip in two days, seven hours and twenty eight minutes, so we should have some time for a couple of leisurely breakfasts along the way this time. My number and email are still the same John, so either will do. Nearer the time I can video link with you on one of the platforms and go through any loose ends. We'll likely spend a few days in Lerwick or sail around the Islands if the weather is conducive. It's been good to speak with you again and I hope that you'll be around at least for a few hours of reminiscing at the Boating Club bar. We'll speak later. Take care and keep sailing!'

Kjell laid the handset back in its cradle and settled back with his coffee. For the first time in a long time he felt as though he had regained his zest for life.

It had been his friend Richard's suggestion, when he met him way back in late February, that the first voyage in Kjell's yacht after he had refurbished her, should be to the old Viking heartland of the Shetland Islands. Egil had been crewing the Naaskel on and off for a number of years, helping him out with her crew of up to six. She had very little room for spare kit on board if six were aboard and in any case it was usually more of a laugh when just the two of them were crewing. Skipper and First Mate, deckhand, cook, rigger and helmsman, all rolled in to one.

That weekend, after his chat with Kjell, Egil headed for the Skipperstuan pub on Torggaten for a couple of very expensive beers. He preferred to drink at the clubhouse at the marina, but today he fancied putting it about that he was going to be off sailing for a week or so with Kjell, in Naaskel.

It was late May and the long days were lighting up the sky. The dreaded darkness of winter was lifted, but the squally showers still battered in from the North Sea. But the pub was warm, with a mixture of locals and tourists. A very attractive, dark haired girl sat on a bar stool at the end of the bar counter, a lovely pair of long legs squeezed into white three quarter length jeans and a cool pale green buttoned cardigan, open at the neck. Her lustrous black hair was tied back in a pony tail and cascaded half way down her back. The tanned hands, face and calves seemed to suggest money and so did the cut of her clothes. Her hands were clear of any jewellery, as was her neck, but she was wearing simple gold stud earrings.

He took a bar stool not far away and called for Magnus to bring him a pint of Carlsberg and a packet of salted peanuts. ‘Put it on a tab for me please. I could be here a while.’ and he winked at the bartender and made a slight move of his head towards the end of the bar. ‘Sure Egil, what have you been up to recently. I haven’t seen you in here for a few weeks. Are you keeping busy with the odds and sods that keep you in beer?’

He took a long draught from his beer, licked the froth from his lips and stroked the blond stubble on his chin. He was a tall, athletic and very handsome Norse man, with a tough Viking exterior that belied his soft centre. His hands were workmanlike but clean, and his full head of blond curls hung loosely over his ears and the nape of his neck.

‘Well I prefer to talk about what the future holds and discuss the world, or crack a few jokes between us Magnus, so I can tell you that – in six weeks – I will be sailing with Kjell Nilsen in his sloop, Naaskel, over to Lerwick’

‘Are you racing? Who else is crewing for you? Are you stopping off in Lerwick for a few days or sailing around the islands before you sail back?’ asked Magnus.

‘No, we’re not racing this time and there’ll just be the two of us. He’s not sure yet what we’ll do when we arrive in Lerwick. We're going to be meeting up with our friend John Stevenson. In fact we might even be staying with him at his house, but that's depending on whether or not John and his wife Katie shoot off to the west of Scotland themselves. If they're gone, there's an apartment at the back of the Lounge Bar in the central part of town that we might be able to book, but there'll always be somewhere, even the Naaskel, for goodness sake, so we'll not be stuck on that account.'

He took another slurp of beer and glanced over to the corner of the bar. He caught her looking at him intently and then her face lit up with a coy smile and she looked away, back to her mobile phone and her guide book.

An hour passed, customers came and went and the two at the bar consumed their drinks alone. A group of four, two girls with their partners, came breezing through the door and passed between Egil and the girl at the end of the bar. Magnus took their order and served them. The group cast their eyes about the room looking for a suitable table but none was to be had. One of the group looked along the bar and discussed their options with the others, before turning to Egil and said, 'Would you mind moving along the bar to another stool and we can then get four together?' Egil thought for a nano second, said that this would be okay and moved along beside the dark haired beauty, with a, 'You don't mind, do you? Or are you waiting for somebody else?' in perfect English, the common language of the world.

‘No I am not expecting anybody else. Please.’ and she indicated the stool next to her own. ‘Hello, my name is Fatima. How do you do?’ He beamed a white smile, hoping that there was not bits of peanuts stuck in his teeth, took the proffered slim hand and shook it warmly, with a, ‘Hi, I’m Egil.’

The ice was broken, for both of them. He was on the lookout for a woman and Fatima was on the lookout for a courier for the packages. Egil was the perfect fit for her, according to his conversation with the barman and she would have to do her duty to get what she wanted.

As the evening wore on Egil and Fatima were getting on famously, much better than most first date couples. He was telling her a little about his back history and recounting a few of the old funny stories, some of the lesser dodgy moments in his life. Fatima listened intently and threw in a few tales about herself, in her cover story alter ego, and at the same time showed interest in his upcoming yacht trip to Shetland. If the whole story panned out then the last piece of the transport puzzle would be accomplished. Ardavan would be pleased. She made a mental note to call him the next day and update him.

By 22:30 Fatima had heard enough for her needs and he was getting closer. She leaned back on her stool, pretended to yawn, and said to him, ‘Well, Egil, It’s been really nice chatting to you, but I’m exhausted and I’m heading for bed. Goodnight.’

Egil was immediately in with, ‘Oh you can’t go yet. The night is young and we’ve just met. Where are you staying? Can I walk you there?’

‘I’m sorry, but I have to get my beauty sleep, you know, but if you want to you can walk me back. I’m staying at the Clarion.’

‘I know it well. We’ll be there in no time. Now I must tell you a funny story. When I was younger I took my father’s rigid inflatable. It was the May Day holiday.........

They agreed to meet again the next day, back at the bar at seven in the evening.

Fatima strolled into the bar on the dot of seven, stood for a moment and looked around. There were a few in, mostly locals by the look of it, judging by the way they looked over their shoulders. Magnus raised his head as he polished some wine glasses and greeted her with a jovial, ‘Hi, nice to see you in again.’ She crossed over to the bar and squeezed between two bar stools, most of which were occupied and said, ‘May I have a gin and tonic please? Could you take it over to the corner table please, as I’ll take it while it’s available. Has Egil been in?’

Magnus replied with a quick, ‘Certainly and no, he hasn’t been in today. Have you arranged to meet him?’

'Yes I have.' He replied, 'Well he'll definitely be in then,' smirked and proceeded to pour her drink. 'Ice and lemon?'

'No, could I please have a slice of orange instead of the lemon, if you have it?'

'Of course,' he replied, and she wandered over to the small table, removed her jacket and sat down.

The drink came, and as she sipped from the tall glass, Egil came through the door, looked across the bar at the bartender and followed his gaze to the small corner table. 'She's here – wonderful,' he thought, went across and sat down opposite her. They both exchanged smiles and Egil started with 'It was a great chat we had last night and I'm so glad that I had to swap seats at the bar. Have you had a nice day, so far?'

She began, 'Well I can see the wooden buildings across the harbour from the Clarion, so I started there this morning after breakfast. They're very colourful. I bought a ceramic model of them to take back with me. I found out that the area is a UNESCO World Heritage Site, with a history going back to the fourteenth century. It's very quaint. I noticed the sprinklers while I was wandering through the narrow alleys and thought what would the folks have done, or what equipment would they have had to fight a huge fire in the early eighteenth century. Did the whole place burn down, Egil? Was it the whole city, or just the area around the wharf?'

He told her a bit about the history of Bryggen, its Hanseatic League influence and the importance of the shops, cafes and outlets now trading, mostly as a result of the tourist industry. He told her about the large cruise liners, which regularly dock in Bergen, and how Bryggen's economy was boosted accordingly. He told her that Norway's own Hurtigruten shipping line runs regularly up and down the western coast, calling in at numerous ports and up into the fjords.

Fatima replied, 'That's one of the things I want to do while I'm here – a short cruise into a fjord. It's meant to be quite spectacular. Which one is best?'

'Well from here, the Sognefjorden, it's the longest in Norway, but only if you like hours of achingly beautiful scenery. You'll get a cruise daily from Bergen. There are lots of companies doing it and you can do adventure tours too. Sometimes I help out with those ones.'

'There are loads of things to do, in and around Bergen.' he went on, 'Especially if you like outdoors. I also help with some of the adventure touring to the high mountain plateaus, some kayaking tours and quad bike tours as well. In winter I can change to ski-ing and snow scooter trekking, so I'm kept busy, but it also allows me to pick and choose what I do, as I'm not employed by anyone directly. I am a free spirit.'

As the evening wore on she learned more about him, kept her own back history on hold and kept the line of conversation firmly on the track of that of a tourist, questioning him more and more on the Bergen to Lerwick trip he had planned and at the same time learning about his personality and traits. The drinks flowed. He more than matched the number of beers with her small gins, watered down liberally with tonic water.

At the end of the evening Egil saw her to the door of the Clarion once more. The timing had to be right for Fatima. She had to work on him, yet not thwart his advances with too much zeal. She suggested that they meet again, for a spot of dinner the following Friday, to which he agreed. They would meet in the bar first, for an aperitif, at seven. She leaned towards him, gave him a peck on the cheek and turned her back.

During the days that followed, Fatima went around all the tourist spots, starting with the funicular up Floyen, the Floibanen. It was an easy walk to the base station and it was a sunny day, just perfect for the open air and the view over the city. After the short ascent in the funicular she stepped out into the nature trails, admiring the sculptures as she went. As she sat on a bench, overlooking the harbour and the maze of islands below her she imagined the yacht leaving to pass the package to the other side of the North Sea. Nearly a month from now and she'd move on to another phase of the operation. She smiled, rose and walked back down the mountain trail and back to the hotel to log her notes. All the information she gathered would assist the Intelligence Chief in future operations.

On another day she visited the Aquarium with its fifty different tanks and aquariums, with beautiful displays and an abundance of species. It was a very rainy day and she was glad to be able to spend some time indoors.

As the rainclouds came and went over Bergen she amused herself building up her knowledge of the region in order to have meaningful, yet superfluous, conversations with Egil. She hired a car, a small Volvo XC40 to allow her more freedom to scope out the countryside.

She visited Troldhaugen Concert Hall and Museum and learned about Edvard Grieg's life and passions. The building had once been Grieg's home, housing his Composer's Hut and Steinway piano. His melancholy music played as she soaked up more information.

The rains persisted and so next on the list was KODE Art museum, for some showings of Edvard Munch, JC Dahl, Nikolai Astrup and others. The rain had cleared sufficiently as she exited the museum to allow her to head for the Fish Market and a snack of raw fish and salad and a black coffee.

On another occasion she drove south, out on the E39 towards Fantoft Stave Church, the uniquely Norwegian architectural style from 1150, rebuilt in its entirely original historical splendour in 1992 after a fire, which was the suspected work of a notorious musician and murderer. She gleaned more knowledge for her armoury.

As she drove around, a plan was formulating in her mind. Ardavan had tasked her with finding a route for the package from the European mainland to Great Britain, but avoiding the crowded ferry shipping lines into England from the continent. There were too many risks involved on those routes, what with drugs and traffickers and migrant checks. His preferred route had been across the North Sea and she could now see a way forward.

One day she saw an articulated truck with a Turkish registration plate, towing a large trailer, pull in to an agricultural wholesaler on the outskirts of Bergen, A light bulb moment stuck her and she pulled over to watch what happened next.

The contents of the truck were ploughshares, manure spreaders and other farm machinery, all emblazoned in a green and red livery with the name HKS. She checked on her laptop when she returned to the hotel later that day and found the manufacturer's location in Turkey. The idea ballooned in her mind.

On the Friday, before she was due to meet Egil again, she drove south west to flatter pieces of land and around the farms until she found, on the S40, the Bergen Llama Farm and noted that down as a likely addition to the plan. In the afternoon the laptop popped up the details of the farm, the name of the owners, their trading details, phone and email details and a few other tidbits of information, which might come in useful later.

She reported back to Ardavan, went through the updated plan, and then went for her shower, dressed and put on her light make up before she set out to meet Egil.

They met in the bar and moved on to the restaurant that he had booked. It was a rare occasion for Egil to dine out, as that was usually reserved for tourists. He had decided to break the bank on this occasion and have a traditional Norwegian meal, washed down with champagne and the obligatory aquavit, or akvavit as they liked to pronounce it locally.

The evening went well. He continued with his pursuit of Fatima and she found out more about the North Sea voyage. He would leave with his friend Kjell aboard Naaskel on the first day of July, their start time being dependent on tides and the wind. All going well they would be in Lerwick by the morning of the fourth, but the crossing time could vary, depending on the power of the wind and the condition of the sea.

She played over in her mind over hearing the co-incidental conversation with Kjell and Richard a few months back. The plan was working and the luck was running for her.

'Tell me more about Naaskel. What size is it? Where do you sleep? Where does everything fit in? I've never been in, or is it on, a yacht!'

He explained about the yacht. 'Well, it's a Bavaria make, type 44, thirteen metres long. It's got three cabins, a master forward and two doubles aft, or rear, a galley, a shower with toilet and wash hand basin. There's a saloon, located midships, with a large chart table and chart drawers between saloon and heads, or toilet. It's quite fast through the water and Kjell's just scraped and refinished her hull and keel, so she'll be nice and sleek through the water. She's single masted, with teak decks. She's a lovely little boat. There's plenty of locker space and as there will be only the two of us then there's a whole cabin free for any additional stuff. There are also sail lockers, rope lockers and all sorts of little spaces to store the paraphernalia you'd need for a long sail. You could go around the world in her. It is usually a good time of year to make the short crossing across the North Sea.'

He saw her back to the Clarion and they had another drink at the bar before she pleaded tiredness once more. This time she took Egil's tanned face in her soft hands and kissed him full on the mouth before asking him, 'See you tomorrow? Are you working?'

'I am in the morning, but I could meet you in the afternoon. By the time I finish and get showered and dressed I could be ready for 2. Would that be okay?'

'Sure. We could go for a drive and you can show me around to places I wouldn't know.'

'That's a date. I'll meet you in the Clarion lobby.' She swivelled and strode fetchingly towards the lifts. He was in awe.

Early on the morning of 30th May, Fatima called Ardavan and briefed him on the actions of the previous evening. He commended her on her work and was surprised that she had managed to do so much in a matter of three days. She said that she had spent more time in bars than she had in a long time, with most of the conversations being about more mundane matters. There were still plenty of boats in harbour that had obviously not been moved for months, and she had struck lucky when her contact, Egil, had walked in. She said, 'The yacht, the Naaskel, would sail on the first day of July. We will have to move on the other aspects as soon as possible.' Ardavan agreed and told her to return as soon as she had finalised her work in Bergen.

Next day, when they met, Egil asked if she knew about the Laerdal Tunnel, the longest road tunnel in Europe, if not the world. She answered in the negative and so they decided to head there in the car. He said, 'I'm not going to tell you much about the tunnel. I'll leave that for a surprise, but I believe that you'll think it's cool.'

The drive was very pleasant as they climbed up into the snow-capped mountains. The day was bright, but not brilliantly sunny and now and again they passed through a small rain shower as they cruised around the myriad of corners. 'You know,' he said, 'The authorities had to put speed cameras inside the tunnel as it is one of the few locations in Norway where the road goes in a straight line for any distance at all.'

By half past four, Egil suggested a break and he pointed her in the direction of Flam, one of the tails of the Sognefjord and said, 'If you take up my suggestion of a cruise in the Sognefjord you would be best to pick Flam as your destination option. From here, there is a narrow gauge railway which threads up the cliffside, doing a complete radial at one point to gain elevation, stops half way up for some music and sprites at a waterfall, and then carries on up to Myrdal, which is a station on the main line between Bergen and Oslo. It's quite a tourist attraction. Some folks do the boat leg, the narrow gauge train leg and finish up with the express back to Bergen. It's a long day but well worth it.'

They stopped for a coffee in a hotel lobby. He thought it would have been better to sit in the microbrewery across the road, but the Norwegian laws on drink driving were very strict and Fatima would just have to sip water. She could try the brewery if she decided to have a tourist day, with no driving involved, next week. 'Next week?' he thought, 'Will she be here next week?'

'Fatima, how long will you be staying in Bergen' 'I leave next Sunday', she replied, 'The seventh of June.'

Coffee came and went and they were back on the road to the tunnel. Straight through the tunnel to Laerdal would be about 40 minutes and then they could return to Bergen for late evening, with a stop along the way for some food.

As they approached the roundabout the sign showed straight on for Oslo and Laerdal. She crossed the roundabout as directed and headed for the craggy bluff ahead and the tunnel system sat directly in front.

She noted her speed and checked the speed sign and all was well. She noted the overhead cameras too. His chatter was just a soft buzz in her head, not really listening. The white light in the tunnel took a bit of getting used to. She noticed the rumble strips at the sides and down the centre, the requirement for no central reservation or barrier system, the amount of vehicles heading in each direction and the gaps between them. She noticed the lack of emergency exits. She was particularly keen on a more detailed view of the brightly lit cavern that they came across, for vehicle drivers to rest, or as some were doing, photo opportunities in the blue and yellow lighting of a Norwegian simulated daybreak. She momentarily heard Egil say that there were three caverns in the twenty-four kilometre tunnel and they passed through the other two before succumbing to the sights and sounds of mother nature's world and another roundabout loomed up quickly. She told him that she was turning round for another look and that she wanted to stop in one of the caverns and he nodded in agreement.

On the drive back through the tunnel, Fatima had already decided that she would use the last cavern, nearest to Bergen to make the exchange of the package, so she said to Egil, 'Let's stop for a few photographs in the last cavern, just for a laugh!' and he agreed. They stepped out into the blue and yellow scene that had been set by the lighting engineers to simulate a sunrise. She wandered up and down looking at the slow stream of cars and trucks passing by. It was mostly cars that stopped, she noted. There was one large vehicle parked at the south end of the cavern and a minibus disgorging tourists pulled in behind her Volvo.

She made a play of getting photographs of Egil, both of them and even ones solely of her that he took, scoping everything that was in the tunnel, the carriageways, the walls, roof, cars, people, the overall scale of things. She had a special interest in surveillance cameras and, without him noticing, paced out the length of the cavern and the depth of the arc from the carriageway. From those details she could model the cavern and decide on a strategy for package transfer at a later date. With a final flourish she grabbed him, drew him close and planted a lingering kiss on his whiskered lips. He noticed her glow and remarked to himself that things were getting better. Maybe tonight he could grab his moment, if she didn't beat him to it first. His laughter filled the cavern and the watching tourists smiled at their view of the happy couple.

Late that evening they arrived back at the hotel and she turned, with a sparkle in her eye and said to him, in a teasing voice, 'It's been a lovely day so far Egil, would you like to come up for a nightcap?' He gave her a big beaming smile and replied, coyly, 'That would be very nice Fatima, but aren't you too tired?'

'I'm only too tired when I want to be Egil. Let's go.'

They spent the night and the whole of the next day together. He showed her around some of the off tourist areas. It turned out to be a lovely sunny day, flowers were blooming, butterflies were flitting around in their random jiggly fashion of flight and bees with nectar bristling on their leg hairs buzzed across their path, oblivious to the huge monster shapes of humans walking ahead, hand in hand.

'Alas,' thought Egil, as he once more scanned the features of the lovely creature before him. 'I've got to work tomorrow and I'm on call, so there's no chance of seeing her again before the weekend, if she's still here.'

'Fatima, I'm having a lovely time here with you. I have to work on my guiding up in the mountains, with a group from Ireland and in the evening I will be on call with the Lifeboat.'

'The Lifeboat? You never told me about that. Tell me more.'

He went on ‘Well I am a volunteer lifeboatman. You know when ships are in distress they call out the Coastguard and they in turn usually call on us with our fast rigid inflatable boats, or RIBs, to deal with any inshore incidents, which are usually small craft or individuals in distress. They deal with the larger vessels, sea going, with deeper draught, tankers, oil service vessels and rigs. I put in a few hours each week. There’s a rota of the retained lifeboatmen, who get paid, and a few locals, who just want to give something back to the community and help out on a voluntary basis. Our group of volunteers has a farmer, a baker, a musician and myself. It can be good fun, especially in the training days, but can be a bit ropey at times when we’re dealing with real distress calls and the few idiots that should not venture out on the water at all.’

‘Ah, Egil, that’s interesting. You say there is a musician in your group. What kind of musician, what does he play? Piano, guitar or what?’

‘She’s a saxophone player, but she’s pretty handy with most wind instruments, piano and drums. She’s a music teacher in the school so her weekends and nights are always free to give a hand with the lifeboat crew or puddle about in her own five metre RIB. A very talented woman.’

She snatched at the opportunity and smoothly came in with, ‘I’ve a musician friend in London, originally from my part of the world. Plays strings. They could start up a band together!’

'Has he - is it a he, this time - ever been to Norway, Fatima?'

'Well to my knowledge he's been to Oslo, but as far as I'm aware he hasn't been to Bergen, but once I tell him about this wonderful place he might be cajoled into coming and playing some violin concertos in Grieg's house, who knows.'

They laughed together and he asked her if she was still leaving Bergen on the 7th June.

'Egil, it's been lovely, but I have to leave at some point during next week, but I promise to come back as soon as I can.' She turned her face up and kissed him again, letting his soft blond whiskers tickle her nose. 'Tell me about your trip to Lerwick again. Maybe I can come back then, to see you off. What date was that again?'

'That would be great. I'd really look forward to seeing you again. Our targeted date is to sail from Bergen on the 1st July, but as I think I said before, that would depend on the tide. Well there will definitely be tides, and the state of the wind and seas. A storm could put us back a few days, but it is highly unlikely that we would be able to bring our departure forward by more than twenty-four hours.'

'Okay, I'm going to try and get back to Bergen before the end of June and we could have some nice time together before you set sail.'

‘What a lovely thought that is to look forward to’ he beamed.

In the next few days, without the anchor of Egil to contend with, Fatima went about the other tasks that she had set herself. The HKS connection would be used for transport to the Llama Farm. The changeover would take place in the tunnel. She needed to dream up an idea that would successfully get the packages to Egil and get his authority to transport them for her, without raising suspicion.

She booked one-way tickets on the Hurtigruten ferry boat to Flam, the Flam to Myrdal railway and the Myrdal to Bergen Express. It would be a typical touristy thing to do and she could plan as she went. She could also see the volume of coastal activity on the North Sea and the route a yacht would take to get out to sea from the marina. She’d have to check out the marina again, where Kjells’s yacht was located and model the characteristics of the Laerdal Tunnel, for the switch.

By the time she had arrived back in Bergen the following evening she had formulated all parts of the plan up to the point where the package arrived in Lerwick. She needed to get there and reconnoitre the lie of the land on the downward leg to the final target location of London. Time was marching on. She decided that she would update Ardavan before she left Bergen. They needed to meet.

She called him and a meeting was arranged for mid-day in Oslo International Airport, where they discussed the plan in depth and the need for her to go on to Lerwick. They parted, on two independent tickets, to Turkey and Bursa. Fatima could then arrange her itinerary to Lerwick, while she waited for the flight after Ardavan's.

She would fly back to Istanbul and on to Bursa and meet up with him there, as they had to put the transport plan in motion. There was a man in Bursa to call. She would initially do it and he would take over. She would then have to travel back to Bergen and place an order. She could be in Bergen before nightfall, email the order from a local hotel, not the Clarion, and be on her way back to Bursa the next day, from Bergen, through Oslo and Istanbul and the drive to Bursa. She would meet Ardavan again later.

Fatima found that there were flight connections between Norway and Aberdeen in Scotland and she decided upon that flight connection as there were regularly oil workers operating between the two cities and she could pass unobtrusively as one of them, or an accountant, suitably attired.

She headed for departures and got a new and not inexpensive business suit, shoes, flat boots, blouse, cardigan and coat, scarf and headwear. Her small case and laptop bag would fit in perfectly.

……….

During another conversation with Bernadette Bucheron, Vicky Douglas was looking for an update on the identification of the foreign national who was shot dead in London. Bernadette told her that there was nothing more to go on as yet, but there was every possibility that he was of Northern Iraqi origin, going by his DNA profile. There was nothing on him of a criminal nature and all other lines of enquiry had turned up zilch.

Bernadette passed on a snippet of information that might interest Special branch in London. 'Word on the grapevine is that a Bosnian munitions expert was awash with cash, which was unusual for him and that loose talk in the bar had determined that some weaponry was being prepared for an attack in Britain.' She had nothing more to go on for the present. 'But you never know when things that do not seem to be in the least bit connected, turn out to be linked, and when they are, they are usually, in our business, very dangerous. That is why we do our jobs, to prevent dangerous things from happening. No doubt we'll speak again Victoria.'

'I'm sure we will Bernadette and please call me Vicky.'

'Okay Vicky.'

8 Out from undercover

In the HKS Makina agricultural machinery factory in Bursa, Turkey, Behwan Fidan was putting the finishing touches to the chassis of a Type 1000 Storm Turbo Atomiser. He had, for the last three years, been an employee, hiding his real identity as a KRG undercover sleeper agent, in the name of Yusef Polat.

It was a typical day, fitting the 1000 litre polyethylene tank, Italian pump, control unit, gearbox and nozzles and all the interconnecting plastic parts to the pre-painted chassis.

Behwan was well liked in the factory and noted as a hard worker with a strong work ethic.

He was half way through his shift that fateful day and as he sat by his workstation, with his plastic lunch box, having his break, drinking his hot sweet coffee, his manager came across and said, ‘Behwan, I am so sorry to tell you this, but I have just had a phone call. It is something about the death of your grandmother. Here is the phone number you must call. It is very urgent. Take as long as you like.’ Behwan’s look of surprise was well justified, as both his grandmothers had been killed in the border clashes between Syria and Turkey long before he had been placed in Bursa. He took the note from his manager and gave his apologies for interrupting his work schedule and strode off to find a public telephone. He had never had a call since his arrival in Bursa. His former colleagues in the PKK had said that they would find him if they needed him, but to stay as a sleeper until then. He had wondered as to when the call would come. This was his daily thought.

He was fed up with his humdrum undercover life and longed for the excitement of the border fighting that was his life before, but he knew that when he was eventually called upon, it would be for the greater need of the Kurdish people. His journey had taken him from the battlefields of Northern Syria, fighting against Daesh initially, at the behest of The West, before the Kurdish forces had been abandoned by Great Britain and their armament agents, when Syria enlisted the assistance of The Russian Federation to claim back the Syrian borders.

The weapons that they were given were usually shipped through the Balkan States and were of Eastern Bloc origin, like the Russian Kalashnikov rifles and RPG7 grenade launchers. The accuracy of the Western arms or more modern Russian arms would have been beneficial, but when there is a need you will take anything offered.

Yusef Polat called the number he had been given from the payphone in the canteen. It rang four times before it was picked up.

'Silav, ki gazi dike?' The voice was female, and he vaguely recognized it but she had asked who was calling. Was it a trick? Should he answer with his Turkish name or his real Kurdish name?

'I was asked to call this number, regarding the death of my grandmother,' he said in Turkish, playing a cagey game. After all it could be the Turkish police or worse, on the other end of the line. But they would likely be male, not female.

'Yusef, you likely do not trust me, but I have been asked by Ardavan Kamandi to make contact with you. My name is Fatima Ardalan. I know that this conversation has to be very quick. I know that you no longer have grandmothers, as they were both killed. I know that you have been under cover for years. Call this number again at eight o'clock tonight and we will give you further instructions.'

The call ended and Yusef stared at the handset for a moment before he replaced it. He carefully looked around him and everybody seemed to be going about their daily business as normal. He had only mentioned his grandmother, nothing else that could be picked up on by listeners. Was the line safe? Were there eavesdroppers? Was his position being compromised?

There were too many questions running around in his head. He walked slowly away from the booth, trying to remember the training he had been given all those years ago. He knew Ardavan. At least he knew of a person named Ardavan Kamandi. He had been Yusef's section commander in the PKK. Was it really him? Had Ardavan been compromised? Was he even still alive? He did not remember this Fatima person. Could she be trusted?

He had around seven hours to wait until he had to make a decision on whether or not to make the call. If he called and it was genuine he would finally get away from this tedious job screwing together agricultural machinery. If he made the call and it was a trap he would still get away from the job, but likely not to a good place. If he didn't make the call he could still be set up in a trap, or he could go back to helping the Kurds on the front line. It was 50:50 as far as he could tell, so in the next few hours he would have to choose.

Later that afternoon after work, Yusef slipped unobtrusively out of his small flat and headed for the city centre. He parked his van on the waste ground close to Akasya Street and strolled the half-hour it took him to arrive at the corner of Aday Street and the main thoroughfare of Lefkose.

He walked on a further one hundred metres, then quickly doubled back and headed for the café in Eker Meydan Shopping Centre, where he ordered Chicken Shashlik and tea. He blended in with the throng of people milling about the café and surroundings. With a watchful eye, he got the impression that nobody was paying any undue attention to him being there. He was also convinced that he had not been followed to the location. He felt happier with the situation and ate unhurriedly.

He left in plenty of time before the centre closed, sticking with the crowds and ambled along a figure of eight route before arriving at the rank of telephone booths he had selected earlier. He decided that he had not been followed.
At exactly 8pm he dialled the number again. She answered with the same greeting and again he asked about his grandmother. Fatima said, 'I will let you speak with your Uncle Ardavan.' Very quickly the female voice had been swapped to that of a male, one that was familiar.

'Yusef, I am Ardavan Kamandi. I know you from Syria. I cannot say more now but meet me at the car park at the head of the Doganci dam, about twenty kilometres south of Bursa. It's at the junction of Bursa to Keles and Bursa to Orhaneli roads. 15:00 hours tomorrow. Take a paper to read.'

The phone went dead. Yusef had little doubt now that his sleeper days were over and that exciting times lay ahead.

The next day, as he left Bursa in the van for the short drive to the Dam, the adrenalin was pumping through his system. He was on edge, still thinking there may be a trap ahead. If the Turkish authorities were involved then it would be a long jail sentence at the least. Recep Erdogan ruled with a very firm hand and there was the underlying loathing of the Kurdish people, like the Palestinians, a nation without a country to call their own.

He took the smooth Lefkose dual carriageway south until he reached the underpass at the point where the Lefkose ended and the Keles road commenced. He thought that his timing was good, as he didn't want to arrive too early nor did he want to miss the 15:00 deadline. His speed slowed as he approached the single carriageway at the 50kph signpost. 'Only seven or eight kilometres to go,' he thought as he checked his watch. It showed 14:40. He was looking good. Just around the corner there was a large truck ahead, one of those bulk carriers for cement or chemicals. He slowed as he caught up with it. The road was getting busier, more cars and trucks ahead and a queue of traffic at the road works in front. Yusef never bargained for this.

He ground to a halt in the queue, behind the cement truck. He glanced in his mirror. 'Shit!' he exclaimed, as the obvious livery of a police car with two up drew to a stop behind him. He looked away and concentrated on avoiding looking in his van mirrors. The truck in front started to pull away and he dropped the clutch and gently started after it. The police did not seem to be interested, but a squeaky moment nevertheless.

The sequence of lights was kind to him and he got through the single section under green, with the police car still behind him. The road twisted around the contours of the wooded valley. The queue was still edging ahead and the police car was still behind. Quite a few cars were parked in the cleared dust at the side of the road and further on the compound for the diggers and scrapers for the road works came into view on the right.

Then the Dam was in view over on the right – 14:53 – it would be cutting it fine, but okay. The blue signposts came into view, straight on for Keles and right for Orhaneli, Kutahya and Balikesir. Yusef signalled right and carried on down the steep hill, dropping through the gears to the 30kph limit, with the police car still on his tail.

The sleek waters of the Dam were suddenly on his left and the watercourse to the hydro-electric station was there and beside it the small car park, just on the left at the corner. He signalled, waited for the break in traffic and pulled over on to the dirt surface, by the rubbish bin. The police car pulled away and disappeared across the Dam bridge. He was alone with his thoughts. The paper was in the door bin so he casually wound down the window on the driver's side, away from the traffic and with a view of the Dam, and pretended to read. The time was 14:57.

He never noticed the pedestrian crossing the Dam bridge, as he was expecting a vehicle to approach him. Ardavan Kamandi opened the passenger door and sat in, startling Yusef who jerked round in surprise. If Yusef had had the inclination to look at his watch at that instant he would have noticed that the time was exactly 1500 hours.

Ardavan started to speak immediately. 'Do not say anything Yusef, just nod your head now and again and look at me from time to time, as we would do in any normal conversation. Do not put away the paper, but listen very carefully to what I am about to say. I take it you recognise me from our time in Syria. We fought well together, but we were both destined for more intelligent roles in the making of a Kurdish Nation, with respected international boundaries. Very recently we were promised this, by the West and especially by the British. They gave us arms to fight Daesh in Syria and when they were beaten they gave us more arms to fight the Syrian regime. We thought that we had a deal. We would take over a large part of northern Syria, up to the Turkish border and the land would become ours, an internationally recognized country, The People's Republic of Kurdistan. In time we would wrestle control of our homelands from Turkey and turn the region back into a land wholly of Kurds and not infiltrators. We sat down and discussed terms with British generals, politicians and diplomats but they are not good at keeping promises. Just look at Palestine, another people without a homeland, another failure to keep promises by the British. Of course when the Russians became involved in assisting Syria, the British backed out of their promises and stitched us Kurds up once again.'

Yusef continued looking at his paper and gave a slight nod of his head, thinking that he knew all this, what is this all about, when will he get to the point, the police are still out there somewhere.

Ardavan continued, 'There has come a time when we have to bite back, in a way that will get us noticed around the world. It will include an act of extreme violence, to enable us to get around a table and talk sensibly about our future. Look how the Taliban did it in Afghanistan. It took years but they had to start somewhere. We are going to hit Britain hard and you have a big part to play in this. You will continue with your job at the machinery works, but in the next few days an order will be placed for two Storm Turbo Atomisers, the ones with the 1000 litre tanks. The order will be from a new client in Norway, a farmer and near neighbour of another presently using the factory equipment. As you will be working on the order, you will see the Norwegian connection. When you have completed it you will ask for some time off, as you have still got underlying issues concerning the death of your grandmother. You will suggest that the time off would involve travel to recover, but as an act of support to the company, you could transport the equipment to Norway. We have something that we want to transport to Norway as well and the packages could be stored within the polyethylene tanks of the atomisers.'

Ardavan carried on, 'The factory will supply all the necessary travel papers, bills of sale and customs declarations to enable the shipment to pass from Turkey into the European Union. You will leave the factory without the packages on board just in case there is a search done at the customs posts in Turkey and Greece. There will be a stop along the way, once you are in the European Union, to enable us to insert our packages into the tanks.'

Yusef smiled, looked up from his paper and looked over the dammed waters with the sunshine glinting on the surface. This was a big part to play. Everything and everybody was depending on him. He wondered about the bigger picture, why Norway and what was in the packages, but turned to Ardavan and simply said, 'I will do it. I will not let you down.'

With that, Ardavan passed a scrap of paper to Yusef with another number on it and said, 'Phone again on this number twenty four hours before you are due to leave with your load for Norway. We will give you the packages collection location then. I am depending on you. Do not let me down.' He opened the car door and left to walk across the bridge into anonymity once more. The police were nowhere to be seen. Yusef relaxed. In fact he was more relaxed than he had been for a very long time. He was back in action. He could not wait to see the factory order appear at his work bench.

....

By early June Paulo had his answer. The shipyard delivery must be made on the 15th June, to the guy in the shipyard in Bursa.

He swung into action, hired the white van and loaded it up with various items of electrical goods, applied some padding between the boxes and checked that the electronics of both weapons and electronic kit merged into one. He was satisfied and sent the pair on their way, with explicit route and timing instructions and at the last second gave them the name of the contact. They had a bit of difficulty committing the shipyard name to memory as it was so long, but they would find it.

On the fifteenth, Guests One and Two drove up to the shipyard security barrier and asked the gatekeeper for Aleksander. In less than half an hour they were back on the road to Italy with an empty van. Aleksander would have a few bits of electronics to sell on in the black market and two bundles, which he would conceal in the lockers in his welding booth. The gatekeeper received a bottle of vodka to keep the need he had from waning.

Paulo met again with Ardavan at The Villa Borghese in Rome and they strolled in the gardens. Ardavan now felt that Paulo could be trusted with some parts of the plan. He acknowledged that delivery had been made, and discussed the ins and outs of deployment of the rocket propelled grenades. Ardavan couldn't tell him who the target was or when, even where the weapons would be deployed, but discussed the ramifications of getting close enough to a target in a secure area in Western Europe and hopefully retreating from the scene without being apprehended.

Paulo's interest was piqued. He had a macabre view of all things deadly and had used various small calibre weapons, as a necessity or as an instrument of threat over the years.

They talked about carrying an assembled launcher and raising it in public, of carrying the weapon and rockets in a broken-down configuration and at all twists, turns and variations they stumbled over the final deployment of launcher and fully assembled RPG.

Paulo had a brainwave. 'Ardavan, I think I have the answer you are looking for.' He went on to describe the Aero Club and the guy flying a microlight. 'Consider the launchers affixed to a microlight. Maybe the aircraft could be adapted to fire RPG's from a fixed platform on the aircraft, like a jet fighter, only slower. It could fly in, fire and fly out before anybody really noticed. They are quite small and pretty agile machines. What do you think?'

The Kurd's face creased into a small smile, then broadened and finally he laughed out loud. 'That is it. You've cracked the enigma. Let's go over the information on this microlight again.'

By the time they'd walked around the grounds of Villa Borghese a second time they had decided that they would need two microlight pilots with strategic flying skills and a bit of Kamikaze in them too. Then they would need to source the microlights and an engineer to modify the aircraft to take the weaponry. They could only do this once. So the target had to be readily available and in the open. It had to be in the open in any case to achieve line of sight for the RPG. The benefit was the launcher and RPG could be readied at a distance, deployed and removed from the scene swiftly. There would of course be security issues to deal with, but there were always those snags to address in any attack.

....

Fatima left the airport for the long drive into Oslo and booked into a hotel opposite the Central Train Station. She caught an express to Bergen the next day. Seven hours later she had changed her appearance with a change of clothes and hat, to the Norwegian style and donned a pair of clear lens glasses before she arrived at the station in her destination city.

She hired a small car and found the Bed and Breakfast she was looking for in the Melkplassen area to the south of the city. She concocted an order form headed ‘Llama Farm, Bergen, Norway’ and was going to send it, but decided to ask the owner if she could use her internet to send the email, which the lady kindly allowed her to do. She got the received ping back from the factory in Turkey and deleted all traces from the Bed and Breakfast system.

Fatima checked out the following day, headed for the station and was on the first train back to Oslo. She caught the only flight remaining that day to Istanbul, through Munich with Lufthansa. It was the early hours of the next day when she finally got to Bursa. She grabbed a few hours sleep and met with Ardavan early the same morning.

They discussed the current situation and Fatima was to make the call to the factory, to initiate the next phase of the plan.

....

When Yusef (now Behwan Fidan again) saw the A4 sheet leave the hands of his supervisor with the address of somewhere near Bergen, Norway, on the heading for two HKS 1000 Storm Turbo Atomisers, his heart leapt in his chest. The day had come and he knew that, within four days, he would have two finished products to pass to final testing and then on to Dispatch. The paperwork and sign off would likely use up another couple of days, so within a week he would be on his way. It was time to sit down and have a chat with his Manager.

His boss welcomed him into his office, with a pleasant smile on his face as usual. He was a hard taskmaster but always fair to all the employees under his charge. He worked on the principle of give a little and get more back in return. The employees liked him for it. When the wife of one of Behwan's colleagues was seriously ill the man got time off to attend to his wife. His colleague more than made up for the time off in unpaid overtime when he came back.

'Well Behwan, what would you like to discuss?' the Manager asked affably.

'Well boss, I don't know if you've noticed, and I hope that it hasn't changed my work output here, but the death of my grandmother has affected me more that I first realised. I think that I need some time off. I know that my holidays are scheduled around the factory shut down in high summer, but I was thinking that I could kill two birds with one stone, so to speak. Would it be possible for me to drive the delivery truck on the upcoming delivery to Norway? The paperwork arrived at my bench and I'll have the units built and cleared by the Certification Department within seven days. I could then have time off, well away from Turkey and my dismal thoughts, but still do work for the company. I'm convinced that a few days in different scenery would be the stimulus that I need right now.'

'Well Behwan, I have noticed that your mind is not quite on the job. There's nothing wrong with your performance, but you are a bit slower than normal. However I believe that your suggestion is a good one and so I will arrange this with the various departments. Go to Human Resources later today and file for secondment to transport. I will have spoken to them by then.'

Yusef was over the moon. His plan, or the plan of the KRG was working. In a week or so he should be in a position to make the all important telephone call.

When Behwan clocked in for his shift the following week he worked on the first chassis, fitting the tank, pump, controls, piping and the all important control pack. He made a mental note to check journey times and likely stopovers with the Dispatch

Department later in the day. That would be critical for the long journey ahead. It would be better if he had access to mobile phones or a computer, but his original instructions on being posted to the factory were to avoid social contact and the internet. He guessed that the instruction still stood.

Six days later Yusef drove away in his little van and back to Akasya Street car parking area and wandered in to the Shopping Centre of Eker Meydan to the telephone booths. During the final week of working in the factory he had memorized the number and destroyed the slip of paper. He lifted the receiver and dialled. After four rings it was answered with 'Silav, ki gazi dike?' The voice was female again, and this time he recognized the voice as that of Fatima and once more she had asked who was calling.

'I was asked to call this number, regarding the death of my grandmother,' he said in Turkish. She replied, 'Yusef, I am Fatima Ardalan. None of this information must be written down. You must commit all to memory. Your pick up location will be in Burgas, in Bulgaria, on the Black Sea. There is a narrow neck of land between Burgas Bay and Lake Burgas. Your destination on it will be a shipyard, in the Southern Industrial Area, called Burgaski Korabostroitelnitsi. The name is long and you cannot miss it. Access to the industrial zone is from the roundabout at routes 9 and 79. There will be two packages for you, one to be inserted in each of the polyethylene tanks and they will be wrapped in bubble wrap and a white plastic sheeting, so that they do not show through the walls of the tanks. Ask for Aleksander Chavdarov, who will fit the packages. They will not be particularly heavy – about twenty-two kilograms each, one for each tank. All the work is to be done under cover, in the confines of the shipyard, within the screens of a welding booth. You will drive in directly to the booth under Aleksander's direction. You will not have to offload the equipment aboard the flatbed truck, only remove the tarpaulin and refit securely once the tanks are loaded. The load will be perfectly safe for you to drive normally on the open roads. Once you are ready you will immediately leave Burgas and continue with your shipment to Bergen. You have to be in Burgas by the end of the same day as you leave Bursa. Call this number again when you get to Hamburg, in Germany.'

Fatima rang off and Yusef checked his watch. The call had taken ninety seconds, and it was a lot of information to recall. He left the booth and headed for the café and a glass of sweetened tea, mulling over everything that had been said. He was not expecting to deviate from the normal route from Istanbul into Europe and away from Sofia, to Burgas. He didn't think that, in the big picture, the time from Bursa to Bergen would increase substantially. It would take him about two or three hours from the main route to Burgas, so he'd have to factor around five or six hours into his route plan back at base. The Europeans were very strict regarding daily driving hours and the factory would expect the load to arrive on the scheduled delivery date, otherwise the 'client' would be calling his boss.

The guy in Dispatch showed him the route on the computer. It would take him right across Europe. His journey would take him from Bursa to Istanbul and then on to Sofia, the capital of Bulgaria, Yusef did not mention the deviation to Burgas to pick up the packages. From Sofia the route would take him out of Bulgaria into Serbia, to Belgrade, then on to Budapest in Hungary and then into Slovakia and the city of Bratislava. From there, the route would be to Prague in Czechia and onwards through Germany, via Dresden, Leipzig, Hanover and Hamburg.

'We tend to avoid ferries,' said the guy in Dispatch, 'as they can sometimes be affected by weather and loading times, so we always suggest coming past Kiel on the 210, on to the 7 and then, it's the main road up into Denmark, past Flensburg to Kolding on the E45, then strike off right on the E20 to Nyborg. After Nyborg you will cross via the bridge link and on to Copenhagen. After that it is plain sailing all the way.'

He showed him the last piece of the travel jigsaw, into Copenhagen, then across the bridge into Sweden, through Malmo and Gothenburg and finally into Norway just past Selater. 'From Selater you will believe that your journey has come to an end, as you will be in Norway, but there will still be another six hundred kilometres to add to the three thousand four hundred kilometres you will have driven from the point of the border crossing. This is not your usual line of work. Are you sure you are up to this long and lonely drive? The European rules are strict. You will only be able to drive fifty-six hours in a week, so work it out for yourself. Four thousand kilometres at eight hours each day is five hundred kilometres daily. Your speed will have to average over sixty kilometres per hour. The truck is limited to one hundred, so you will be driving steadily for the whole journey. By the way the eight hours do not include breaks. You will have to take a break every six hours or less. Most of our drivers drive for three, rest for half, drive for two, rest for one and drive for a final three, so their day on the road takes nine and a half hours. Starting at 07:00, you are finished by 16:30. The truck is a flatbed type but does not have a laydown bed in the cab so you'll need to find cheap accommodation along the way. The stops will depend on what distance you have managed to clock up on a particular day. Speak to some of the other drivers who'll steer you in the right direction regarding roadside stops, fuel stops and accommodation. And then you've got to do the same all over again in reverse. I'll see you in two weeks Behwan!'

As he closed down the screen he said to Behwan, 'Be sure to take a camera along with you and get some photos of your journey, as I'll bet you won't want to do it again!'

His alter ego, Yusef, thought to himself that it might be unlikely that he would want to return to Bursa and his humdrum job, sticking pieces of pesticide sprayers together. He had been asked to respond to bigger and better tasks that would help the cause of Kurds greatly.

Behwan said, 'Thanks for all that information. I didn't think the journey would be as long as it is. But the change will, hopefully, put my mind back in order. I will buy a small camera and I will take some pictures to show you when I return. Now I'd better go to Certification and arrange for my travel papers and export documentation for the atomisers, to get me across the border from Turkey into Europe. See you later.'

Yusef, the Kurd, in his identity as Behwan, had his Turkish national identity card and a forged passport, which he had never needed to use up to now. He had a bank account in Bursa that he needed to get his wages paid into, but he had never travelled outside of Turkey in his three years as a sleeper. Now was the time to find out if his identity would be sustained as he crossed over into Europe in a few days' time.

The two Atomisers were completed, certified and export paperwork was finalised. An email message had been sent off to the purchaser advising that delivery was scheduled for the following week and that arrival of the products could be expected within ten days thereafter, just to allow for the vagaries of the delivery route.

The Manager called in Behwan and said, 'Hi Behwan, nice to see you again. Sit down please.

Well this is not what I ever envisaged doing – taking one of my line operatives away from their important place in the production line – and putting one into delivery. Usually it is the other way around. I promote delivery drivers to line workers, but we are in a crazy world and I appreciate your honesty regarding how you were feeling and a suggested way of fixing the situation. So here we are. The two Atomisers that our Norwegian customer has ordered are ready to go. They just need to be loaded on to the flatbed truck and you can head off. On Monday please report to Dispatch and they will give you all the paperwork. Supervise the loading of the two pieces yourself as they will be your responsibility from now on. Ensure that the loading straps are tightened around the packing spacers so that no damage is done to any of the equipment. It is only the chassis that needs to concern you for tie down integrity, as the rest of the machine is designed sturdily enough for a life being hauled about fields. The tarpaulins on the truck are new so eyelet holes will be fine, to protect against the elements on your journey. So….I wish you all the best for your travels. I will not see you before you set off, so enjoy yourself touring across Europe, but don't like it too much as I want you back here on the production line. Okay?'

They shook hands and Behwan turned and walked out the door with a small smile on his face. Underneath he was ecstatic and could have jumped up and clicked his heels. That would have to wait for another day. He returned to the telephone kiosk in the shopping centre and made the call to Fatima.

9 Interpol calling

The morning came. Yusef packed his carry bag, shovelled his breakfast down his throat and left his flat in his little van to the factory and into the yard for his new beginning.

The flatbed was there, a Fiat Ducato, liveried in the company colours of red and green. He went to Dispatch and the keys were handed over, together with a fuel card. It was a diesel unit, a flatbed with small folding sides and back. He then went to the factory entrance and fitted the tow truck to the first of the Atomisers and moved it round to the flatbed and repeated the process for the second Atomizer. There was a small crane affixed to the chassis of the truck. Yusef extended the stabilising legs on the truck and he attached the slings at the lifting points. He moved back to the control panel and watched carefully as he made the lift on to the flatbed. The second one followed and he tied down both machines between the lifting points and the D rings on the flatbed using the transit spacers to prevent damage on the journey ahead. The sides and back were hinged back up and the tarpaulin was lashed down to the hooks on the flatbed chassis. All present and correct with the load. Just the sign-off procedure to be completed at the Dispatch office, a quick dash inside to freshen up and 'Behwan' would be on his way. It was 08:45. With luck he would be going around Istanbul by 11:30.

As he left Ali Osman Sonmez Boulevard from The North West Industrial Zone and turned on to the D575 he imagined the route he was about to take. A series of road numbers were to follow and large cities to either encounter or bypass. He hoped that the signage would be easy to follow and in language he could understand. He had never been to Europe, just read about it. At least they all drove on the right, apart from the British of course. They always had to be different. What was it about them? Why did they think that they were so superior and could change their minds like the seasons? It was no wonder that Ardavan Kamandi wanted to settle a score with them, for the good of all Kurds.

Yusef made good time to Istanbul and was through by 11:45 and on the route that would take him into Bulgaria. As he steadily purred along the E80 he passed under an overhead gantry just before his turn off on the E87 into Bulgaria and the shipyard in Burgas. The gantry warned that the E87 was closed at the border due to technical difficulties and advised all drivers to head further up the E80.

He arrived at the border between Turkey and Greece, having followed the diversion directions. The Meric Nehri river flowed alongside and the signage warned of two border crossing stops, one in Turkey and another in Greece. Drivers had to stop at both. More delay.

The first hurdle was Pazarkule Sinir Kapisi and Pazarkule Gumruk Sahasi border post and customs on the Turkish side. The guards checked his passport, the vehicle identification papers, looked at the VIN number and asked to see below the tarpaulin before signing off his paperwork. All was all in order and they waved him on his way. 'Phew' Yusef breathed 'That's the first over.'

About seven hundred metres away, across the border, lay the Greek border post and customs at Kastanies. It was a short distance, but a major leap in his eyes, to arrive into Europe. Would all his paperwork stand up to scrutiny? Did European entry involve more technical security equipment, which would seek out his hidden credentials. He was still the Turk, Behwan Fidan and everything he said now depended upon him recalling his whole new persona.

He climbed down from the truck and went into the office. The officer took his papers and scanned his passport, without looking up. He said, 'First time in Greece, driver?' He confirmed that this was the case and added a friendly, 'In fact, officer, it is my first time in any place in Europe, so I will have to take a picture.'

'No pictures at the Border Post, sir. Wait till you're inside Greece. First time you say. Well in that case just wait here a minute while we make further enquiries. Leave your truck keys on the desk. We will be giving it a spot check for contraband. How many cigarettes have you with you? Any alcohol?'

‘I am not carrying any of these items. I do not smoke or drink, in any case.’

‘Are you carrying anything else with you apart from the consignment load? Are you carrying anything for somebody else? What do you know about the load you are carrying?’

‘No’ said Yusef, ‘the only items are the two Atomisers that I have to deliver to Norway, just as the papers state. You can check anything you want.’

‘How long is your visit and where will you be staying while you are in Europe. Do you intend to work while you are here?’

‘No, officer, my only reason for being here is to take the load from my factory to our customer in Norway, at the other side of Europe. My only work will be driving the truck there and back, which will take me about two weeks,’ he replied.

At that point he noticed that the guards had untied the tarpaulin and a large black Labrador dog was in the cab, under the flatbed and on top of the flatbed, sniffing everywhere as he went. The guards signalled to the officer and he stamped his passport and waved him on his way, with a quick reminder to ensure that his load was fully tied down before he left the Border Post.

He was through, into Europe and there was nothing else to stop him from completing his task. Next stop was the shipyard in Burgas, to collect the mysterious load. He turned on the cab radio and spent the next few moments fiddling with the tuning control until he found some Greek instrumental music. The presenter had said that the folk music being performed was from Northern Greece and a number of instruments were to be played during the rendition – the bouzouki, laouto, oud, souravil and toubeleki. Yusef listened intently, had understood none of the language but his fingers started tapping the steering wheel as he drove along the dusty road.

....

Within the interior of the Border Post at Kastanies, the duty officer Barak Alexopoulos was starting his break, having just waved through the Turkish truck, the one with the agricultural load. Something was not sitting well with him. What was it? His papers all checked out. The manifest matched the export licence. The sniffer dogs had had a good search of the truck cab and the load, so what was niggling him?

A few moments later Barak shot up in his seat, having had a Eureka moment. He had these from time to time, but after all, he was Greek! It was the driver. What company in their right mind would send a driver all the way across Europe, if he'd never been out of Turkey before? It was idiocy. They'd surely try the guy out on a smaller journey first. There must be something dodgy about one or more of the load, the truck or the driver. He must be stopped and a fuller process gone through.

He dashed into the corridor and headed for the door marked 'Interpol.' His colleague in Interpol, Theo Adamos, looked up from the load of work already piling up on his desk with a pained look on his face. Every time the officer entered the room it was only adding to his workload, but he said 'Well what can I do for you today, Barak?'

Barak said 'I have just stamped for a truck heading out of Turkey, bound for Norway, at the other end of the European Union and I have one of my feelings. We need your authority and that of the State Police to stop it and make another more detailed search.'

'Well, if there is something being carried, like arms or drugs or contraband of some fashion, like cigarettes or alcohol, the search would surely have pinpointed them. Could they have been hidden, in the frame of the truck or in behind door panelling, or even within the payload?'

'Well maybe,' said Barak, 'but we can't check everything, just act on our hunches and I have a hunch about this one. I'll speak to the dog handler again and see if he thinks the same. I'll be back in a minute.'

The dog handler had not noticed anything suspicious in the load. He'd looked in the tanks and opened the control panels. He said, 'The dog would have picked up anything, so if there was something it had to be embedded in the truck. Look, there's another dog handler who is based further up the road at the old border post, you know the mothballed one, at Sironiakos as the road passes into Bulgaria. It's about thirty minutes away. How much time have we got? We could have another look there, just to be safe and even fit a satellite tracker.'

Barak rushed back into the Interpol Office and went over his findings. Theo told him to make the stop. It would be tight but hopefully they'd catch him, make another search and then wave him on his way again, but this time with a satellite tracker fitted.

'We can then sit back, relax, and watch the dot move across our screens. Every stop he makes can be monitored and if we hear of any tie up along the way, through our European wide intelligence, we can do something about it, wherever and whenever. I'll also give my controller, the delectable Inspector Bucheron, a quick shout. I'd normally email headquarters to let them know but her French accent drives me into naughty thoughts every time she calls.' said Theo.

....

He nearly didn't notice the officer running across the road, signalling him to stop, just as he approached the old border post at Sironiakos. He jerked himself back into fully alert mode and braked sharply to a halt some ten metres beyond the officer. 'What on earth? I should not be getting stopped here. What is happening? I have nothing to hide. The last stop was thorough.' Yusef thought. 'Maybe it's my passport!'

The officer walked towards him, right hand on his hip by his pistol and left hand on the leash of the straining black and tan Alsatian dog.

Yusef wound down the cab window and looked meekly at the officer.

'We are carrying out random stops today, driver, and so I would like to check all your documentation and your cargo. Pass me your papers please, the cargo documentation and your export licence. There is no need for you to get out of the cab just yet, but if I call on you to do so please follow my instructions,' said the officer.

Yusef looked at him blankly, shrugged his shoulders and lamely asked, in Turkish, 'What are you saying? I don't understand.'

The officer sighed and repeated the instruction in Turkish, Yusef nodded and smiled at the officer.

The stop had worked. The officer looked at all the paperwork, as though he had a real need to, walked all round the truck, looking up and down, undid the tarpaulin and briefly inspected the load at each side, then at the rear of the truck, out of sight of the driver's wing mirrors. He let the Alsatian off the lead and the dog patrolled all around the cab and flatbed, sniffing hurriedly as she went. While the driver was distracted by the dog he removed the matchbox sized magnetic tracker, set it to 'ON', checked the code of 2020GR312 was flashing a dim red on the screen and attached it to the underside of the truck chassis, beside the rear light cluster.

He asked Yusef to step out of the cab, which he did and ordered the dog into the vacated space. He let the sniffing continue for a minute, then called the dog back out. He handed all Yusef's papers back to him, thanked him for his patience and sent him on his way.
The tracker would be blinking on a screen on a computer somewhere in the world, another statistic for law and order.

....

In her office in Interpol headquarters on Quai Charles de Gaulle, in Lyon, France, Bernadette Bucheron's attention was brought to the red light on the top of her handset. She knew that this would be an external call patched through the switchboard. She lifted the handset and answered the call.

'Oui, this is Bernadette Bucheron, how can I help you? Will I continue the call in English, French or some other language?'

The caller replied 'Bonjour Bernadette, and if it's all the same we could continue in English. It is Theo Adamos, one of the Greek representatives. I think that I have something for you. I happened to be in one of our offices within the border post between Turkey and Greece, at Kastanies. It is a busy crossing point for Turkish freight passing to the European Union.'

'Yes Theo, I am familiar with the location.'

She was never one to stand on ceremony or chat about the time of day or other fritter. She dealt in facts and logic. Nothing else seemed to excite her. Bernadette was a very attractive woman, early thirties, athletic build, with soft, fair shoulder length hair and intense pale green eyes. There was always a man ready to seduce her, but she was more interested in solving crimes. Some in the office said she didn't sleep, never mind having enough time to sleep with a man! Her dedication to her role was held in awe. Once she was on a case she followed it doggedly through to the end, to whatever part of the world it took her.

'Well', said Theo, drooling at her accent, 'One of the Border Post officers called on a hunch regarding a truck leaving Turkey, bound for Norway. To be more accurate it is destined for Bergen with a manifest of agricultural machinery. There was nothing unusual about the load and it came through with a clean bill of health after the usual search and action by the sniffer dog for contraband or drugs.'

‘So why are you making this call Theo? What disturbs you so much that you interrupted my busy day?’ Bernadettte said grumpily.

‘Well the officer who brought it to my attention said that the driver had a clean passport, unstamped, and had never been outside of Turkey before, never mind all the countries he would cross to get to Norway. He wondered why a company would send a greenhorn all that way. On reflection I thought the same, so I ordered that he be stopped again at the Bulgaria / Greece border, even though we do not need to, being inside the EU. We’ve gone over the vehicle again to see if we could flush something out, and under the cover of the search, fitted a satellite tracker to the underside of the vehicle. It’s a flatbed truck, red and green livery, Fiat Ducato standard cab. It’s carrying two agricultural Atomisers, according to his manifest, fully built. He is carrying a small bag for clothes and other essentials for his journey. He is not carrying a mobile phone, laptop or other electronic device, just a European Road map. His cab is not fitted with a company tracker either.’

‘Okay Theo, thanks for the information. Nice and precise, just how I like it. Why did you not just log it electronically and we would have picked it up from there?’ said Bernadette.

‘Well I thought it better to speak with you in the first instance, then log it later.’ replied Theo, as he thought, ‘Oh how I do love that sensuous accent of hers. You don’t get that in an email, and anyway, if this kicks off into something worthwhile chasing, then we'll speak again, hopefully.'

'That's fine Theo. I'll check the tracker on screen. What is its tag?'

'It's 2020GR312, Bernadette.'

'Merci beaucoup Theo,' and she replaced the handset. The light went out and she returned to the caseload on her laptop.

Yusef inwardly sighed, fastened his seat belt, started the engine, engaged first gear and gave the officer a quick wave. There was really nothing to worry about, but the guy back in Dispatch hadn't told him about any random stops along the way, and neither had Fatima or Ardavan. He hoped that this would be the end of checks for the day, as he still had the detour to Burgas to make.

Three hours later he drove up to the shipyard entrance barrier. He dismounted from his cab, stretched, then ambled over to the guard in the gatehouse and asked for his contact, Aleksander Chavdarov. The portly gatekeeper, combed his fingers through his dark, greasy hair and gave him a lazy look, puffed out his cheeks and blew slowly through his lips, before turning around and making a call from the handset sitting next to the steaming coffee cup and the small bottle of vodka.

He turned back around, pointed to the truck, made a walking sign with his fingers and then pointed at the clock above his head and put up three fingers.

'Okay,' thought Yusef, 'I guess that I'll go sit in the truck again for a while.' The barrier remained down.

Aleksander arrived at the barrier a few minutes later, signalled to the gatekeeper to open up and climbed into the cab. He said under his breath in Kurdish 'Welcome Yusef, we will not speak any more. I will use sign language, as I cannot be seen to speak Turkish or Kurdish and you know nothing of Bulgarian lingo.' They drove forward through the upraised barrier.

Yusef's companion in the cab steered him right and left through the shipyard and into a workshop lined with plates of steel, all kinds of piping and trolleys of welding bottles and hoses. There was a curtained welding booth at the back of the workshop and it was to that point he was finally directed.

Aleksander hopped out of the truck, had a quick look around, then drew back the front curtain of the booth and beckoned the truck in. Yusef inched forward and the curtain was drawn shut behind him.

'Come out,' whispered Aleksander. 'Remove the tarpaulin quickly. I have to get to the two tanks and insert a package into each one.'

Yusef complied with the instruction, unlashed the tarpaulin and threw it back a bit for easy access to each tank. His fellow Kurd jumped up onto the flatbed and opened up both tank lids and pointed to the white plastic wrapped bundles lying on the floor on a piece of clean marine plywood. 'Give me those up, one at a time.' Again, Yusef complied. Each bundle was not particularly heavy and he stretched up to hand over the first package. As Aleksander placed it into the vessel Yusef noted that they were virtually invisible in the white polyethylene shell. Aleksander turned back for the second package, inserted it, then closed each lid firmly. He jumped down from the flatbed and they both swiftly re-arranged the tarpaulin and lashed it down to the chassis. Nothing looked different. The lashing looked the same all round. The load would pass a surface inspection quite easily, but if somebody opened up the tanks, what would they find?

Aleksander waved Yusef back into the truck and they tracked through the shipyard again, back to the greasy gatekeeper's lodge. Aleksander hopped out, produced a small bottle of vodka from his overalls pocket and entered the lodge. The barrier rose and Yusef was on his way again. The two men remaining in the gatehouse gave small waves and the gatekeeper raised his coffee cup in salute. The whole process had taken a little under thirty minutes.

As he left the shipyard confines and headed back through the industrial buildings he saw the sign pointing to Sofia and headed on to the main road. He knew that the city would be about four hours away. He had left at 09:30 that morning and it was now 19:30. He'd managed to have a bite at his first border post stop, while they checked over his truck. He'd kept himself watered and dewatered on his journey. He was tired, but he realised that he had been in Europe for just two and a half hours of the eight hours allowed in any one day on the road under the confines of EU rules. He could still make up some of the detour time lost if he continued towards Sofia. He decided to put some more kilometres on the flatbed odometer and see how he lasted, but he would need fuel soon.

He stopped at a fuel station and then motored on along the A1, which was beginning to shed traffic left and right as the commuters went home from Burgas. Just under an hour later he took a right off the main road into the sleepy enclave of Zavoy and found a small pension, close to FTV Enerdji, for the night.

When he awakened he ate a hearty breakfast, paid the little old lady and walked out to the truck for another leg of his European journey. He was thinking that in this flat agricultural landscape they could be doing with two spray Atomisers. It was eight o'clock in the morning. He walked around the truck, checking tyres, for any fluid leaks, and the tarpaulin covers. He even slackened one strap off and looked under the tarpaulin, just to make sure his load had not been tampered with.

……….

Back at her desk in Lyon early that morning, Bernadette Bucheron sat down with her black coffee and croissant ready to start her day. She checked the logs that had come in during the night watch and noted down those that were of interest to her. There were numerous logs, some of which were noted within her speciality of drugs, people trafficking and smuggling, using any form of transport. The remaining actions would be processed by her colleagues.

She had a daily routine and so she went methodically through the tags on the satellite trackers spread across the European Union. There were hundreds, and each one could be a separate crime, a linked series of crimes or simply a hunch that turned out to be a completely innocent incident. By mid morning she had scanned them all and set out to try and computer match the top twenty. There was also one that stood out, a fresh one. That was 2020GR312, tagged at the Turkish / Greek border on a hunch. The route was from Bursa in Turkey to Bergen in Norway. She investigated if the route was a normal one and found that there was trade between the two countries and that loads did travel between them in the type of agricultural machinery listed in the manifest. But the tracker had shown that, instead of taking a direct route from the border to the West, it had deviated from the normally defined route, to Burgas, a coastal town in Bulgaria. Why would it do that? There was nothing on the manifest that needed a second pick up. She checked the log again to be sure and then took action to move the tracker up into the top twenty. She had a hunch, just like her colleague at the Border Post.

....

Back on the A1 headed for Sofia, Yusef passed Plovdiv by 9:45, half way to Sofia, and stopped at a truck stop. He got out and stretched, locked up his cab and went to the toilet. He ordered a couple of pastries and coffee from the stall and sat on one of the benches to eat and rest his eyes. It was a bright sunny morning. He was pleased that he was travelling West and not East, with the rising sun in his eyes. He thought that the road was always looking more scenic when the sun was shining from over his shoulder, but it did affect the view in the cab's wing mirrors. He saved one of the pastries for later, then he carried out his inspection of the truck again and decided that a truck check should be repeated from now on, at every stop he made. The cargo was crucial, after all.

He jumped back in and set off out of the truck stop, joining the traffic fluidly and hit his steady maximum cruising speed once more. As he made his way to Sofia, the traffic intensified and his speed had slowed to accommodate the slower and larger trucks and the lack of overtaking opportunities afforded to him, even though the Ducato had a decent acceleration to squeeze into the breaks in traffic, as his load was not particularly heavy. The time was twelve noon as he made his route change on to the ring road to the south of Sofia, the Bulgarian capital city. He decided to give it another hour at the wheel and have another break. He'd covered three hundred and fifteen kilometres so far.

An hour later he had reached Pirot in Serbia. The journey from Sofia had been easy, with another ninety kilometres below his belt. 'Another one to two hundred kilometres would be possible today,' he thought. 'That would put me on track at the least and maybe a little bit ahead of schedule, if the guy back in Dispatch was right.' He pulled in to the first truck stop that he found and turned off the engine.

His journey from Bursa, through Istanbul, the corner of Greece and into Burgas, to Sofia and to his stop in Pirot had covered fourteen hundred kilometres and he'd been in four countries so far, three of them European and he still had not taken his promised photographs for the guys back in the factory. He sipped from his water bottle and chewed a couple of sweets, went for his time behind the bush and then checked his load once more. It was fine, no straps to tighten. 'Time for a pastry and an amble out of the cab to give my legs a stretch,' he murmured to himself, looking up at a crow, beadily eyeing up his pastry as he munched away.

……….

The log showed Bernadette that the tag was moving along the route first spoken about by the trucker. Maybe the trucker was just visiting somebody in Burgas. She decided to pass it on, in the log, and mark it for a clandestine search later in the planned journey, if there were no other deviations, otherwise she would instruct a fully detailed search of all component parts, and the physical elements of the truck itself. Whatever was maybe in, or on, the tracked vehicle there was nothing to show that 'it' was being hidden. But she had often discovered that things were often hidden in plain view, so to speak.

……….

The next leg of his journey, the one hundred and sixty kilometres to Cuprija took him two hours, passing along the trunk road swiftly and just stopping for the tolls. He was tired and so he headed off the fast road, looping up and over the main A1/E75 route, on to route 160 and in to the town. He noticed the fuel station on the right, Lukoil Autoput, and he drove into the forecourt and stopped at one of the many diesel pumps available.

He selected the nozzle and filled the Fiat up to the brim. As he went to pay he asked the cashier, using his usual sign language of his head and hands resting on a pillow, of any pensions in the area.

The girl behind the counter was very helpful and shouted to one of her colleagues, who relayed to her a couple of names and proceeded to write them down for her. As she handed Yusef the paper he thanked her, then pulled his map from his pocket and pointed in all directions of the compass. He offered the map, but she saw that it was at too large a scale to be of any use, so she drew a quick sketch of how to get to the first on the list. With that, she looked over his shoulder, saw that a queue was beginning to form, pointed to her right and sent him on his way.

The place that she had indicated was not far off down the road, on the right hand side. As he pulled in it seemed a bit more upmarket for his needs and parking the truck would not be easy, but he'd simply find somewhere else for the truck close to it. There were a few cars already slotted in to the parking area directly outside the small hotel and he drew up in the truck, half in and half out of the roadway. He locked up and went in with his small travel bag in hand. Reception advised him that a room was available for the night, with a bathroom and he would be able to park his truck out back in the service yard for the business there. She would phone the boss and tell him that he would be coming in the next five minutes. Yusef was shown to the room, laid his bag on the bed and hurried back outside to attend to the Fiat's bed for the night. Where his room was situated he could look directly out on to the yard.

He laid down on top of the bed and fell instantly asleep. He woke with a start after napping for a while, rose and showered, changed his shirt, pants and socks, washed his sets of the last two days and hung them over the bath. Maybe a hotel was a good idea after all. He rummaged for his small camera in his bag, grabbed his wallet and sunglasses and headed off down, picked up a town map in Reception and out of the door, turning right, to find somewhere to eat. A short stroll took him to a pizza restaurant, just what he was needing after his long drive. Day two was done. He'd check the route map later, back at the hotel, but for now Cuprija was his to tour and maybe the opportunity for a picture or two, before the light faded.

He wandered through town, past the stadium, opted to turn left down a side street onto a street marked Ive Lole Ribara, which took him out close to a bridge with yellow metal railings. 'A photo opportunity, maybe.' mused Yusef, but no, nothing exciting to see there. Over the bridge he took another right, which took him past a School of Nursing and then across another bridge over the stream towards a school, and eventually back on to route 160 and back to his hotel. All light had faded, to hide the nondescript town. And still no pictures.

Day three of his journey commenced earlier, at 07:00, with a quick shower and breakfast, before he picked up his truck from the yard. He had woken up twice in the dark hours of the night to visually check his load from the hotel room window on the first floor and all had looked fine. He would give it the once over before he drove off though. From his map reading the previous night he reckoned he would pass through what was left of Serbia, and be heading through Hungary. His first stop of the day, for his morning break would be in a truck stop just past Belgrade, the Serbian capital.

He was enjoying the drive better as he passed through Serbia, It was more appealing scenically than the plains of Bulgaria. Traffic was steady and there had been road works not far north of Cuprija, which had held him up for a short time, as the lights sequenced between red and green. That would eat into his daily drive time, he thought, even though for much of the time he was stationary. The music on the radio was changing as the signals from the previous stations on his journey faded, crackled and hissed.

Yusef had to re-tune frequently to get musical broadcasts, as the talk shows were meaningless and none seemed to be in Kurdish or Turkish. Four hundred kilometres from Cuprija he arrived for another stop in Szeged. He'd decided for a change to drive into the town, rather than look for a truck stop and be away from the continual hum of the traffic. He hoped that he could make Budapest, the Hungarian capital, by nightfall.

He hooked off the E75 Euro route on to route 55 and headed into town, past a small airfield where a two-seater plane was taxi-ing to the end of the runway, alongside the rusting railway tracks and across the main line level crossing. On his left a water tank rose high into the air. He passed some industrial units and then he was into suburbia with flatted developments. The rusty rail track gave way to a modern suburban system, with station platforms, alongside the road. Still he headed in and a tram passed on his left down the centre of the dual carriageway.

The centre of the town was nice and the heritage could be seen in the buildings. The facades were neatly painted, the stonework nicely pointed, a feeling of wealth about the place. He'd gone as far as he could. He'd reached a dead end, at a river promenade, the river Tisa, as he would later find out. There was enough room to park the truck and also a short drive to an ornate entrance gateway, which he could use to turn and get back to the E75 route.

Yusef looked forward to an hour of a break. He had spotted a baker's shop a short distance back and he locked up, gave a cursory glance around his load and set off for his lunch-time snack.

....

The buzzer on Bernadette's desk alarm went off in her ear. There was a tracker movement that did not ring true. She glanced up at her computer from the mountain of paperwork in her In Tray and looked at the screen. Tag 2020GR312 was flashing. It had indicated a stationary vehicle, but Bernadette noticed that it was off the main highway and off on a side road in the centre of a town.

Szeged was the location, when she zoomed in, just by the river. Why the stop? Why not use a truck stop? Was it another pick up or a drop off? She logged the incident right away and marked it 'URGENT – COVERT CHECK REQUIRED'

Colleagues in Slovakia and Germany noted the log and asked their bosses what should be done. The Slovaks decided that they could not cope with that particular track at the time and handed it over to the Germans, who had better resources for covert checks.

....

Yusef returned to the truck, went past it and on to the promenade, by the river. It was gloriously warm in the sun but cooler in the shelter of the buildings.

The street was lined with trees and birdsong filled the air.

As he walked with the sun on his back, he felt good. This was photogenic and he was glad that he had grabbed his camera and stuffed it in his jeans pocket as he left the cab. He climbed the steps on his left, thinking that the bridge up ahead would be accessible. As he poked his head above the bridge parapet wall it was clear to see that pedestrians could cross and there was a sign saying 'Erzebet Liget Park, 200m.' He took a chance that it was a park for leisure and not some kind of industrial park and crossed the bridge, taking a couple of shots north and south as he went. A burst of greenery appeared in front of him as he topped the camber of the suspension bridge and he strolled down. Directly in front of him the roadways split left and right and the gate to the park was in the centre.

The foliage was dense, but interspersed with pools of sunshine beaming down, their rays catching the insects as they floated around between the trunks. He found a quiet spot in the sunshine and sat down on the grass and had his lunch. An hour later he was back in his cab, having checked his load, the radio was on and his next and last stop of the day, EU hours rule permitting, would be in or around Budapest.

The final piece of his journey that day went to plan, without interruptions to his journey. The E75 was thankfully clear of road works and he made the one hundred and seventy five kilometres in a little less than two hours. His stop at Szeged had refreshed him considerably and he felt that he could maximize his journey time allowed. His bed for the night was at a roadside lodge for truckers, just before Gyor. There was a fuel station with the CMV logo he'd seen on his travels, a small shopping mall and some night beds with communal toilets and showers. He was still in Hungary, but would certainly get through Slovakia and hopefully Czechia and into Germany in the course of the next day, day four of his long and wearisome journey across the continent of Europe.

....

In London, Vicky Douglas had seen the marker put on a vehicle passing through Europe and logged it in her own system. She made a mental note to discuss the three events in her head with her dear husband, Paddy, the next time they had free time together.

She had three entirely different things to consider, but as Bernadette Bucheron had said, they might be linked. She had a potential killer following her husband's second-in-command, a Bosnian munitions expert talking about an attack on London and a tracker on a vehicle heading from Turkey to one of Britain's neighbours, Norway. Was it far fetched? Time would tell.

11 Tracking the package

It was nearly two months before Felek received the second call, advising him to travel to Lerwick, in the Shetland Islands, by train and ferry, under his trade as a musician and arrange accommodation in a Bed and Breakfast. He replied that he could do better than that. He could enquire if he could stay with his friend, who he had met at a festival of music, a fellow violin player whose home was in Lerwick, a major hub for violin players, or fiddlers as they were known locally. He knew that his friend was not travelling for at least six weeks as he had just texted to tell Felek that he had been on the wrong end of a bullock and had a broken leg. He'd laughed about it and said that it was a good thing he didn't play drums, but he'd manage the fiddle sitting down.

The idea was good. Felek would travel up and spend some time with his friend Michael Lawson and play a tune or two together on the fiddles. Maybe they could compose something together, music for violin and a fitting reflection of this strange world.

The call came to Felek with a date to arrive in Lerwick. He had already investigated the travel arrangements needed and so went immediately on line and booked a train to Aberdeen, and a matching ferry onwards to Lerwick.

....

Yusef rose, washed, ate a breakfast of porridge and toast with coffee, then checked his route and his load, loosening and tightening all the straps and was on the road by seven. He would have until four thirty in the afternoon to max out his time. He didn't know that the little box magnetized to his vehicle's chassis was still operational, putting his every move over the ether and showing as a small red dot on a screen, quite some distance away, in Lyon.

As he pulled away into the slipstream of the articulated lorry as it swept by he wondered how his day would turn out. 'Would I get a free and uninterrupted run through Slovakia and Czechia today? I'd better not wish or something will happen,' he thought.

Was it fate that morning? The clouds had rolled over about one hundred kilometres into his journey, the skies darkened and the rain poured down out of the heavens. The rain turned the road into a river and Yusef could feel the drag on the steering as he drove on through it and the lightness on the wheel from time to time as the Fiat aquaplaned. He slowed his speed, ever watchful of the passage of vehicles in front which were all slowing down to suit the conditions.

Between the darkening of the day and the continual spray, driving was getting more treacherous and his speed was slowing further. Suddenly he was aware of hazard lights ahead and traffic blocking all carriageways. He swiftly braked to a stop, pulled in to the verge as far as he could and applied his own hazard lights. Thankfully the traffic behind him was just as alert and not speeding and didn't crush him. Traffic was at a standstill and so he switched off his engine and waited. In time, through the gloom of his misting windscreen he made out the uniform of a policeman striding purposefully up to his cab. He rapped on the window and Yusef rolled it down far enough to hear what the officer had to say but not enough to let the worst of the rain in to the cab. The officer, upon realising that the driver was not conversant with his own language, indicated that there had been a crash and pointed to his watch, circled the dial and raised two fingers. Yusef took it to mean that he would not be going anywhere for two hours, wound up the window and settled down in his seat for a long wait. At least the officer didn't want to check his load.

'So much for my schedule today! I can still do the hours, but I wonder if the EU rules will allow me. Better to be safe and take off a couple today. I don't want any reason to be impounded for disobeying the rules. They're bound to look at the load then,' he muttered. He was getting used to his own mutterings, after all he had nobody else to speak to. He made a mental note to telephone the factory at his next stop to let them know of the delay.

He was stuck somewhere on the road, just past Bratislava in Slovakia, as he'd chosen to miss out the eastern corner of Austria. He'd go there on the way back.

As it happened, it was nearer eleven o'clock before the traffic was moved on slowly past the scene of the problem. An articulated truck had veered across the carriageway and shunted two passenger cars head on. The emergency services were still there in the form of police and fire engines and the essential metal cutters. The roofs of both cars were off, the occupants already taken away. The convoy of vehicles slowly gathered speed, marshalled in the front by a car with blue flashing lights. The heavy downpour had abated into steady rain, but nothing that would prevent him motoring on at near top speed for the truck. He had not prepared for such a long stop so he needed a toilet break and something to eat, buy some more water and some sweets.

....

The tracker had set the alarm off again. It was set to monitor any stops, as well as any deviations set. Bernadette was on to the two hours of no movement in the middle of the day in a flash and logged the event as 'URGENT _ CONDITIONAL STOP _ REPORT REQUIRED IMMEDIATELY'

Her colleague in Slovakia noted her alarm and, despite what his boss had said, went to check. He was aware of bad weather forecast for the region and within minutes he had an update from the local emergency services about an accident at the position on the highway. He chose not to log the incident but phoned Interpol in Lyon. He was patched through to Inspector Bernadette Bucheron and said, 'You posted an alarm on 2020GR312. I can advise that it has been checked and I believe that the tracker is likely caught up in a traffic incident at the location. Do you want us to check first hand on whether the tracker is involved in the incident?'

Bernadette thought for a moment and then replied, 'No. I will check for movement shortly and then get back in touch when and if needed. Thanks for your quick response.'

....

Brno was too far away and getting to Prague that day seemed too distant. Yusef passed a roadside sign indicating a fuel station in thirty-five kilometres, so he stuck it out and pulled in. He checked his load and tyres, cleaned the mirrors, checked under the hood for windscreen water, saw that it needed to be replenished, so added some screen wash to his list.

The first thing to do was to find a payphone and he found a row of them in the corridor to the toilet block.

The factory receptionist took the call from him and patched him though to Dispatch. 'Hello this is Behwan here, Behwan Fidan. I'm on my way to Bergen in Norway with a load. I think that I've been making good progress, but I lost two and a half hours today as there was an accident.'

‘An accident? Are you hurt? Is the truck damaged? Is the load in one piece?’ said the voice at the other end of the line.

‘Oh nothing like that. There was an accident that stopped the traffic and held me up, that is all. The load, the truck, and me are all fine. I just wanted to tell you that I have been delayed, that’s all. I thought that you might have to let the customer know that I might be late with the delivery.’

‘Ah well, Behwan, don’t worry about it, these things happen all the time. Where are you, as a matter of interest?’

‘I’m at a place called Malacky, in Slovakia,’ he replied.

Once he had done all that he had to do he went back to the truck, replenished the screen wash and water, re-fuelled the vehicle and checked the engine oil. Ready to go once more he accelerated along the entry slip road, back into the traffic stream, back to the mundane life of a trucker.

However, with good speed and no further delays, he saw the boundary signs pass by between Slovakia and Czechia and the sign for Prague came into view. He’d driven up the E50 from Brno and now he needed to get on to the E55, to head into Germany the following day. It was nearing the end of day four. He decided to get on to the route E55 and make a stop at the next available pension or truck stop. He’d travelled another five hundred and fifty kilometres in a little over five and a half hours, but he'd been stopped for another two and a half at the accident.

His maximum shift of eight hours was complete. He'd passed over the Vitava river, by the bridge over the Stivanice island, and then crossed back after the great bend in the river. He saw to his right the beckoning tower of the AandO hotel. He had to go past it, cross the motorway and swing back into the hotel street, but it stood out high on the skyline and already there were a few vans and small trucks parked in the car park. The sign above the door said it was a one star hotel. He firstly carried out his regular check on his truck, booked in at reception and then ate in the hotel café before taking the lift to the thirteenth floor and his bedroom, where he found the amenities basic but comfortable. He relaxed on his bed and checked over the map for next day.

Day five saw Yusef pass into Germany, on to route 14 and on toward Dresden and Leipzig, switching to route 2 at Magdeburg and on to Hanover. He chose to bypass the city and stop on the outskirts. He'd stopped for fuel and once again checked over the truck and his load just before Hanover and had regulated his breaks to the EU rules. He'd another hour of driving time.

After Hanover he would have to head north towards Hamburg on route 7 before crossing into Denmark, the first of his three Scandinavian countries. He felt as though he was on the homeward stretch. The weather had cooled considerably since he'd left Czechia, but the day had brightened. 'The Mercedes', BMW's, Audis and Porches speed past as though I'm standing still,' Yusef mused. 'Was time that important? Could they not look around them as they drove?' He glanced again in his wing mirrors, nobody on his tail. All was going smoothly.

There was a Parkplatz not very far up route 7 with an accommodation block and fuel station. 'That will do nicely,' he thought. He jumped down, stretched and checked all around the vehicle, easing a strap and peeking under the tarpaulin. All was in perfect shape. He tied down again and strode off into the accommodation block with his little bag in one hand and map in the other. The room he asked for was on the second floor, overlooking the parking bay. He decided to wash his smalls in the basin and hung them on the line in the shower and went downstairs to find food, taking his map with him.

It was nearly eighteen hundred kilometres to Bergen. He couldn't do that in a day. He was going to be way behind schedule. The deviation to Burgas and the accident on the motorway had delayed him too much. Ardavan would not be pleased when he made the scheduled call from Hamburg. He had a restless start to his night's sleep. He couldn't fail Ardavan. He had to take a chance on driving more than the permitted hours. He might make it then. He was in dreamland and had no idea what was about to happen.

....

Bernadette had ordered a covert check by her German colleagues at precisely 03:00 hours. Three black clad officers with hoodies, balaclavas and night vision goggles went to work on the truck. They checked firstly that the tracker was still functioning and the serial number was indeed 2020GR312. They had the right truck and proceeded to look under and around the vehicle itself and, from the information in the full maintenance manual that had been scanned before the raid, there were no untoward parts, or additions. Any bodywork changes would have to have been made before the vehicle left the Border Post at Turkey.

They took a note to check the rolling vehicle weight at the next opportunity by a standard vehicle excise stop. By knowing the load weight and the unladen weight they could see what had been done, if anything.

Two got under the tarpaulin, while the third stood watch from a hidden spot close by. They looked at all the machinery and could not, again, see anything different from the component parts in the manual that they had downloaded.

They could not, in the confined space they had to work in, get the tops off of the polyethylene tanks, but their night vision goggles showed up nothing of interest.

They left all as found and returned to base to write up their report on the covert search.

....

Yusef decided to get up very early the next morning and showered, breakfasted and re-fuelled the truck. He was on his way towards Hamburg. It was ten past four. His target was to get over the Norwegian border at the very least. As he rounded Hamburg on the final few kilometres of Route 7, coming to the Elbe river, to the west of the city, he noticed the tower cranes at the docks in the distance, rising higher and higher as he closed on them. The white building of Eurokai loomed up on his left. The overhead gantry warned him to cut his speed to eighty. All along the route, to his left and right were racks high with steel containers and then the blue entrance to the Elbetunnel was ahead.

12 Delivery to Bergen

Egil met Fatima again. She'd phoned him as he was busying himself with the provisioning of Naaskel for the North Sea crossing to Lerwick.

'Hi, what are you up to?' she asked. 'I'm doing my shopping for our trip over to Scotland, Fatima. It's really nice to hear from you. Where are you?'

'I'm in Oslo right now. Remember my friend Felek, from London, the musician?'

'Yeah, I remember you saying something about him. What's the story?'

'Well, I was wandering round Oslo and I had a call from Felek, just for a catch up. I told him what I was doing and he'd said that he'd left his two violas for some repairs, after a concert he played in the city. He'd heard that the guy at Urs Wenk-Wolff in the Frogner area was a particularly good repairer and left them with him. He was going to get them DHL shipped to London when Urs had finished them before he heads to Lerwick with his trusty violin, to meet a friend. I told him that the co-incidence was amazing, as you were also going to Lerwick. I suggested that you meet up. I hope that's okay.'

'Of course, I'll make time to catch up with him. But I don't know him. How would I recognise him? Describe him to me.'

‘Well he’s dark and handsome and plays the violin. He’s a Kurd, like me. I’m sure that he said he was looking forward to playing some traditional music with local musicians in, I think, The Lounge. It’s a bar.’

‘I know The Lounge, Fatima, if he’s there I’ll see him.’

‘I’ve just had another thought! No, a brainwave! Instead of sending his precious violas by DHL to London, why don’t I get them to you before you leave for Lerwick and you can deliver them to him?’ That would be a right surprise and he could even whip up a concerto or two for the locals, as well as play their traditional music.’

Fatima’s soft and alluring tones washed over Egil and he found himself wanting to bend to her every need. He thought that another few hours in her company would be fantastic.

‘Mmmm, well I could, but you would have to bring them to me in Bergen, before Kjell and I set sail. Can you manage that?’

‘Yes of course. That would be wonderful, my darling. I’ll make sure I’m there and in plenty of time to meet the departure time. Are you still leaving on the 1st July? We might even have a bit of time for ourselves too,’ she purred.

‘Yeah Fatima, still the First. Make sure that they are wrapped and protected against any damage and that both are fully waterproofed. I've got some spare dry bags that we can put them into anyway. I presume they are in instrument cases, but bubble wrapping and plastic taped covering would make each thing totally watertight. It can get rough aboard the yacht and water has a habit of getting into everything.'

'Okay I'll do that. I'll also put some manuscripts into the cases, as a surprise for Felek. He just loves to get his hands on new music. There's some Edvard Grieg stuff that I found in Oslo. I'm very grateful and owe you a big hug when I see you.'

While Kjell and Egil had been busying themselves with Naaskel's provisioning, Fatima had motored to the package pick up location in the Laerdal tunnel and worked her timings to perfection. The pick up had to be successful and every rehearsal would help to ensure the success of the operation.

....

Yusef dropped down into the gloom of the Elbetunnel and rose on the northern side, leaving the brown brick façade behind him. His eyes scanned for the next fuel station. He passed the airport turn off and noticed that the gantry speed limit had been cancelled as he left the road works behind. Arrays of white industrial buildings and warehouses followed him along his journey, over railway lines, below flyovers, a myriad of junctions with vehicles leaving and joining his stream. There was a sign ahead for fuel and food and he drew into the slip road and headed towards Marche Restaurant, Holmmoor Ost.

The fuel station was first and he stopped to top up the tank. His nerves were beginning to tug at him. He wondered about his load. What would he say on the phone? A squad car lay up ahead by the restaurant. It was empty.

'Do I look anxious,' he thought, 'Will they be close to the phones? What will I do if they are? Wait? Check my load again? I can't chance looking under the tarpaulin, can I?'

He went to pay for his fuel and as he joined the queue he noticed the newspaper rack. There were copies of the Turkish Hurriyet and Sabah dailies on sale, so he grabbed a copy of both, some more sweets, bottled water and a couple of pastries and paid. No sign of any police, but there was a woman watching him. He kept his head down as he passed her to leave the kiosk and the woman said, in Turkish, 'Hello, are you Turkish?' Yusef was taken aback. How did she know he was Turkish? 'I'm sorry, but I saw your truck, then I saw you buy the newspapers? I'm Turkish too. I've been living here in Germany for a few years now and occasionally I see a truck or car with Turkish plates. I get curious as to where they come from, that is all. I didn't mean to bother you.'

'It's no bother, really. I am Turkish and from Bursa. Do you know it?' replied Yusef. 'Well I have heard of it but I'm from Ankara originally, well, just outside

Ankara. I'm here now, working as a freelance photographer. Do you have time for a chat over coffee?' said the other Turk. 'Not today, I'm afraid. I'm already late with my load delivery due to accidents and traffic, but I have to make a phone call and let my boss know how I'm getting on. It's been nice meeting you. Now I must go,' he said, as he drew away.

He re-parked the truck in the parking area and as he headed for the phones he began to look furtively about him, then realised what he was doing and attempted to get back into the persona of a trucker enjoying his break. He found a booth and proceeded to make his call. After four rings Ardavan answered with his usual line. He replied with 'You know about my grandmother. I have been a bit delayed on my journey, but I am now just past Hamburg, heading for Denmark. Is everything okay?'

'Yes Behwan, all is well with your grandmother, so no need to worry. But there has to be a change of plan. We will work on it and let you know. As you head north, leave the main route towards Denmark and drive in to Kiel. As you do so a red car will follow you, flash you three times from behind and you will pull over. The driver will pull in behind you and ask you to check the rear lights of your truck. While you do so you will be passed a slip of paper with your new instructions. You will shake hands and watch the car drive away before you read the instructions and go on your way. Is that clear?'

He replied that it was and the call was cut at the other end of the line. He made his way back to the truck. The other Turk was sitting on one of the benches outside. He gave her a wave and looked around for the police car. It was gone.

He checked the map. It was nearly seven o'clock and Kiel was two hundred and twenty kilometres away, so he should be there around half past nine. 'I wonder how many red cars I will see before I get there?' he muttered to himself. He thought of a game his father used to play when he was a child. It was called 'I Spy'. He thought it a tad ironic as he journeyed on with a watchful eye.

As he left route 7 for route 215 into Kiel, his regular inspections in his wing mirrors intensified. He'd counted twenty-three red cars on his journey, some had pulled off, some had passed him but for the moment there were none in sight. He passed a couple of interchanges and was then on Schutzenwall. A red car pulled out from a side street into the traffic behind him and a few seconds later he saw three flashes of its headlights. He indicated right and pulled off the main road onto a side street and the red car followed.

The driver got out. Yusef was terrified. It was the woman from the halt outside Hamburg. She strode up to the cab and pointed to the rear of the truck. Their eyes met for an instant. He jumped down and followed her around, where she pointed at his rear light clusters, while she shook her head. 'This must be the signal, but how did she manage it?' thought

Yusef. As he bent down to check the lights a hand was thrust out as if to shake his hand. He noticed the folded paper in her palm and took the shake, smiled, nodded his head and the paper was transferred to his own palm. The woman went back to her car, pulled out from behind the truck and sped off. Yusef got in and out of his cab a few times, looking as though he was checking that his signalling worked and then drove off to find a route back on to the main road, retracing his route into the city.

His mind was racing as he drove in a square to get back to his route, crossed the carriageway and proceeded back along Schutzenwall, slipped on to the route 210 taking him back on to route 7.

....

In the office in Lyon, Bernadette Bucheron had noticed the tracker signal again, and on zooming in to the area saw that there had been another, small, deviation. It had not been enough to bring up an alarm but something was still niggling her. She had read the report from her colleagues in Germany and had concluded that it must be the truck itself and asked for the weighbridge stop to be initiated as soon as possible.

....

The paper had instructed him to arrive at another stop before Bergen, indicating a specific time to arrive. The pressure to get to Bergen was off. He had another day to arrive at his new checkpoint.

On he drove, into Denmark, around Flensburg and Kolding to Nyborg, some five hundred and twenty kilometres from his set off point in the morning. He'd kept to the scheduled EU regulations and had not been delayed, other than his detour into Kiel. He needed to rest but Copenhagen flashed past on his left as he motored on around the city. The Oresund Bridge between Denmark and Sweden beckoned and maybe he would make it to Malmo, by the end of day six of his European journey.

As he approached the causeway there was a police cordon ahead and all commercial vehicles were being ushered in to a side road. Another issue to hinder his travel. As he slowed down and got nearer he saw that each truck was only stopping for a couple of minutes, so he thought that his delay would not be crucial. As he crawled forward it became apparent that it was a weighbridge, presumably to check vehicle weights before they drove on to the causeway.

His turn came and the scales were read. He was waved off without any conversation at all. Everything was still okay. He breathed another sigh of relief.

He crossed the causeway aware of the speeding express train as it sped past him on the adjoining tracks. He passed through Malmo just as his seven hours driving was coming to an end. He would look for a stop for the night. He left Euroroute E20 and continued along the E6 and swept around to the east of the Swedish city. About five minutes on his journey north, away from the city, he saw in the distance, and just off the main route a couple of fuel stations and assorted buildings and soon saw the road signage showing fuel, accommodation and food, so he followed on along the off ramp and turned for the bright lights ahead.

He stopped in the car park of a small travel lodge and went to check out the accommodation. A room was available, again his choice of room overlooking the car park could also be arranged. He took his room key, took the stairs to the first floor to stretch his legs and along the corridor to his room, which was fitted out in very sleek Scandinavian style. He dropped his travel bag and headed downstairs again to check over the cab and load. All was well and he left to return to his room, blissfully unaware that a little red flashing light had disappeared from a screen and showed instead as an orange rectangle with a nine digit code within.

Yusef relaxed, ate and slept well that night. He'd checked his map and had nine hundred kilometres to go to meet his next enforced stop, in Norway, the stop that had been noted on the slip of paper, back in Kiel. The journey would take him around eleven hours to cover the distance through the mountains.

....

In France it was a public holiday, but not for Bernadette. She only had time for a couple of weekends off in a year. She was a workaholic. She was lost in thought when she saw the log pop up on her computer. The search had not proven anything and the weighbridge check had just come up with the answer that the vehicle weight was within range. Any discrepancy could be in the fuel weight or tools on board. Despite that she still had a hunch that kept pinging in her mind.

....

The following day saw Yusef cover six hundred and twenty kilometres to the settlement of Honefoss, in the seven hours available to him. From Malmo he took the E6 Euroroute to Oslo, the Norwegian capital, with the city of Gothenburg in his wake. He'd skipped along the shores of Tyrifjorden as he'd left Oslo and crossed the bridge over Steinsfjorden at Sundvollen. He left the flat farmlands and began to rise from the coastline into Honefoss and to a Youth Hostel that he'd noticed as he drove in. He carried out his usual inspection after he had booked in to a dormitory style room for six and headed in to the centre to find food. He'd check his map as he was eating. It was day seven, Sunday 28th June.

On Monday morning he was back on the road, with a full fuel load, his drinks and snacks and with a must do target of the last leg and his next meeting point at 14:00, give or take 5 minutes. He'd allowed for a full six hours of driving if needed, to cover the remaining distance, so that would mean an average of 45 kms/hr on the calculated two hundred and seventy kilometres distance. It was going to be quite a twisty journey but he should maintain at least 60 kph. Nevertheless, Yusef was determined to see it through when he set off at eight that morning.

He'd decided to take the shorter Route 7 out of Honefoss, rather than the faster, but longer Euroroute E16. He stopped every hour, to check his map and re-calculate his timing. He was ahead of schedule after one hour. Two hours into the journey he joined route 52, which joined with traffic from route 51 and he was still ahead of schedule but the zig-zag bends and the slower heavy traffic was taking its toll on his average speed. After three hours he was well behind schedule and his concentration levels were dropping, so he pulled over to stretch, snack and catnap. When he awoke another hour had passed and he still had ninety minutes run time to the tunnel.

He entered the Laerdal Tunnel, a wonderful feat of engineering, the longest road tunnel in the world, 24.5 kilometres in length. His instruction was to head for the southern exit, but to stop in the third cavern, or rest point, in the tunnel, the one nearest to Aurland on the south side, nearest to Bergen. The tunnel was a tourist attraction, a twenty minute drive, very colourful and with a good flow of traffic passing through daily. Nobody would particularly heed a couple of packages being transferred from a truck to a car boot. The stopping point would be about 15 minutes in and the stop itself would be less than 5 minutes and he would be free to take a proper break and allow the other vehicle on its way. The car would be a dark grey Volvo XC 40 and Ardavan had told him the registration plate details.

....

The tracker alarm went again. This time it had disappeared from the screen. Bernadette's instincts flew up the scale by a number of notches. She immediately zoomed in to the screen position and the tracker blip had disappeared just south of Laerdal in Norway. She checked back the route and noticed that, while she had been at a Regional Crime meeting there had been a number of small disappearances from the screen, but nothing of any significance. The truck had been hidden momentarily as it made its way under the river in Hamburg and she thought it might be signal interference again, due to the mountainous nature of Norway. As she probed further she found that there was a tunnel system, a long one and that was likely the answer. She checked the time of the loss of signal. It was 13:43.

At the designated maximum traffic speed within the tunnel, she quickly calculated that the tracker would be on target at the south end of the tunnel at seven or eight minutes past the hour. She switched on the timer on her phone and watched steadily as she sipped from her coffee cup.

She also made a call to her colleague in Oslo, who told her that his man was actually leaving Bergen, heading for Oslo. He would check exactly where he would be and call back. Within five minutes he had called Bernadette back and said, 'My guy should be at the tunnel entrance on the South side at around 14:00, so we should meet the target coming the other way. I've told him to make all haste.'

'Good. Keep me posted,' said Bernadette and rang off, all attention back on the screen in front of her.

....

The tunnel was brightly lit with the caverns a blue hue with yellow at the fringes. Yusef noted the inspection cameras as he entered, the speed cameras as he went along and the lack of emergency exits. He kept his speed at 60 kph, within the maximum speed of the truck and that which the tunnel authorities had prescribed. His targeted arrival time was 14:00 and his watch showed 13:45. He was on schedule.

He passed two caverns and noticed a fair amount of traffic stopped, with some groups getting out and taking photographs of the scene. Five minutes to go. 'I hope my contact is there,' he breathed. 'I have no other instructions to follow, other than to deliver my load to the farm.'

He motored on and very quickly came across the third cavern and on the right at the tail end of the resting traffic was a grey Volvo. As he neared it he recognized the number and signalled to pull over, drew up behind the Volvo and killed the engine. A bead of sweat trickled down his forehead and into his eye. It was not warm in the tunnel, he thought, and he casually wiped it away.

A woman walked along from the front of the parked cars. She was kitted out in a grey two-piece jogging suit, bobble hat and black trainers. She wore frameless glasses. As she carried on past the truck cab she rapped twice on the window, passed to the end of the flatbed and turned around. Yusef wound down the window and enquired with a shrug of his shoulders. 'What did you tell me about my grandmother?' he said in Kurdish. The girl replied, 'You know they are no longer alive Yusef,' and moved to untie the tarpaulin straps on the side away from the traffic. She then went to the Volvo and opened the boot, scattering some clothes to one side.

He jumped from his cab and leapt up to pull the tarpaulin back from the loosened straps and unscrewed both Polyethylene tank lids. He removed the first package and the woman took it from his grip and placed it carefully in the car boot, returning to retrieve the second of the pair and also placing it in the boot. Her final act was to cover both packages with the spare clothes. The nearest security camera was at the end of the cavern and its line of sight was shielded by both the open hatch of the Volvo and the open cab door of the truck. To the casual observer the driver was checking his load, a very sensible thing in the twisting and winding roads of the region.

The woman closed the boot, gave a cheerful wave to Yusef, got in to the Volvo and drove off down the tunnel, towards Bergen, about two and a half hours away.

He replaced the lids, pulled back the tarpaulin and once more secured his load, breathing a big sigh of relief. He had done his bit, had helped the cause and wondered about the load he had transported once more. After another twenty minutes, his scheduled EU Rules break was over and he was off out of the tunnel on the Ausland side and heading for the farm beside Bergen.

....

The Interpol driver did not pay much attention to the grey Volvo as it passed by on the opposite carriageway. A couple of minutes later he had come across the red and green truck in the first cavern and he had pulled over on the opposite side to take a stroll and see what was up. All that he had witnessed was a trucker with his eyes shut, a typical scene on any road he had driven. He returned to his vehicle and drove off down the tunnel, reported to Oslo, who in turn reported to Bernadette. Nothing was amiss.

The tracker lit up again. 2020GR312 was back in action and heading for Bergen. It was 14:31. The truck had taken forty eight minutes to travel a little over twenty four kilometres. Bernadette thought that to be very slow. She needed to check the previous stationary plots on the tracker log. She was tired. She needed to refresh and start again later. It would be at least a couple of hours to Bergen.

13 Package aboard

The following day Fatima arrived back in Bergen and in the evening shared a dinner table with Egil. She asked about his planning for the sail across the North Sea and enquired about Kjell, what he was up to and if his end of the preparations were as far advanced as Egil's.

'He will have had all this worked out in his head. He'll have charts marked up and plans of action written down and stored in the chart drawers, just in case the worst happens, which never does. There's a bit of commercial shipping to miss, some oil rigs and rig supply vessels to negotiate and then some fishing boats and sometimes cruise liners. We'll be kept busy, but the equipment on board will be the latest technology. He's always one for getting the best, but he can afford it.'

'I'll be quite busy with him over the last couple of days as June comes to an end, but if you could get the violas to me at the marina that would be great.'

'I don't want them lying around in the marina just waiting to get damaged so I'd rather you picked them up from the hotel on the 30th, Egil. Also, they're a bit heavier, with the manuscripts inside and the packaging all around. I'll collect the dry bags from you and put the parcels into them and you can pick them up on the 30th, to suit your timescale.'

‘Okay, it’s a deal.’ he said, as she leaned over the table and stroked the back of his neck.

‘Are you seeing me back to my room tonight? I’ve missed you.’

‘I’ve missed you too Fatima,’ said Egil, his mind wandering far, far away from the parcels.

....

At her home in London that evening Vicky pulled up her chair to the long table and looked across at her husband Paddy. ‘Darling, this might interest you or it might not. Funny thing is I’ve got one of my hunches and I’d like to talk it through with you if you don’t mind. We don’t usually do this over dinner, but I feel that, if it’s not over dinner then it will never be talked through.’

‘Go right ahead, my love, it will make a refreshing change to what is going on in my head at the moment.’

‘Well, you know the old adage that things come in threes? There are three things which, taken in isolation I can deal with, but something is irking me on the matter and I can’t fathom out why. You see, it was brought to my attention that – and you might already know about this one – there is a Bosnian munitions expert who was shooting his mouth off about coming into some wad of cash and that the weaponry he’d been working on was destined for this country, and particularly London.’

‘The second is the attempt on Russell Murdoch’s life that went sorely wrong for the perpetrator. He definitely picked on the wrong guy, but was it meant to be you? You were the chosen speaker for the RUSI dinner, not him. He was Director of SAS, not you, so would you have been ready for him in the same way? I’m afraid for your safety Paddy, on this one. The third weirdo in the bunch is a truck that’s travelling from Turkey to Norway with some agricultural gear on the manifest. A colleague, Bernadette, in Interpol, has a hunch about the truck, and you know us girls, once we have a hunch and all that.’

‘She arranged for a tracker to be fitted to the chassis, as we do, and also had arranged for a covert stop and search with sniffer dogs and hand searches in the middle of the night, but nothing is turning up, other than the trucker goes out of his way now and again to deviate from a normal delivery route across Europe. She thinks he’s picking up or dropping off something.’

‘Well Vicky, Military Intelligence has heard about the Bosnian weapons guy. Russell knew of him from his Bosnia deployment. He has a habit of changing sides, as long as the pay is good. He’ll step across any boundary to do a job. In fact we’ve used him ourselves. He’s very good at what he does. The trucker would not have come into my domain. Your point about me and not Russell is a fair one and we are taking steps to raise the bar on personal security.’

‘Do you think there’s a link, Paddy?’

‘I really don’t know Vicky, but I’ll leave that marker up to you. If two merge into one then I’d take immediate action to prevent the third merging, if I could.’

‘Yes, Paddy, that was my take on it, but I’ve issued an ‘Upscale’ ticket on all of them just in case. Better safe than sorry, eh?’

‘Now Vic, I was fancying an early night tonight, maybe a candle-lit soak in the bath to start. What say you?’

‘Another bottle of Chateau Musar red from the Bekaa Valley, please hon. See you upstairs in five?’

....

It was fifteen minutes past five o’clock when Yusef crawled up the farm road toward the farmhouse and neat farm buildings. A black and white sheepdog was waiting for him as he drew to a stop, barking and nipping at the tyres, one ear lopsided and the other erect. A young man in dungarees and waterproof jacket strode out from an outbuilding and strolled to the truck. Yusef wound down the window and offered him the delivery papers, written in Turkish, English and Norwegian. The young man looked at the papers and then back to Yusef with a quizzical look on his weather beaten face, stroking his wispy beard.

....

Bernadette noticed that tracker 2020GR312 was stationary again. She ordered a full piece by piece open search as soon as possible. Oslo was back on in a few minutes. Their man was now two and a half hours beyond Laerdal on his way to Oslo. Bernadette insisted on him returning immediately and involve the local police force as necessary. Oslo replied that they would but that a break would be needed for their colleague as he had been on the road for over five hours. He would also contact the local Bergen Police force, which he did immediately. A Constable on the desk took the call and as nobody else was in the Station he logged it in the activity book. He went off duty later and the log was still active. No colleague had actioned the event, but not through malice, just through over work, as usual.

....

The lad said in Norwegian, then repeated in English that he had no idea what this was about. He didn't know of any load of equipment expected but he would speak to his father, who was having supper. Yusef understood nothing of the statement, other than the worldwide sign of shrug, shaking of head and making off. The load was for here. He had no doubt. He jumped out and started removing the straps holding down the tarpaulin.

The father came out walking gingerly with a stick in his right hand and the papers in his left, waving them in the air. He repeated in English 'No, no, not for me! Take it away!' He kept on shaking his head vigorously.

Yusef took the papers back, shook his head and pointed to the delivery address and the farm name, then pointed to the telephone sign at the top of the delivery note and suggested by hand signals that the farmer phone the factory.

It was 17:30, but 18:30 in Bursa, and the factory would be closed. Yusef decided to leave the farm and telephone the factory the next day and resolve what he should do with the load. The Manager was not going to be happy. He signalled to the farmer that he would do so by imitating a handset and pointing to his chest. The farmer nodded a few times and they went their separate ways. Yusef turned the truck around and retreated back down the farm road to find a bed for the night.

Early the next morning the farmer woke to find the two atomisers at the end of The Llama Farm road. Yusef had decided, without contacting the factory, to offload the cargo in any case, to avoid unnecessary questioning when he returned to the factory, if he ever returned to Turkey. He'd tried to contact Ardavan, to no avail. He concluded that the atomisers were only a screen for the packages and did not hold any value to the mission any more. The farmer would likely take the machinery in any case, once he realised it was not costing him anything.

He also decided upon a different route back, a more scenic route back through Norway. He wasn't on a schedule and he had photographs to take. He never went through the Laerdal Tunnel and never passed the unmarked Interpol car on any part of his return journey towards Oslo.

....

Later that day the farmer was flabbergasted to discover that the machinery had been dumped at the end of the Llama Farm road and so, after he'd checked on the llamas and done all his other chores, the farmer talked the matter over with his wife after dinner. They both decided not to accept the delivery, although it would be a nice gift and they could certainly use them or sell them on. He decided to contact the police in the morning regarding the matter.

....

Ardavan and Fatima never knew that the eyes of Interpol had been on Yusef, ever since he crossed the border from Turkey into Greece. They never knew that Interpol had been checking on the consignment as it passed through the European Member States. They never knew that Interpol had lost the signal in the Laerdal Tunnel for some crucial minutes and they never knew that the Interpol unmarked car, when asked to check the tunnel, passed a small grey Volvo travelling in the opposite direction. They didn't know if Behwan, aka Yusef, had delivered the agricultural goods to the

Llama Farm and that the local constabulary in Bergen were soon to be investigating the load. The tracker had shown that the truck was stopped somewhere south of Bergen.

....

Egil was busy with his provisioning for a round trip and some time around the islands, so water, gas, food, and the inevitable beers and akvavit were loaded and stashed in the lockers. He went to the bank and withdrew the Pounds Sterling they would need while away and stored them in yet another waterproof bag. He checked over the two sets of short cruising boots, bright yellow Helly Hansen overjackets and overtrousers, the offshore trousers, edge boots, hoodies and buoyancy aids. He ensured that their race caps, beanies, sunglasses with lanyards and sunscreen were to hand.

Kjell checked and rechecked Naaskel's instruments. The compass, the auto-pilot, AIS sytem, Raymarine plotter, Speed log, VHF radio and GPS were all listed and ticked off. The safety equipment was next. The two liferafts, danbuoys, flares and fire extinguishers.

Kjell worked away, moving from piece to piece, the warps, fenders, boathook, the inflatable was pressurized and secure, the Yamaha outboard was fired up and mounted to the back board.

He moved down into the saloon again and tested the electrical and mechanical bilge pumps, navigation lights, gas detector and foghorn. The sprayhood and dodgers were ready for use and the final pieces of upholstery and decking safety netting had been placed in position.

The anchor chain, anchor and windlass were lifted and dropped before reseating in cruising position once again. The diesel tank was filled to the brim with two hundred and sixty litres of fuel and the fresh water tank was replenished. The waste tank had been emptied while out of the water and it was checked over too.

Kjell turned over the engine a couple of times and Egil gave him a hand to raise and lower the foresail and mainsail and refold the spinnaker and store it away in the sail locker.

....

The unmarked Interpol car was already chasing down the tracker again as the vehicle sped towards Oslo.

A couple of days had passed before the Sergeant in the local force in Bergen got around to speaking with the farmer and paying him a visit. The Sergeant decided that a crime had not been committed and that the farmer was free to do as he wished. He logged the incident on the office computer when he got back to the police station, remarking to colleagues that he'd never come across something like this before in all his days policing.

The log of other events over the previous two days was then investigated. The Sergeant came across the one about the red and green truck and made the connection. He put out an all points bulletin and the truck was stopped before it had left Norway. Yusef was pulled in and interrogated in a local police station. The truck was X-Rayed and all the panelling taken apart. Nothing was found and the trucker was allowed to get on his way back to Turkey.

....

Late on the afternoon of the 30th June, Kjell gave a nod to Egil and with a flourish raised a bottle of akvavit above his head, two shot glasses between his fingers and shouted, 'That's it, I'm finished. I've broken into the stores already. Let's drink to far away friends and the cruise we're about to do. May Odin watch over us and keep us safe.' He poured out two shots, handed one to his sailing companion and they both shouted at the top of their voices 'Skol .... To Odin... and to Ran...Goddess of the sea....may her daughters, the waves, look after us.' The glasses clinked, the contents rushed down in a big swallow, they leaned towards each other and hugged, a man bear hug.

'Now that only leaves Fatima's parcels. I'll get them now, as Kjell will be off the yacht, looking for a few beers and some dinner,' thought Egil. 'Kjell, I'm going to catch up with Fatima this evening, so off you go and enjoy yourself and I'll lock everything up so we'll be ready for the off tomorrow. How is the weather looking, by the way?'

'Oh the weather is looking reasonable for our crossing. We'll have to tack a fair bit as we start sailing, with the onshore breeze that's forecast, but it will veer in the high pressure and we'll get a good North Easterly that will push us south of the Troll oil field, and above the Frigg gas field. It looks like it's going to change as the high pressure moves, to south easterly. It should take us close to the Oselung and Tune platforms, so we'll have to keep an eye out for oil and gas traffic, but after we've passed them we'll have a bit of clear sailing to Lerwick. Have a good evening, you lucky sod. I wish I was you right now. I'm off for a few lonely beers. See you tomorrow. It's best if we set off at 10:35 to catch the best of the ebbing tide. Night!'
'Night Kjell, don't drink too much and I'll see you at the marina at ten.'

He slipped his mobile from his jeans pocket and dialled. 'Hi Fatima. Can I come round to the hotel and collect the parcels now? Kjell's away to have a few beers at the marina clubhouse and this would be a good time to store them.'

'Yes, of course, that would be great. Just come straight up to my room. See you soon.'

He strode over to his car and headed for the Clarion a short distance away. He raced up the stairs two at a time, rather than waiting for the lift. He thought that he would pick up the parcels in

Reception, but the thought of the bedroom lengthened his stride. He knocked on the door and it was tentatively opened and Fatima peered around the edge.

'Come in, I've been waiting for you,' she provocatively murmured, as her black glossy hair tumbled down over one eye. She put out a hand and pulled him quickly through the door. She feasted on his lips and backed away to the bed and pulled him down on to the softness.

'Mmmm, I thought I'd come here to collect something Fatima! I should get back before Kjell starts looking around in the yacht again. He has a habit of double checking and triple checking. I can get the parcels stashed and then I can be back here without a care in the world…and you can have my undivided attention!'

'Oh Egil, if you must, but be quick about it.' She kissed him again and let him rise from the bed. She pointed to the corner of the room and there were the two dry bags he had given her earlier. He went over and picked the first up. It was heavier than he expected and he looked wonderingly at Fatima. She pursed her lips and with a little shrug of her shoulders said 'They're a little bit heavier than I thought and the manuscripts are a bit bulkier than I imagined once they're all tied up, bubble wrapped and sealed with tape. I hope they'll be okay. I've told Felek that you'll be bringing them to him. He was over the moon. He'd been worrying a bit about how DHL would package and transport them. He said that he'd see you in The Lounge Bar in Lerwick. I've described him to you, but he doesn't like fuss, so no hugging and stuff. Keep that for me.'

He grabbed each bag and Fatima showed him out with a 'See you later. I'll be waiting for you,' and planted another kiss on him.

He arrived back at the marina, removed the packages and stashed them in the under bunk locker in the spare cabin. He carefully locked up and then returned to Fatima and spent a very delicious evening, before hunger of another kind took over. Room service was ordered and they ate, drank and continued where they left off.

....

That same evening, despite that nagging feeling and against her better judgement, Bernadette signed off on the 2020GR312 tracker that had been removed covertly from the truck. The log was complete. 'NO FURTHER ACTION' was recorded in the file. The trail was cold, but her mind still held on to its coat tails. She might use the information on another day.

Vicky Douglas picked up on the tracker log and took a mental note to ask for a list of all the truck stops, planned or otherwise, on the tracker log and discuss them with Bernadette Bucheron in Lyon.

14 To Lerwick

Naaskel cleared her mooring at the marina and motored away from her berth with the ebbing tide. The sailors were on their way.

They passed a mixture of small craft whizzing up and down the channels going about their daily business with easier access to all the little villages hidden away in the coves, some only accessible by water.

The main sheet was loosened, the boom rose and Egil set his feet to pull back and down. The sail rose and the slack was taken up. It was a clean raise first time, there were no wrinkles and a tight enough finish on the winch.

They had set a two hour rota for daylight hours and a four hour rota for sleep, so Kjell had taken Naaskel out of Bergen and Egil alternated with him.

The skipper's preferred route in the onshore wind was on a northerly heading, before turning to port on a north westerly heading, keeping the island of Askoy to Naaskel's port side. Kjell threaded her through the narrows between Askoy and Holsnoy and she was out into the wider sea as they passed the old airfield at Herdia. He ordered the fore sail to be unfurled and Egil set about the task with his usual endeavor. Naaskel continued sailing parallel to the coastal islands to port and then turned into the wide expanse of the North Sea.

As they started their first tack to the south west the yacht began to pound and bang through the stronger waves and Kjell attached his safety line and called for Egil to do the same. He shouted 'Sure, Kjell' but firstly went below decks to get some sandwiches and coffee for the two of them. After a few minutes he poked his head above the saloon stairwell hatch. 'Do you want a break for your grub or will I bring it up to you?' 'Up here will be fine. It's too nice a day to be sitting about down below. And I've got to keep an eye on those two vessels out there, the oil supply vessel and the tanker. We'll have to keep well away in our tacks, especially with one vessel going south and the other going north. Can you keep an ear open for any radio transmissions? I'd like to know that they've seen us in the water, or on their ship's radar.'

Once they were clear of the coastal shipping channels Kjell fixed the Autopilot and they settled into a regular tack on their westward course. The Fulmars, Kittiwakes and Herring Gulls were left behind and they had the sea to themselves. The wind was steady and the log showed that Naaskel was making 15 knots. He reckoned that once the wind veered and was following Naaskel, the next day they would pick up to nearer 25 knots. They were on schedule for a two to three day crossing.

As night fell, the sky cleared of cloud and the half moon lit the sea around them and each wave danced and sparkled. Egil pointed out various constellations above them and his skipper was again amazed by his friend's knowledge of nature. He enjoyed the technicalities of sailing but had relied on instrumentation to tell him where he was. He thought of Egil as a bygone age Viking sailing his square sailed longboat, with a ferocious crew behind him, as he gazed ahead from the dragon's head prow.

Kjell had the first night watch and Egil went below for some sustenance, a couple of beers and a shot of akvavit before retiring to his bunk. His thoughts turned to Fatima and the wonderful night he'd spent in her arms. She hadn't been there to see him off, which he was quite disappointed about. In no time he was fast asleep, knowing that the ever alert Kjell was at the helm.

....

When he roused from his slumber Felek was passing Sumburgh Head and he showered and breakfasted. He'd let Michael Lawson know he'd be coming and Michael had promised to meet him off the ferry and take him over to his house on the Island of Bressay, just across the Sound.

The morning passed incredibly quickly, with Michael and Felek catching up on old times. Michael's wife got them all lunch then Michael revealed that he had a routine appointment at Gilbert Bain Hospital back in Lerwick, so Felek would have to fend for himself for a few hours. He decided to go with Michael over to Lerwick on the ferry.

He wandered about the town, searching out local delicacies, knitwear and silver-wear from the local craft shops, before finding his way again and recognizing some of his haunts from previous trips.

He met up with Michael after his appointment and they had a coffee in the Peerie Café before catching the ferry back over to Bressay. Back at the house, as the clock ticked on through the non-stop chatter across the dining table the talk of music and violins was uppermost. While Michael's wife cleared up, the violins were brought out of their cases and the jamming began. Later, she accompanied them on the squeezebox as Michael introduced Felek to three traditional Shetland Reels, Da Forfeit o' da Ship, Aandowin at de Bowe and Faroe Rum, which they all played with some gusto before the evening was out.

Michael said that they'd have to get over to The Lounge, just up from Victoria Pier in Lerwick the following night and take part in one of the many traditional music sessions that are held in the pub, to which Felek happily agreed.

It was a great session in The Lounge. The pints were flowing freely and the crowd in the bar were exhausted, with hands red and stinging from both applause and keeping time to the music. A few local folk songs were suggested by those wandering in to the bar from time to time. Felek thought that traditional themed music sounded much better than the more choreographed classical pieces he was used to playing. The warmth of the atmosphere was much better than earlier in the day, which was spent on a trip to Scalloway on the Atlantic coast, with the squally rain showers belting in from Iceland.

....

On the dot of four hours Egil was up and out on deck. The air had turned colder and small clouds were moving into view across the horizon. A distant glow in the sky showed the position of a flare stack, way off in the distance.

As they passed over the watch Kjell said, 'Naaskel is on to wind vane steering, so the course tacking will be at its most effective. We'll need to don our wet weather gear come morning as the forecast is for showers or more persistent periods of wet weather. We'll hopefully get a good cooked breakfast inside us before then though. See you in the morning.'

'Okay. Sleep well mate. By the way, any radio traffic to think about?'

'Well there's the usual sporadic stuff from a rig now and then but nothing of any concern. And there's no shipping movement showing up on the radar in our chosen tacking width within thirty kilometres. Enjoy your watch. Goodnight.'

Another day came and, as forecast, so did the rain and battered the sea and Naaskel. Visibility dropped and they strained their eyes as they both watched through it and kept a good look at their instruments. Their cruising speed had picked up in the log to over 20 knots and, despite the weather overhead, they were enjoying the freedom of the seas. The rigging was slapping, the yacht was gently rolling and there was very little banging and crashing from stowed equipment and the waves.

There was a break in the clouds and shafts of sunlight dappled the waters. Egil pointed out a small school of dolphins as they raced in to the yacht and then swished in and out below the prow, their dorsal fins breaking the surface as they took deep breaths before diving away on another fishing mission.

Further on they crossed in front of a large trawler with the LK designation and number, which identified her home town as Lerwick. Their journey was more than half way completed and a couple of beers were broken out to mark the occasion. They passed within a short distance of a number of oil rigs. Their sentry safety boats were sitting idly in the water and their flare stacks clearly visible, sending wisps of heat haze and smoke into the sky above, as it was blown away in the prevailing wind, which was now clearly coming from directly behind Naaskel.

There was no more need to tack, just use full sail and add the spinnaker to further generate speed. Before long the log was showing a rate of 25 knots and the sea had smoothed in front of them as they danced along. More beers were taken up from the locker below and the shipmates broke into song.

At the next shift change Kjell decided that they should take down the spinnaker, as they were going to arrive into Lerwick in the middle of the night. They did that and later took down the fore sail and slowed Naaskel down even further. If the wind held they would be in Lerwick after sun up and could anchor in the Sound of Bressay until it was safe to move into harbour or berth alongside the pier.

As dawn broke smaller fishing boats began to appear and some slight changes of course were needed. The Shetland Islands hove into view and as the isle of Noss drew closer, Kjell decided to use the wind and come up into the Sound of Bressay from the south, so they tacked away to the south west and turned to starboard. They were both out on deck as they rounded Bressay, taking in the rocky stack of The Giant's Leg as they sailed under the mainsail.

As they sailed on to a north west heading they covered the straight run towards Mainland Shetland before dog-legging round The Knab and into the channel. The mainsail was dropped and clipped and Naaskel was brought in under her diesel motor. Kjell knew of the sailing school, which launched from the small beach not far from the lifeboat station and he steered Naaskel towards it, cut the motor and dropped anchor about fifty metres from the shore.

The two sailors tidied and stored all their gear, switched off their instruments and headed to their cabins for a snooze. The harbourmaster and customs would no doubt be checking up on them at the start of their working hours. It had been a good crossing and Kjell thought that it was a lot easier than racing. Naaskel had come through unscathed, too.

Later that morning the harbourmaster called and offered Naaskel a berth on the outside edge of Victoria pier, which Kjell accepted. He was also informed that a Customs official would come aboard before skipper and crew disembarked. The anchor was winched aboard and Naaskel was berthed at the pier. There was a waiting Customs official standing there with a Labrador dog by his side. Kjell was on deck and the official asked him if he was skipper.

....

From across the Sound, on Bressay, a twitcher, a bird watcher, had set up her tripod and camera with its powerful lens. She held a pair of large magnification binoculars to her eyes. It wasn't Snipe, Curlew or Tern she was spotting. She was more interested in what was happening at the yacht, which had berthed earlier. She saw the skipper speaking to the officer with the dog.

....

'I'll get my dog down to you skipper, then I'll come aboard and carry out a search. Then you can get on with your day.' The dog was gently lowered and the officer climbed down to the deck. 'Now firstly, why are you in Lerwick, skipper? Business or pleasure?'

'It's pleasure. In fact it's always a pleasure to come to Lerwick. We've been here on a few occasions, for the Bergen races over the years, but this time it's just a pleasure cruise. We'll likely sail around the islands before we head back to Bergen. But before that we'll meet up with old friends that we've met over the years. John and Katie Stevenson are two of them and he's to meet us at the boat later.'

'Ah, you know John, do you? Well be sure to have a great time. In the meantime I'll have a look round below with Corrie. Anything you're carrying that I should be aware of before I start? He has a very good nose for cannabis and anything stronger!'

'No officer, there's nothing on board that would come anywhere near that sort of thing. He might get a scent of the sea and fresh paint, but that's about all.'

....

The watcher on the far shore continued her vigil, her heart momentarily racing.

....

Kjell shouted below. 'Egil, there's a sniffer dog coming below. You'd better come on deck out of the way. At that, a head appeared and the dog and officer went below. After some tail wagging and jumping up and down the dog detected nothing and the officer disembarked up the gangplank that had been affixed.

....

The twitcher breathed a sigh of relief. Fatima was pleased that the only possible hiccup, apart from the sea crossing, hadn't happened.

....

'Kjell', came the shout from the pier, 'I thought that you'd been arrested, you old bugger.' 'John, Katie, it's great to see you! Wait till I come up to you! Egil! John and Katie are here with a welcoming band!' Kjell laughed.

....

Fatima had one last look at Egil as convivial embraces were made on the far shore. She folded up her tripod and packed away her gear into the satchel. Just another twitcher, going about her business that morning, thought Michael Lawson, as he watched from the bay window on the higher ground behind.

....

The four said their greetings, kissed and hugged and wandered off to John's place for morning coffee and scones. As they walked up John said, 'I saw you come in the Sound earlier. As you know I'm an early riser. I love mornings like these. Come in, we've a lot to catch up on.'

....

Later that day, Michael and Felek were on their way to visit the Viking archaeological site on the south tip of Shetland, at Sumburgh. They'd agreed to pop over to the Lounge again in the evening. He'd arranged to meet some friends there, John and Katie Stevenson.

'I usually meet them in the Boat Club, but when I mentioned that you were here, John suggested that we meet in the Lounge. They'd love to hear you play and you might also be encouraged to play some of your classical or Kurdish Folk stuff as well. I think that would go down a treat. It would be a real surprise for the regular traditional music players too.'

'That sounds like a great idea and I so enjoyed last night. I can't wait to go back.'

The journey to Sumburgh in the big automatic SUV was not very long, but a bit bleak, The occasional green fields were interspersed with brown mossy and heathery hills, with black faced small sheep busily munching whatever nourishment they could get from the treeless landscape.

They arrived at the Jarlshof archaeological dig close to the airport and spent a good hour wandering through the Viking settlement abandoned over one thousand years previously, before returning back up the bleak winding road. By this time, some miniature Shetland ponies had trotted over to the barbed wire fence beside the road so Michael stopped to let Felek take another one of his tourist pictures. As he was doing so his phone rang. It was Fatima.

'Your package has arrived. Arrange the transfer with the guy I told you about.' The call was cut. Michael had not noticed the quick call, as he sat in the car.

....

The two Norwegians had a great morning with the Stevensons and Katie prepared a lovely roast lamb lunch with all the trimmings. Later the three lads headed down to the Boat Club for some beers and yachting chat. John then took the two Norwegians to see his yacht and they pored over it for a while, talking techy stuff.

Katie had arranged to meet up with them later in the evening, for a bar supper at the Boat Club and then they headed over to The Lounge bar to listen to some traditional Shetland music.

'Michael Lawson will likely be here lads. He said he would pop across with a musician friend that he has up from London,' said Katie. She smiled as the three lads weaved their merry way along the narrow street to the bar.

....

Michael and Felek arrived at The Lounge, which was initially quite quiet, but as the evening wore on some session folks came in and settled opposite the bar, ordered some drinks and started to tune up their instruments. A couple of slow airs were played, then a change of tempo into rather maudlin tunes, which were greeted with various nods of approval from the surrounding players, before a short intermission for drinks refills.

Just as everyone in the bar was milling about John and Katie Stevenson arrived in the company of two tall men, one rough and ready looking, sun tanned and blonde and the other older looking and greying around the temples of his dark hair.

'John, Katie!' Michael shouted over to them and they threaded through the throng to their side of the bar. 'Don't get up Michael,' John said, 'I heard that you'd been in the wars. How are you doing now? Are you healing well? Oh I forgot my manners, may I introduce you to two of our sailing buddies from the Pantaenius races, Kjell Nilsen and Egil Hansen, they're Norwegians from Bergen, but you'd likely guessed that already, Michael, by the look of them. They have a great resemblance to Kirk Douglas, don't you think?' he laughed.

'Yes John, their names are Scandinavian at the least. Pleased to meet you both.' He snaked out his hand and shook warmly with them, before turning to Felek, 'and this is Lucky, a musician friend of mine, from Iraq, but he prefers to be known as a Kurd. By the way he also answers to his Kurdish name, don't you?'

'I do indeed Michael, but you know, I've never known how I got the name 'Lucky'. Nice to meet you guys too. Kjell. Egil. I am indeed 'Lucky'.'

The pleasantries continued for a few moments then Michael gave the bar attendant a shout and ordered up pints all round for the boys and a red wine for Katie.

'So what instruments do you play Lucky?' asked Egil.

'My instrument of choice is the violin, but also the viola, cello and some Kurdish instruments. I've also been known to tinker with a piano now and again, but I'm far from proficient in it. I prefer to stick to my strings. I think my fingers are more suited to them and I have a big chin for holding on to them, well maybe not the cello!'

With that, the Trad session got in to full swing again and continued for some time before the compere asked if there were any takers for the visitors spot and Michael answered with a big shout of 'Over here Ally, my friend is a great fiddle player, but he's also Kurdish and I think you'd all love to hear him play some tunes, wouldn't you?'

There was a chorus of acceptance from the gathered musicians and then a hush as Felek prepared his violin, tuning it to the chemistry of the humid bar. He played three numbers of Kurdish folk melodies and totally enthralled the listening musicians and casual drinkers, who gave him heartfelt applause as he ended. More drinks were called for and more variations of scores were played. Michael suggested that Felek and himself, and others who may care to join in, all play the three Shetland Reels that they had practiced together, to a rousing finish and mass appreciation from the non-playing congregation of the bar.

As they left the bar at the end of their wonderful evening Egil whispered in Felek's ear, 'I have a parcel for you from Fatima.' Felek turned towards him and gave a thumbs up and said 'When?'

'To suit you, Felek.' was the reply.
Felek noted that Egil knew his real name, even though Michael had only mentioned him as 'Lucky'. He responded to him, 'I leave Michael's for the Aberdeen ferry tomorrow evening. We have to do it before then.'

'Kjell's yacht is just off Victoria Pier, so I think that, if I give you the parcels there, you can take them with you directly to the ferry. I understand that Michael lives on Bressay, so you'll land at the pier from there anyway, and it's only a short taxi hop to the Terminal.'

....

The next day, Kjell had gone off fishing with John Stevenson and Egil was left alone with Naaskel. He'd seen Felek board the ferry through his binoculars and was already at the top of Naaskel's gangplank with the two packages, removed from the wet bags. He wondered again why they were so heavy, but really thought not to worry as the sniffer dog would have brought them to the attention of his handler, if there was anything untoward.

Egil waved to Felek as he stepped off the Bressay ferry, with a small shoulder bag and his violin case strapped over his back. As they met, the Norwegian asked him where he was headed.

'After I drop these at the Holmsgarth Ferry Terminal, I'm at a bit of a loose end until the ferry sails to Aberdeen at five o'clock. So I'll just wander around for a bit. Come with me if you wish, if you've nothing else to keep you busy.'

'Yes, let's do that. I was going to be doing much the same as you anyway. I'll just secure Naaskel and we can get a taxi from the end of the pier.'

The taxi drove them the short distance to the Holmsgarth Ferry Terminal and Egil helped him to deposit his baggage and the packages with the customary security questions. He baulked internally at the 'Have you anything dangerous in your luggage?' query, but stated categorically 'No.' And 'Are you carrying anything for anybody else?' And again 'No' was his reply. He was told where to store the luggage and picked up his receipt from the purser.

They headed back into town for some browsing, a coffee and scone in The Peerie Café, then a visit to Fort Charlotte up on the bluff. They walked as far as Knab Head before turning and finding themselves walking back by the shore to the Kveldsro House Hotel, for a bite of lunch and a few beers.

They talked about life in their countries of birth, politics, religion, sport, their respective professions and the general ways of the world. Finally Egil got round to asking about Fatima, and how Felek had first met her. Felek mentioned that they were brought up in the same village in Northern Iraq and that they had kept in touch over the years. He avoided every probing question on the subject, but very skilfully steered the conversation away before Egil's persistence always brought it back. By the end of the afternoon Egil knew some more falsehoods about his gorgeous and beloved Fatima. It was time for Felek to get on his way, so they both strolled to the pier and said their farewells before Felek continued the walk to the Terminal and boarded the ferry bound for Aberdeen.

15 Warehouse

Felek's cabin had been allocated, so he collected his luggage and deposited it there. He needed two journeys because of the narrow aisles and the size of the packages.

....

Earlier that day a solitary twitcher boarded a flight from Shetland's airport at Sumburgh Head to Aberdeen airport and had gone on to deposit her equipment in Jury's Hotel by the railway station.

....

Felek's overnight ferry trip went without a hitch, the sea conditions were fair and he slept peacefully. He awoke to the announcement on the ship's tannoy that they were approaching Aberdeen Harbour and that all passengers should get ready for disembarkation. He got up from his bunk, showered and went on his way to the access ramp with the first of the packages. He followed with the second and used a trolley to take all of his luggage down to the waiting taxi rank. The driver took his luggage and placed it into his boot and asked Felek where he wanted to go. 'The railway station,' was his reply.

'The railway station?' The driver pointed to the large building across the dual carriageway. 'The railway station is over there! Are you serious? You could walk there, mate!'

'Cabbie, I cannot walk there with these packages and my hand luggage, so please take me there. I know it is not a good fare for you, but I will recompense you for your troubles. Now please go.'

Within two minutes Felek was deposited along with his luggage. He found a left luggage locker and placed the two packages, his precious violin and his small bag inside.

He set off for the shopping mall and a breakfast to his liking.

....

The twitcher had strolled from her hotel and sat bird watching at the ferry terminal. She noticed the packages being placed in the boot of the taxi and then went back to her hotel.

....

The express train to London King's Cross Station was scheduled to depart on time. After breakfast he wandered the shopping mall to while the time away, then collected his baggage and stepped aboard the Express, taking his seat in First Class as instructed. The car attendant assisted him with his luggage. The twitcher saw him pass through the barrier on to the platform, then headed for the Station Taxi Rank

and asked the driver to take her to Aberdeen Airport.
Fatima was in King's Cross to meet the incoming train from Aberdeen. She greeted Felek, as he passed through the barrier, carrying two heavy parcels, one in each arm and violin case over his shoulder. He was with a young girl who was carrying his personal bag.

'Felek! It's wonderful to see you again. Let me help you with those.' She took one of the packages while he thanked the young girl, as he took the small bag from her.

The two of them headed for the taxi rank and jumped in to the first black cab that was available.

After Fatima had re-taken control of the packages in London, she and Felek went to her hotel and took up the luggage to her room. When she had first checked in she had told Front of House that her partner would be arriving later. They took the elevator up to the ninth floor and stepped out into the lobby and along to the end of the corridor to their suite, 9012. They congratulated each other on a job well done. They had moved the packages across Europe and safely to London, without so much as a hitch.

They left the packages untouched and stacked them in the bottom of the wardrobe and decided that they would be better transported in a wheeled bag, so Felek went out to buy a couple from a luggage store nearby while Fatima phoned Ardavan to update him.

He answered at the fourth ring 'Hello, how can I help you?'

'It's Fatima, and I have an update for you. The delivery has arrived safely at the postal address. What do you want me to do next?'

'Take the delivery to this warehouse,' and he read out an address in Wapping, on the north bank of the Thames in East London. 'Keys will be delivered to you. Where are you staying?'

She told him and he carried on, 'I suggest that you might be in London for some time so rather than stay where you are, you should look for an apartment, an unfurnished one and you can arrange to fit it out while you enjoy the city. I still require you to suss out possible ways of using the goods to our advantage. Take a two or three bedroomed flat within a reasonably central location, suitable for you and one or two colleagues. We will cancel the arrangement with the warehouse later, when the time suits us.'

She spent a good night in the large double and Felek had slept on the couch. In the morning they breakfasted together, then he checked out and went back to his day job as a musician. Front of House had left a message on her room phone to say that an envelope had been delivered for her. She collected the envelope, removed the set of keys and asked the porter to trolley down the packages. The porter hailed a cab and helped Fatima with her luggage. She took the packages to the Wapping warehouse. She left the packages in the back office, locked up, making sure both the door lock and the padlock were secure.

She then headed for the first flat address on her long list.

Most of what she saw were located in narrow streets, had no parking, were overlooked or had other features that were not in keeping with her specific needs. The listings in one estate agent came up with quite a few possibilities and after two days whittling down the list she found a suitable one.

She plumped for a two bedroomed corner flat on the top floor of Riddell Court. It overlooked Burgess Park, on the south side of the Thames, but was within reasonable travel distance from the main sights of the city. It was on the third floor, with a service lift and close to an emergency exit stair to ground level. The rate was higher than usual but it was available on a short-term lease and was unfurnished. She phoned the agency later in the day and put down the deposit using her American Express card. The keys would be available at reception at the estate agent at the Elephant and Castle later in the day.

At the office within the Elephant and Castle Shopping Centre she agreed the terms for a three month lease, with the option on another three. Service charges were agreed and the three months rent paid up front, with her credit card. She took the keys, hailed a cab and headed for Riddell Court. The flat was at one end of the block, with a round lounge overlooking the park. There were two allocated parking spaces for the flat.

By the end of that week she had arranged bedroom and lounge furniture from a local Ikea store, arranged for collection by a local haulage company and had taken delivery in the flat. She had shopped at Waitrose for necessities and was ready to move in.

She hailed another cab from the main street nearby and headed for the warehouse in Wapping. She asked the cabbie to drop her off a short distance away, at The Grapes pub overlooking the Thames, for some food. Then she headed for the warehouse, where she set up a chair on top of a desk, outside the small office. The packages were where she had left them. She grabbed one and hauled it up on to the desk, stepped onto the chair and heaved it up on to the office roof, out of sight, where she felt it was safer. The second package followed. She telephoned Ardavan and updated him.

'Well done! I will arrange to cut our ties with the warehouse in due course but in the meantime you are now tasked with finding out the whereabouts and the normal movements of the targets, which will not be easy. There will always be security around the two members of the British Government we are targeting, but the pair of Generals should be easier to track. Use your cover as that of a photographic journalist whenever possible, or that of a tourist, with a decent lens on the camera. I do not yet have a plan for final delivery. I will call you.'

She sat down and started to compile a list of persons, places of work, home addresses where available and schedules where possible. Persons of these ranks would not be easy to follow. It would need a canny approach and a step by step philosophy to put all the ingredients together and get the cake to rise. 'One good thing though, my days of incessant travel are on hold for a while. I have a base, a home to call my own, for a while at least,' she thought.

She spent the next few weeks moving between the seats of power for the targets, The Ministry of Defence and The Home Office. She was able to study journeys or parts of journeys and work out some, but not all of the routine daily movements of the targets. It was a frustrating time for her, but then she received a call from Ardavan.

16 Test flight

In early August the plane from Dublin landed at Aberdeen Airport.

Lorenzo Russo walked across the short piece of tarmac and into the concourse, hunched up with his hands in his pockets. His little tote bag was crammed full of his wordly possessions. He had sold the house in Carrick and all the furniture, fixtures and fittings, his RAV4, Lucy's Fiesta and Michael's Peugot van. Those had brought in a few more thousand euros, but he had been guarantor for Pietro's business so some of the cash had to go to settle that, once he had sold the coaches and cleared the loans.

'Lorenzo!' came the jovial shout from Euan. His Italian brother-in-law had arrived at Baggage Reclaim. Lorenzo raised his curly head of hair and a faint smile appeared on his weary face. 'Euan, it's good to see you man. How are you doing?' 'I'm great Lorenzo, but more to the point, how are you getting on these days? Don't answer that because I guess I know. How was your journey up? Did everything go to schedule?'

'Yeah,' said Lorenzo, 'the bus to Dublin airport was the worst bit, that was nearly two hours. It was pissing rain in Carrick as usual, so I got soaked, in fact we all got soaked waiting for the bloody bus. You know how it is, waiting on buses in all weathers. Why can't they put up a shelter? Down to money and politics likely! All these politicians are the same, just out for what they can get. Never mind the ordinary folk on the street, as long as they're all right, rolling in taxpayers cash!'

'But anyway the flight was good and we seemed to fly over some hills as we came in. It would be great to be an eagle right now, soaring in the thermals.' He looked thoughtful. 'I thought we came in over the sea the last time Lucy and I came over.' At that he stopped, looked down and a tear rolled down his cheek.

'If there's a south wind the planes will land into the wind from the north so the route takes you inland and over the low hills to the west. On those days they don't overfly the house so we have more peace when we sit out in the garden. Mind you, it's hardly like Heathrow over our house, even when they're flying in from the south. In fact it's quite nice at times, but our mobile signals seem to come and go every time a plane or a chopper flies over.'

Euan was aware of the silence as Lorenzo's eyes searched the baggage carousel, as it started delivering the Dublin inbound flight luggage. 'Come here Lorenzo,' he said, and drew him into his arms and hugged him. The luggage could wait. Over his shoulder Lorenzo could see the black case with the red nametag coming into view through the rubber curtains, disengaged himself from Euan and squeezed through the other waiting passengers to grab his bag.

Euan had parked the Discovery Sport in the short stay car park, even though it bugged him every time he did so. The rates were extortionate but the taxi queues were worse. Anyway, better to have the car today, as a detour could always be taken on the way to the house in Mannofield on the south side of the city.

'I'll just text Michelle and let her know that you've arrived safely in Aberdeen. She's looking forward to seeing you again,' said Euan.

He pulled out his phone and texted, then rummaged in his pocket for some change for the car park. He had just got used to his preferred cash again after using nothing but swipe during the pandemic. 'Here we go Lorenzo, all set. My car is just at the end of the first level, to the left.'

'It's a gorgeous day, not a cloud in the sky. It's nice to be away from the wet days in Carrick, but it feels quite a bit colder. But I do prefer a sunny day to a rainy day any time. It reminds me of the sunny days in Napoli, but the humidity was a killer in summer time, if you'll excuse the pun. Are you still getting away to the hills or doing a bit of cycling?'

'Yes, but I've been a tad curtailed during the spring and early summer, as you could guess. I was going to be cycling a lot more but I punctured my rear tyre last autumn and never got round to fixing it. When I did want to go riding again, it was of course still punctured and I couldn't get the blinking tyre off the rim to get at the inner tube. It's only last week that I got it to the bike shop in George Street to effect a repair. They gave it a full service too, so it's ready to rock and roll.'

'Well that's good. Has Michelle still got hers? Does she use it much?'

'Not a lot, but maybe, if you're up for it and don't mind the girly cross bar we could take a ride out along the old railway track towards Banchory.' 'Hey man, that's a great idea and if I fell off at least my goolies wouldn't get a crunching. We might even see some eagles. That would be fecking awesome!'

'Well maybe not eagles, but likely some buzzards circling their territory, looking for some carrion or rabbits or whatever.'

Michelle was at the lounge window when they arrived and she rushed out into the drive to greet them. Lorenzo threw open the car door, stepped out and into a massive embrace. They were both in floods of tears. 'Oh Lorenzo, my love, it's so good to see you. I've been sick with worry over you. I'd hoped that you could have come over earlier but at least the restrictions on both sides of the Irish Sea have now been lifted. My, but you've lost a lot of weight. You're almost lean. Have you been working out? And sun tanned too. It must have been a good summer so far.'

'It's good to see you too, Michelle,' said Lorenzo, as he looked down on the petite figure. 'Right now you remind me so much of Lucy. There were times when I never thought that I would see this day. I thought that I'd end up the same way as Pietro, but something pulled me through it all and here I am,' he muttered, through his choking voice and tears.

'Enough of that Lorenzo, in you come. As it's a lovely day I've set up some food down in the garden room and we can grab a bite and a nice glass of red, sit out in the sunshine and chat away. We've got a helluva lot to chat about,' Michelle sang out.

'I'll grab your luggage. Anything you need out of it right now? If there isn't, I'll drop it in the spare room and you can unpack later!' Euan shouted.

'No Euan, there's nothing I need right now. Thanks,'

The days went and turned into weeks. Lorenzo was beginning to relax and was enjoying the company of Michelle and Euan. One day Euan said to him, 'Remember when we went cycling to Banchory and we spotted the buzzard above the tops of the fir trees in the plantation? You said again that you would like to soar like an eagle! Well guess what, if you are up for it, I have always fancied a trip in a microlight, the ones with a wing and a rigid body, which is manoeuvred through a lightweight aluminium triangle, a bit like a powered paraglider. I've wanted to do it ever since I had my second gliding lesson and the pilot that day actually flew me alongside an eagle at about six hundred metres up. We were both looking for the same thermals.

The eagle was hunting and we were just…well….flying. It was over Aboyne, out of Deeside Flying Club, not far west of where we are now. I felt at the time I wanted to feel the breeze on my face, just like the eagle, and not be stuck in the cockpit of the glider, amazing though that was. There's a company, near Edinburgh, which offers tandem flights, out over the Firth of Forth or over the Pentland Hills towards the Borders. What do you say?'

'I think that's a brilliant idea, but would I have the bottle for something like that. What's the script? Is it totally safe? Do we need parachutes? Do we need a licence?' he asked.

'Well, I don't know the exact details at this stage but I can phone or email the company and see what they can offer.'

'That's good enough for me so let's go with that.'

Euan phoned one of the mobiles listed on the website and the call was picked up immediately. 'Hello, you're speaking to Dan at Gorebridge Flying School. How may I help you?'

Euan told him who he was and that he had seen on their website that tandem microlight flights were available, at various prices, depending on the package ordered. Dan explained the three trial packages available and stated that as business had been obviously quiet recently they were offering a ten per cent discount on flights taken within the following two weeks. At the moment any of the options could be arranged. He checked that both clients were below the weight limit of one hundred kilograms each, which Euan confirmed. Euan chose the two hour flight option as the one hour gliding flight that he'd experienced had just been a bit too short.

When he confirmed that they both wanted to do this Dan was over the moon and said that both of them could be accommodated, as there were two certified pilots and each had their own tandem QuikR Microlight. The two pairs could fly out in a squadron half V formation and enjoy the rapport on the wing. Euan called on Lorenzo, relayed the conversation and received a vigorous nod of approval and so Euan read out his credit card details to Dan. He selected the Thursday of the following week at 13:00 and then proceeded to ask about clothing and all the other sundry details.

Dan advised that all he needed was an email address, which was given over, to send on more information and the call was ended.

Lorenzo was eager to learn of all the details and his brother-in-law responded, adding that it would be an easy day trip. It would take them about three hours tops to get to the airfield at Gorebridge, Midlothian, just outside Edinburgh. If they left at around nine o'clock they would be there for a spot of lunch before the flight, then head back up the motorway at some time after three and be back in time for a nice dinner at home.

‘At long last,’ thought Lorenzo, ‘Something to look forward to. To fly with the eagles. What a thought!’

On the following Thursday Michelle saw the two guys off from the front door and the lads headed for Edinburgh and on to the airfield at Gorebridge. The day had started off with cold showers blowing in from the North Sea but had brightened as they motored south. The sun began to blink through the separating clouds and the day was turning out nice for their inaugural flight.

As Euan drove along the Edinburgh City Bypass and turned on to the A7 towards Gorebridge he mentioned to Lorenzo that he knew of a café in Newtongrange, just short of the airfield. He remembered it as being called the Wheelhouse, which he thought would have been more associated with the coast. Lorenzo remarked, ‘It must have been some tsunami to wash up this far from the Firth of Forth. We might see a couple of masts and some sails, instead of the wings we are looking for!’

A nice leisurely lunch ensued, of chicken sandwiches and broccoli and Stilton soup. Lorenzo had his usual black coffee with two shots and Euan plumped for an Earl Grey Tea with milk. Then it was time to hop back in the car and head for the airfield.

Dan welcomed them as they stepped into the little Portacabin with a warm firm handshake and introduced his partner. ‘This is Charlie, my colleague in arms and your other instructor for today. Here's some information fellas. You should take time to read all about what you are about to do, sign the disclaimer, just in case you fall out of the cockpit, or we decide to jump for our lives. Only joking fellas, but the safety briefing is of paramount importance and I'll do that just after I give you five minutes to do your reading. I'll also tell you a little about the aircraft in which you are going to enjoy your flight this afternoon. I'll take you through this as Charlie checks over the aircraft. We do check them regularly, as a matter of course, but we always re-check them immediately prior to a flight, to be doubly sure.'

As Dan walked through the door into what appeared to be a kitchen, store-room and general back office, Euan and Lorenzo were left to look through the handout. 'Fellas, I'm just away to make a cuppa. Can I get you anything, tea, coffee?'

Euan declined but Lorenzo opted for a black coffee, two shots. Then he glanced and said quietly to his friend 'Is there a toilet on the plane?' as a smile broke across his face.

A few minutes later Dan came back with two cups of steaming coffee, plonked himself down on the tatty high backed leather armchair and said 'Right fellas, let's start with safety.' He went through the drill and finished with, 'And now the parachutes. Yes, we will be wearing parachutes fellas. I've never had to use one yet, but they are unpacked and re-packed on a monthly basis, by an ex paratrooper friend of mine, so you can expect them to open and hopefully save your life, if the worst was to happen. There are three elements to using these. One – never pull this handle, unless you mean to use it. Two – If I say 'leave the aircraft', you will unbuckle your harness and throw yourself out. Three – count to three and then pull the parachute release handle. The aircraft will be on its merry way. You, as a passenger, will be out before your pilot, who will follow swiftly behind you. I say there are three things, but maybe I should mention a fourth – If you do not do all three you will find me standing on your head, as I leave the aircraft before you! Got It fellas?'

They laughed at the thought. The tightness in their stomachs that they were feeling was dissipating.

'Now fellas, let me tell you a bit about the aircraft. There are various forms of aircraft, from ones which fly at supersonic speeds, to ones such as the type we will use today. They are called Microlights in the UK and sometimes they are called Ultralights, for instance in the States and France. As we say here there are two types, the first is usually an enclosed vessel with capacity to change direction from side to side or up and down, using fixed ailerons and rudder. The second uses a fixed hand bar and the pilot pushes or pulls, or swings it from side to side to change direction. There are no foot pedals. It is a very simple process.'

As Dan passed over a couple of photographs, Euan and Lorenzo could readily identify the difference between the two models.

'Now for some technical jargon about the fixed hand bar type we use so you get an idea what our particular aircraft can do,' said Dan as he continued. 'Our machines are both tandem PM Aviation QuikR 912S. This means that they can fly two up, passenger immediately behind the pilot, with a view slightly over the pilot's forward view. PM Aviation is the manufacturer and QuikR is the model type. 912S indicates the engine size and type. Any questions so far?'

Lorenzo piped up 'Hey Dan, do you need a licence to fly one of your planes, or should I say microlights?'

Dan went on to explain that if he wanted to gain a licence to fly, but not to instruct, he would have to pass the BMAA Flexwing Microlight Pilot Licence flying course. 'But Lorenzo, you've just arrived. Let's take one step at a time fella.'

'Now, more technical stuff so you don't get worried when we're ready to fly. I will be last in to the aircraft, after ensuring your parachute and harness are both correct. You'll need to wear warm gear, with gloves. You can wear a liner under the helmets we give you, but your ears need to be kept clear for the head mikes. It will get pretty noisy back there, right next to the engine. On no account can you have long hair or loose clothing, as anything that can flap could get in to the propeller and stall the engine. These machines are not built to stay in the air without engine power. We can glide downwards without power, but a safe landing close by is imperative.'

Dan continued, 'We always have takeoff into the wind and land into the wind. During flight is when the microlight is at its most stable. We will need around two hundred to three hundred metres of runway, the shorter being on a hard surface and the latter on grass for instance, but I've done it with a light load, no passenger, in one hundred and fifty metres. I will refer at all times to kilometres per hour, even though air speed is usually referred to in knots. One knot is about 1.15 miles per hour or 1.84 kilometres per hour, just for info. We can taxi in winds up to 37kph but need a wind speed of less than 20kph for takeoff. The wind sock over there and the anemometer reading on this here console I am pointing at are very important. If it's too windy we are grounded. Fertig. Fini.'

Lorenzo chipped in again, 'Dan, how fast do we go for takeoff and what is the maximum speed we'll fly at?'

'Well Lorenzo, it's obviously the Italian stallion in you....you are Italian, are you not? I was just coming to the speedy bit.'

'Well I am Italian, from just outside Napoli, but I've stayed in Ireland for a long time. I met my wife in a youth hostel in France. We stayed on for a few years before we moved, lock stock and smokin' barrels to Ireland when the family started to come along,' he said, as his voice dipped into a whisper.

Euan broke in 'Lorenzo has recently lost all his family to the COVID19 thing, so this is one of his ways of getting release from those terrible events. He's always wanted to fly like an eagle, so here we are.'

'Well Lorenzo, let's get you into dream land and get you up there. You asked about speeds. Takeoff speed today will be 75 kph and the craft is capable of maxing out at 160 kph, close enough to 100mph, but with two up we'll be a bit short of that. However, that's enough of the techy stuff, fellas. Let's get you kitted up and ready for the off.'

Charlie came back in and told Dan that he'd checked both aircraft and logged flight plans for the two QuikR's. 'We'll go up over the hills to Jedburgh in the Borders, roughly following the A7 and A68, then take a left turn towards the coast and Berwick-upon-Tweed, another left up the coastline to Cockburnspath, then turn inland again to home, where we'll loop the airfield, to check on wind force and direction before we land.'

Once they were all suited and booted and had donned their helmets, Dan went through the weighing process, overall weight including fuel and radio clarity with Lorenzo. Charlie did the same with Euan. Their flying codes would be Tango Echo and

Tango Foxtrot during the flight. Internal chatter would be as their real names.

Lorenzo was amazed by how small the microlight was and Dan explained that it was only 3.8 metres long, 2.75 metres high and the wingspan tip to tip was 8.45 metres.

They all climbed aboard, with Lorenzo in the lead aircraft. They raced down the runway, Dan making slight adjustments to the A frame controlling the wing and then the runway was below them. They'd headed off to the east and Dan took a long look over to his right as they climbed to two hundred metres, then banked away to his left at about forty five degrees. Lorenzo looked over his shoulder and yelped with joy as he saw Tango Foxtrot take off and follow him up and around. Once Dan had her back on a straight course he explained that they were flying at about three hundred and fifty metres above ground level and at a speed of 120 kph, roughly motorway speed on the surface.

Lorenzo's mind wandered into eagle mode and he watched as birds flew below their craft, cars sped like ants along the main road and tractors worked the fields below. He was aware that Dan was vigilant and sometimes took a moment to answer his numerous questions, always levelling before diverting his conversation back to Lorenzo.

Dan pointed out the villages as they flew and then pointed ahead to the Abbey at Jedburgh, which marked their way-point for Berwick and the coast.

Euan and Charlie flew behind and to the right of Tango Echo, keeping clear of his left turn ahead. The airwaves crackled as he let Air Traffic Control know where he was in relation to incoming flights into Edinburgh Airport. Then the QuikR banked at another forty-five degrees and they spun around the Abbey and headed east towards the coast, over the purple, heather clad hills.

Dan said that he'd take the aircraft further up and a quick climb later they were at one thousand metres. Then Dan radioed to Tango Foxtrot, 'Let's have some fun now Charlie. These guys seem as though they're ready for it.' 'Roger that Tango Echo. I will follow at one hundred metres.'

At that Dan said to Lorenzo 'Take a good arms-in position Lorenzo. We're going for a dogfight, to let you see what she can do. I'll take it easy at first then liven it up a bit as we close on the coast. We only have to maintain one thousand feet over towns.'

Dan went into a descent quickly and spiralled in quite a tight circle, came out and climbed again at a shallow angle, then twisted to the right, then left, up again, then down, with Tango Foxtrot in close pursuit. 'We're flying under visual flight rules, so as long as we can see around us we can safely have a little play. In this area towards the coast there are no jet fighters liable to burn us out of the sky and the commercial stuff is too high over here. Don't worry, you still have your parachute, Lorenzo!'

Lorenzo was having the time of his life, but Euan was beginning to feel a little queasy, so he used his helmet mike to pass his fears of the need of a sick bag on to Charlie. 'Roger that Euan,' Charlie said and levelled off the flight. 'Tango Echo, I have called off pursuit, as Euan is showing signs of air sickness and I don't want it down the back of my flying suit! I'll straight line it to Berwick at twelve hundred metres. How's your lad?'

'Tango Foxtrot. Understood. My fella is whooping it up behind me. He's more like the Red Baron that the soaring eagle he wanted to be like though.' With that he swooped, circled, rose and fell, while Tango Foxtrot rose up to twelve hundred metres and settled at a leisurely pace behind and above them.

Once they reached the coast they passed out over the sea and hugged the coastline about a kilometre off shore, until their way-point came up again and they made the turn left for Gorebridge and the airfield. As he made the turn he pointed out Fife across the Firth of Forth and told Lorenzo that he could fly to there but would have to climb to around sixteen hundred metres, so that if there was an engine failure en route the QuikR could glide all the way and still achieve a soft, controlled landing. The parachutes were not needed.

Lorenzo was already beadily looking for the tell tale sign of the windsock and declared to Dan 'The windsock is pointing in the same direction but it looks like the wind has dropped a bit Dan.'

‘Yep, Lorenzo, we’ll just take a wide loop left again, with Charlie still behind and right. We’ll land into the wind and head for the hangar to carry out the post flight checks for the aircraft and refuel her, so she’s ready for the next eagle.’

‘Roger that’ said Lorenzo, as he mentally worked the controls in his head. He was already hooked and had decided that he wanted to do more of it. He’d talk to Euan later, and of course Dan.

‘That was great, Dan’, Lorenzo said, barely able to contain himself. ‘Hey, what kind of fuel does she use? Aircraft high octane stuff? How many miles to the gallon do you get?’

‘Well, the fuel she burns is normal unleaded car type, either Premium or Premium Plus. We have a fuel tank of sixty-five litres capacity, but useable is just over sixty-three. Consumption varies, just as in a car. If just cruising, with a light load she’d do about sixteen kilometres to the litre at one hundred kph. At takeoff and initial climb we’d suck up about eighteen litres. Let’s fill her up and find out. We transfer from jerry cans using a hand pump, as it’s safer than automatically filling and maybe overfilling. We’ll let the engine cool down first though. Let’s go and de-water ourselves and get another coffee down us. You obviously enjoyed that. Enough to get you excited about putting in the hours and getting a licence? We could do with your enthusiasm in our fraternity.’

Euan and Charlie wandered in to the office and Charlie said ‘I’ll hand Euan over to you now Dan, so you can get their flight certificates sorted out and I’ll go and re-fuel. The engine on yours will be cool enough now, so I’ll do that first and mine should be ready thereafter. See you lads! At least the green has gone from your face Euan!’

‘Were you feeling a bit odd up there Euan?’, Dan asked. ‘Yep, I was okay on the straight, the climb and the landing but the weaving about was not for me. How did you get on Lorenzo?’

‘It was brilliant man! I thought it the best experience I’ve ever had. Dan was even calling me the Red Baron, you know the German tri-plane ace from the First World War. I’d really love to have a bash at the controls though. That would really be ace.’

‘Well Lorenzo, you can always take lessons and see how you get on. We do these a few hours a week or can provide an intensive two week training course. If you’re very good at it, especially the book work, then I think you’d do well,’ said Dan.

‘What do you think Euan? Do you think that I could do it? Or am I living in dream land?’

‘Well Lorenzo, you’re good technically, you’ve got an engineering background which would no doubt help you with the technical jargon. Let’s talk about it on the way up the road. Best be on our way. Remember that Michelle is cooking dinner tonight

and the bridge traffic will be a bit slow into Fife. After that we'll cover the distance in no time.'
With that, Charlie popped his head in the door and said, 'Tango Echo's used just over thirty-three litres and Tango Foxtrot, with our straighter and slower run from Jedburgh to Berwick has needed a fill of just under thirty litres.

'There you go, Lorenzo, the fuel loads that you asked for. Enjoy the boring ride home fellas.'

On the way back to Aberdeen Lorenzo had made up his mind. As he always did he was loath to think things through in any fine detail, he liked to act spontaneously. He was going to learn to fly in a microlight.

Next day he phoned the airfield and spoke to Dan. 'Hey Dan, I really took the flying bug. What kind of deal can you cut me for an intensive training course? I'd have to find accommodation near you, so I have to factor that into my costs and I would have to rent a car to get me to and from the airfield. So all in all it'll mount up.'

'Well Lorenzo, it involves a minimum of twenty-five hours flying, the last ten of which would be solo. Then there's fuel for twenty-five hours, and instructor time for fifteen hours, so all in all it will be around £3.5k. If you're not as good as I think you'll be, then it will climb from that as you'll need more lessons and a test or two. Allow £4k maximum to cover it.'

‘Can I do it all in a week then, Dan?’

‘Well you’d better allow for ten days here, with some time between flying, as you’d have to learn the techy stuff as well, fella.’

‘Okay, adding a room for ten days, a hire car and other expenses I’m likely looking at over £5k. I’ll have to do it for under £5k all in, so I must pass in minimum flying hours allowed. I promise to be a good student. How do I get this thing done Dan?’

‘Simple Lorenzo. All I need is a credit card and a start date. Rest is up to you.’

‘Okay here are the details,’ said Lorenzo and he read out the numbers. ‘By the way Dan, do you know of any Bed and Breakfasts around there?’

‘No I don’t, but I’ll speak with Charlie. He might. I’ll ring you back. On this number?’

‘Yeah, that’s fine Dan. Speak later.’

Lorenzo turned to Michelle and Euan and said, ‘Well, that’s me going to flying school. I just need to check when I could start, get me somewhere to stay for the duration and a car to rent. It’ll be a bit funny moving on. But it’s been great staying with you. You’ve helped me to look forward to something again.’

Michelle and Euan replied in unison, ‘It’s the least we could do Lorenzo.’ Michelle went on to say, ‘I hope you've made the right decision, Lorenzo. It is a lot of money and what will you do after that? Will you be able to hire microlights now and again, just like car rental?'

'I just don't know Michelle, but I'm sure Dan will keep me right. I just wish he wouldn't call me 'Fella' all the time.'

Dan phoned Lorenzo back later in the afternoon. 'Charlie told me that there's a place just on the outskirts of Gorebridge, like a camping site, with wooden pods, with bed, chair, table and electric light. There's a communal toilet and shower block and the whole place is quite new. According to reports it's also very clean and tidy and the owner doesn't take any youths or same sex parties. He looks for family groups mostly, but a fella your age on his own should be okay. Here's the number and website details if you want to look on line first. Charlie also suggested that you take the train down to Haymarket station in Edinburgh. You can pick up a hire car there.'

'That's great Dan. Thanks. And Dan, can I start on Monday with you? That's assuming I can get fixed up with accommodation.'

'Jeepers Lorenzo, you're a fast worker. Well I know that I'm free on Monday and Tuesday, thereafter I can check the bookings diary and get something fixed up. I'll book you in and see you at 09:00 Monday. Cheerio.'

Dan looked across at Charlie, told him the good news about the booking and Charlie gave a cursory pretend wipe of his forehead. A booking was a good thing at any time, but especially now when things were a bit tight.

17 Lorenzo goes home

Ardavan said, 'I have a new target site in mind Fatima, one which will strike at the very heart of those politicians and army chiefs who let the Kurdish nation down so badly last year. To do it, I need you to find an airstrip in or around central London. I consider that an air strike will best suit our needs.'

'But we could not possibly get anything remotely like an aircraft hi-jacked and especially from a central London location. The nearest would be London City.'

'We only need a short strip, maybe two hundred metres for our small aircraft. Find somewhere.'

....

The United Kingdom Minister for Culture, Media and Sport brought the meeting on the third day of September to order and read out the agenda for the parade. She discussed the physical timing, the order of proceedings and the dignitaries and others who would attend. There were no real surprises from the previous one held, except that the heads of government for France and Italy would be in attendance, to mark their dead from COVID19.

She went on to say where they would fit in to the proceedings, in terms of pecking order, and a heated debate among those present ensued. There were some who believed that the event should be recognised for what it stood for initially, before the pandemic took hold. There were others who sought to politicise it for their own or their party's political gain.

The Minister stated the position with security and the need to cater for enhanced airport type scanners and bag searches at the perimeters, where the general public would be accommodated. The secondary line of security would be by the beat Bobbies at regular intervals and their armed presence at various points along the route. She went on to discuss the use of CCTV, Special Branch of the Metropolitan Police Force and, if necessary the use of Strategic Forces personnel.

There would also be a requirement for emergency first aid services to be accommodated. Their location stations for rapid response would also be crucial. Barriers in various formats would be required to be positioned prior to the event. The BBC would be covering the parade and they would have their high reach cranes with the telephoto cameras raised in the usual places. There would be a need for a sound booth for commentators and allowance for the press and associated television opportunities.

The Culture Secretary added that this was a world stage event and it showed the absolute best of what Britain could do. It would show the pomp and splendour associated with the country and draw the millions of visitors back after the desolation of the pandemic.

'I will leave the detail to my aides in my Department to sort out the minute details and the official invitations. I will liaise with my colleagues in the Cabinet Office regarding the Military and Police requirements for Defence and Home Office matters. All correspondence shall be in the form of email and will be passed around on a need to know basis. Is all that clear?'

There was a murmur of assent around the oval mahogany table, except for one lone voice, which asked, 'Madam, do we know of any security issues which are liable to disrupt the proceedings? What is the word on the street? What are our intelligence services aware of?'

'The answer to that one is negative sir, and even if it was affirmative there is no way the Prime Minister would allow the cancellation or postponement. This event WILL take place, and if there are circumstances that come to light, then these will be dealt with at the time in our usual professional and calculatingly cold manner. Is that all, people?' Without waiting for a reply she rose from the table and said, 'The meeting is closed.'

Vicky Douglas had been given the task of building and checking the security arrangements for the parade. She had wanted to ask the Minister a few questions, but had realised in the short space of time that the meeting had lasted that these would have to come later. She had still decided that the answers she would likely be given would not be factual, but spurious or downright lies in any case. She would do it her own way. If she covered the detail then everything would look after itself. She had to go for prevention rather than cure.

....

On Sunday, Lorenzo said his farewells to the Halls and caught an early evening train to Edinburgh, picked up his hire car and was soon tucked up in the bunk in his little wooden chalet, dreaming about soaring like an eagle.

He found the course pretty intensive but technically and physically manageable. Dan demonstrated flight diving speed, best angle of climb, limits to angle of turn, stalling procedures, differences between cruising and manoeuvring speeds, the need to apply power in the climb and how to trim the wing.

The machine was proving to be a highly manoeuvrable aircraft and lots of fun too. Lorenzo applied himself to his studies and by the end of the first weekend he had logged an hour more than the twenty-five hours of tandem flight necessary. Now he had to do it all again, by himself. He planned for the ten hours solo being done in the next three days. Charlie would go up in the other QuikR and fly close by to start with, just to give him some support.

By the following Wednesday he had done it, flown 36 hours and passed all the oral and written exam work. He was a qualified BMAA pilot. His chest burst with pride and he wanted to fly some more. That would have to wait until he'd more cash to fritter away. He still had the insurance policy payment on Lucy's life, but wanted to live within the strictures of the cash he had cobbled together in Ireland first.

During his daily chats with his instructors Lorenzo learned a lot about location of other microlight flying clubs and their exploits touring. It was mentioned during the course of one conversation that they knew a flier who had hopped all the way to Italy, using various airfields along the way. The airfield for his final destination was on the Amalfi Coast, at Salerno. Lorenzo was in awe and had retorted that the place was a stone's throw from his birthplace in the suburbs of Napoli.

He took another spur of the moment decision. He was going to go to Napoli, find the airfield and try to get at least a tandem flight, but hopefully a solo one, if he could find a rental company. The lads had said that they did exist, but didn't know exactly the locations of them.

Lorenzo cleared off his bill, deposited his hire car back to the station and checked into a nearby Travel Lodge. He had decided to stay in Edinburgh for four nights and then take a flight to Napoli.

....

Ardavan had discovered that it was always the second Sunday in the month of November. It had to be for good reason. It was always the closest Sunday to the eleventh day of the eleventh month. It suited his purposes perfectly. The attack date was fixed in his head. The British politicians in the form of Prime Minister and his Cabinet, together with the heads of the Armed Forces and the two Generals in particular, would be in attendance, out in the open, where a rocket attack could be effective. He had less than three months to put the final preparations in place.

....

Lorenzo found Edinburgh to be a lovely city. He walked the tourist attractions, down the Royal Mile, to the Castle on the clifftop and Observatory. He ate in historical pubs and listened to all sorts of music, milling about with the tourists, lots of them in family groups. He was feeling a bit lonely, especially after the friendship and hospitality of the Halls and the nerve tingling excitement of the flying lessons. He needed a new buzz and he hoped he would find it back in Napoli.

He found an Easyjet flight direct from Edinburgh to Napoli, leaving in the early afternoon. After he'd made his flight reservation he'd phoned an old friend from his school days and had arranged to meet him at Arrivals. He hopped on the urban tram system to the airport and was in Napoli International by 18:00.

When Paulo Esposito got the call from his old school friend and teenage delinquent in arms he was surprised. It had been over ten years since he had last seen him, for some dinner in London. Paulo had always been the instigator of trouble but Lorenzo had readily followed in their youthful exuberance. If Lorenzo had not met Lucy in France on one of the boys' summer escapades they would likely have still been the best of mates, but Lorenzo had moved away and Paulo had got deeper into trouble. That was before he'd met up with Andrea. Now he got others to do the troubling things, at the behest of Andrea. He had good money coming in, Andrea's Maserati Quattroporte to run about in and sometimes the use of his motor cruiser too, which sat in the marina at Capri.

Paulo parked on the upper level and walked to Arrivals to wait for Lorenzo. As Lorenzo came through from Customs they saw each other and they embraced warmly and air kissed both cheeks. Paulo stretched Lorenzo out at arms length and looked him up and down before saying 'You look not too bad for an old guy, Lorenzo. Quite fit, if I may say.' 'You're looking pretty lean and mean yourself, Paulo. Nicely tanned too. Still keeping out of mischief?'

'Well you know how it is Lorenzo, still doing a bit of this and that.'

They wandered off to the car, Lorenzo's case dragging along behind him, catching up on gossip and reminiscing about the old times, getting into trouble together.

Paulo took him to a local hotel, the Belsito in Nola and left him there, saying, 'I'll see you in the lobby bar and we can decide what to do for food after we've had a few beers. There's a lot to catch up on Lorenzo. See you in an hour or so.'

Lorenzo settled in and went down to the bar and ordered himself a long cold beer and some olives. He propped himself up on a stool and waited, musing over the last couple of weeks. He thought that he would have to find out about the Salerno Airport thing shortly.

Paulo arrived. He'd dropped the suit, white shirt and black slip on shoes for some dark blue slacks, a pale blue linen shirt and tan loafers. Lorenzo was in denims and a tee shirt and he thought, as he looked at Paulo, 'I've lost my Italian style. I'll have to get some tips from Paulo.'

'So bring me up to date, Lorenzo, what have you been up to since I last saw you? No, forget that, what have you been up to that brings you back here?'

Lorenzo looked down at the floor and started. He mentioned COVID19, but the whole world knew about that. But his voice dropped to a low hush as he explained about Michael, then Lucy, Linda and the baby. He took a deep breath and tears rolled from his eyes and his voice broke as he recalled finding Pietro, the last straw. Paulo was visibly moved. He had known a few who had passed away but they were old people and had had good lives.

'I know a guy at the Aero Club who lost his parents, a sister and brother. They were some of the casualties in Bergamo, but he was working around the Amalfi Coast at the time and we got off quite lightly in comparison.'

'The Aero Club?' asked Lorenzo, wanting to change the subject quickly, 'What Aero Club?'

'The one in Salerno, about an hour from here. I sometimes use it for work. It's quite small and easy to get in and out of, without too much activity from the authorities.'

'That's funny, not in a hilarious way, because you'll never guess my real reason for being here. Apart from seeing you, Paulo, it is to see if I can get some flying time.'

'Flying time, Lorenzo? What are you speaking about? I thought you were an engineer on cruisers or something like that. Have you switched to plane mechanics?'

'Well, you're not going to believe this Paulo, but when all that stuff happened to me in Ireland I decided to cash in everything I had and start a new beginning. I went over to Scotland, to Lucy's sister and her husband for a few weeks. I was getting bored and to be honest a bit depressed. Euan, my brother-in-law, suggested a trial flight in an aircraft. Not just any old aircraft, but a microlight…It's a…'

'I know exactly what it is Lorenzo. I fly tandem with Felice, the guy I was talking about just a few minutes ago. He's got his own machine and he takes adventure tourists around the Amalfi Coast. We'll have to go down there and I'll introduce you to him. You'll have loads in common and the Club is quite nice, but a bit quiet still.'

Lorenzo spent the next few days refreshing his knowledge of Nola. He went in to the centre of Napoli, down to the ferry terminal and up to the headland overlooking the old prison in the bay below. He mixed with other Neapolitans in bars and coffee houses at frequent intervals, enjoying the warm sunshine as it streamed through the small openings in the stretched parasols above him.

He interspersed his days in the city with trips on the coastal ferry boats down to Sorrento, Praiano, Amalfi and Maiori, pretending that he was merely a tourist, eavesdropping on what the locals had to say about their clients and any other gossip of the day.

Paulo took him down to the Aero Club at Salerno Airport one evening to meet Felice, which proved to be a great evening. Paulo was just on soft drinks and a small Campari with soda, but both Lorenzo and Felice drank till their boots were overflowing, through mirth and the depths of despair. Felice brought into the conversation his connection with Bergamo and his recent losses.

They talked about their joint suffering at the hands of COVID19, their astonishment at the actions of politicians, the health service, religion, billionaires who pleaded poverty and the fall of the economy. They both complained about the armed forces and their need to hold NATO exercises when their nations' people were expiring left right and centre. They both thought that the armies, navies and air forces would have been better employed to fetch and carry protective equipment for the medical and nursing professions.

It was well into the early hours before they had exhausted all talk of depression and revolt and had moved on to the subject of microlights. An hour later Paulo stood up and said, 'You'll have to finish this another day, guys. I have a bed that awaits me. Lorenzo, we're off!'

Felice and Lorenzo said their good nights and arranged to meet up in a couple of days. Felice would take Lorenzo for a jaunt in his aircraft, and that turned out to be a QuikR, just like the one Lorenzo had learnt to fly in, just a short time before.

When they met again, Felice took Lorenzo on his regular flight pattern, over the Amalfi Coast, to Castellammare, then inland to Salerno. They had lunch at the Aero Club and Felice offered Lorenzo the opportunity to take the hot seat and he would be the back seat driver. All that had to happen was that Lorenzo had to pay for fuel and the additional insurance. Lorenzo jumped at it and the insurance agent resolved the additional cover over the phone. In turn, Lorenzo handed over a bundle of euros to Felice and thanked him for the privilege. They took the same flight plan but in reverse, so that Lorenzo was flying more or less without advance knowledge, although he'd seriously done his homework on navigation and had checked over the microlight most thoroughly.

As they put the aircraft back into the hanger Felice expressed to his companion that he thought that he was a very good pilot, but he needed to work on building up his flying hours in more challenging weather conditions. It wasn't always going to be warm and sunny, with light winds. There would come a time when he would have to take action to prevent putting the craft and himself in danger. Felice promised to help him over the coming days, flying over more mountainous terrain.

After his chat with Ardavan, Paulo had to take the idea to the fliers. He knew that they were anti-establishment, had a grudge in general about life and had nobody and nothing to lose. They were two lonely men with a need to do something for their development and they had the skills to fly aircraft. That is where the idea sat.

Another evening at the Aero Club came about and Paulo steered the conversation onto the technical capabilities of the QuikR and how tight it could turn, its diving and climbing prowess and the ability of two airmen to tackle difficult flying routes to tight parameters.

The two fliers gave their opinions that they were both ace pilots, both describing their glowing reports from their original instructors. Lorenzo interrupted with ‘You know Paulo, I want to buy my own QuikR. In fact I’d buy a flying school and spend all my days up in the air. How do you fancy that Felice? The two of us flying in formation every day, nobody a back seat passenger any longer?’

‘That’s just the perfect job for me Lorenzo! Where will we go though?’

‘Well I know of a flying school in Scotland, the one I trained at not so long ago. Dan and Charlie, the owners, might be interested in selling. They’ve got two QuikR’s, trailers, a host of spares and they rent their hangar space beside Edinburgh at the moment. I could give them a call.’

Paulo’s brain, in its sober condition, took the information in and took the plunge.

‘Guys, I have a proposition for you, one which would get you the flying school of your dreams. There is a catch, though, one that I cannot disclose for the present time. I need to speak with another person, but does the first idea, the one of a flying school in your hands, appeal to you? If you did me a great favour in return, then I, or my contacts, would be due you a great favour and that could be the flying school,’ said Paulo.

Felice cut in with, 'Well Paulo it must be one hell of a favour if we end up with a flying school! It must be at the very least a little bit dodgy. There must be money involved somewhere. I'm certainly not going to get mixed up in drugs. You know my feelings on that. What do you say, Lorenzo?'

'Sounds like we're back in the old days, Paulo. A flying school would cost tens of thousands of euros. What on earth would you want us to do for that? I agree with Felice, if it's not involving drugs then I'm up for it, but it must be dangerous. I've led a peaceful life for a long, long time and maybe a little bit of danger would spice things up a bit. What do you think Felice? A little bit of spice then our own flying school?'

'A little bit of spice would be fine, Lorenzo. In fact a big bit of spice would be great. Speak to your contact Paulo and let us know how you get on.'

Paulo took Lorenzo back to Nola that night with thoughts racing through his head. Could he handle Andrea on this one? He reckoned that the Kurd would be all ears.

The following day Ardavan took a call after four rings. 'Hello, how can I help you?'

'Ardavan, it's me, Paulo. I think I may have found an interesting solution for you. Can we meet?'

'Okay, I'll meet you again at Villa Borghese, in Rome. Two days from now, at noon. Where we met before. Okay?'

'Yes, that will be fine,' replied Paulo.

Paulo called Andrea and asked for a meeting. Andrea asked to be collected at the port and they would go to Bar Nico in Nola.

Later, in Andrea's preferred choice of venue for a business discussion, Paulo told him of his idea to use the two pilots, to purchase the flying school and then to pass the whole mess over to the Kurd. Andrea replied that he would be more than happy to pass the matter over, but there was no way that their funds could be used. If the Kurds want the flying school, then the Kurds pay for the flying school. If Italy gets a slice of the cake for use of resources again then that was business. By the end of their meeting Paulo was in need of some fresh air away from the nervous puffing on the tobacco while Andrea could feel the itch of money in his palm.

Paulo decided that he could make a play for the flying school and manage a cut for Andrea, which would then filter down to him. It would be a win, win situation. Once the flying school was in their hands then he would apply pressure on the flying twins, if needed.

Lorenzo took a call from Paulo, wanting to meet him and Felice at the Aero Club that evening.

Lorenzo accepted and told Felice 'Paulo wants to meet us again. It's about the flying school. Are you up for this Felice?' 'Yeah, sure, what have we got to lose realistically Lorenzo? We're both in the same boat and to be honest, if I were to die tomorrow, nobody would miss me.'

'Nobody would miss me either Felice. Let's do it, whatever it is. And if I just own a flying school for a day I can at the least say I've accomplished something.'

The fliers were nursing their small beers as Paulo entered the Aero Club and ordered a Campari and soda from the bar.

He ushered them over to a table away from big ears and proceeded to tell them his plan. He then questioned Lorenzo.

'This flying school of yours, Lorenzo. What's it called and how do I find it?' 'It's in Gorebridge, just south of Edinburgh in Scotland.' Lorenzo went on to say, 'It's owned by two lads. Dan and Charlie are their names. I can check their last names from their website. From what I could gather they own it outright and there are no sleeping partners. If you like I could give them a phone first.'

'No, Lorenzo, don't do that. This offer has to be business like and come from a legitimate source. We can use our legal guy to get a law firm in Scotland to make the proposition and then all would be good and proper. I'm presuming that they will not ask for silly money and that they are as desperate as you made out. Once we have the deal in place then you and Felice can travel over and sort out any technical details with the sellers, if strictly necessary, but at the moment we have a need for secrecy. This will be a chance to get back at the billionaires and politicians that you were railing against just a few short days ago. You will be the Red Barons. Just think of that, guys.'

....

Paulo and Ardavan agreed that they would purchase the Gorebridge Flying School and that would enable Lorenzo and Felice to carry out training without fear of detection. Ardavan would arrange a design of some form of carrier for the armoury to affix to the microlights. They would also need to purchase two towing vehicles for the trailers. Then they would be ready for an attack anywhere on the British mainland.

Ardavan met with Andrea and arranged to transfer the cash into a Swiss bank account. Andrea would draw down any monies to carry out all the purchases and leave a management fee for the Neapolitan.

18 Microlights as fighters

The firm of Strachan and Fraser, Solicitors in Edinburgh, took on the purchase and made first contact with Dan and Charlie. The offer was to purchase the Gorebridge Flying School and all its component parts, including aircraft and trailers, with no strings attached. The proprietors of the Flying School were not in a good position financially after the lockdown and jumped at the chance when they were asked to put a valuation on the company. When they did, they allowed a bit of leeway for negotiation, on the advice of their own lawyers. In return they did not expect a figure in excess of their valuation. The deal was completed in just over a week to an unknown buyer.

....

Paulo met with Lorenzo and Felice at the Aero Club once more. He started 'Guys, you are now joint owners of The Gorebridge Flying School. Happy?'

Lorenzo was in first with 'Are you joking, Paulo? I didn't think you were serious about that. But I should know you by now. What are Felice and I meant to do now?'

'Well guys, the first thing you have to do is pack up everything that you have here and disappear from Italy. Dispose of your vehicle, Felice, but you'll need to get another couple when you get to Scotland. Don't worry, I've got the cash for you to make the purchases and a float to keep you going until you hear further from me. I'll garage your microlight for the moment too, unless you want to dispose of it before you go. All you have to do is get there and get the sale documents and keys from a legal firm in Edinburgh, Strachan and Fraser. You'll find them on the internet. Buy a couple of second hand vehicles that can tow the load, like a Hilux or something similar. Pay with the company credit card that we'll have set up for you by the time you arrive in Edinburgh. Okay, I have other things to see to now but in the meantime make sure that you stick to all the laws of the land. Ciao.'

The pair took a couple of days to settle everything. Felice got Paulo to store his aircraft and trailer. They bought train tickets to Rome, then the express to the airport and a flight to Edinburgh. The cab they hired took them to the lawyers' offices and they signed for documents and keys, then hailed another cab to take them to a hotel near Haymarket where they booked two rooms for four nights. Their other tasks were to pick up their company credit cards and take a good look around Gorebridge. Lorenzo hired a small car and pointed out all the places of interest that he had seen on his previous visit. It was Felice's first time in the city and he was overawed by the grandeur of the place.

As they approached Gorebridge, Felice suggested that they might be better to stay close to the airfield and save the daily journey to and from Edinburgh and so it was agreed.

There was a rush of excitement racing through the veins of the two fliers as they first drove in to the airfield and saw the sign over the small building stating ‘Gorebridge Flying School’ and below that they saw the names of Dan and Charlie. ‘We’ll have to get some paint Lorenzo and over write the sign with our names, or at the least just paint over their names.’

‘Yeah, Felice, but that can wait. I must see the QuikR’s just to make sure that they actually exist. Maybe Paulo’s pulled a fast one.’

They went in to the building and started to look through paperwork and tried various keys to open desk drawers, a small safe and a filing cabinet. The filing cabinet and desk drawers were empty, but the safe held the security details for the hangar keypad and the sets of twin keys for each of the QuikR’s. Lorenzo felt his pulse quicken and noticed a slight flush appear on Felice’s cheeks.

They were out of the office and on their way to the hanger in double quick time, a bunch of keys in each of their hands.

Both QuikR’s were sitting there in the hangar, their towing trailers alongside each, their Ifor Williams trade labels shining. The lads had left the place spick and span and all the spare parts were tagged with ID and a date. ‘Which one do you want Felice?’ ‘The one on the left, Lorenzo’ ‘Why that one? What’s wrong with the other one?’ ‘Well they both look the same to me but you asked me to pick one, so I did!' Felice said, bursting out in laughter. Lorenzo returned the laugh and said, 'We've done it! I know that you still have an aircraft back in Salerno for sale but this is my first one. Who would have thought, a few months ago, that I would be standing here with my own microlight and a pilot's licence. It's amazing, really amazing. Let's get these beauties checked out and get up in the air.'

A couple of hours later they had checked both aircraft over, according to the manual provided by the aviation company and were taxi-ing along to the end of the runway. The wind was good and they'd logged a flight plan to take them on the headings that Dan had used on Lorenzo's test flight. They'd picked the call signs C for Charlie, or Capasso and R for Romeo, or Russo.

They enjoyed their flight, especially when they had their dogfight on the Jedburgh to Berwick leg. Lorenzo had led and Felice, with more experience, had hung on to Lorenzo's coat tails up and down, side to side, all the way. They laughed with the pleasure of it and even did so as they landed back on the tarmac strip.

They carried out the after flight checks, refuelled and locked up the hangar. They would check out the trailers next day, but before that they had to trawl through commercial and private vehicle sales sites to find the units they would require for the tow.

There were a number of double cab trucks for sale and they decided on a pair of Hilux units from a local dealer in Edinburgh. Lorenzo made the call and arranged to see the salesman in the morning.

On inspection, the vehicles appeared to be in good order, with no bodywork damage and reasonable mileage for their model year. One vehicle was in need of new tyres, so the arrangement was made with the garage to fit new tyres all round.

The credit card was presented and Lorenzo drove one of the vehicles away. Felice would follow him back to the hire car depot and they could pick up the other vehicle later in the day.

They drove up to King Arthur's seat in their new purchase and sat eating their take-away lunch with a view of the city spread out below them. They walked along the crags and discussed how close they could fly to cliffs and other natural obstacles. They vowed to try some close manoeuvres over the Borders Hills in the microlights.

That evening Lorenzo got a call from Paulo. He asked him to arrange for the microlights to be colour changed to a matt grey, so that they would not be so readily identified in the sky. Lorenzo consulted with Felice, who said that the fuselages would be no problem. They could be done by the fliers in the hangar, but the wing was manufactured and delivered as a selected colour of fabric and couldn't be changed. He went on to say that he had to order his own one, back in Italy, from a set list of colours.

He would check with the manufacturers and see if they could produce such a wing and find out how long it would take. The factory was very accommodating. He could have two new wings within ten days.

The colour would be a standard grey for the small wing underside and large wing underside and the leading edge would be white. The factory could supply the paint for the fuselage in a similar grey to the wings and the trike and wheel covers would be in a mottled grey, as applying a flat grey would be messed up by stone chips at landing and takeoff.

The fliers had taken the two Hilux cabs to get tow bars fitted and went back to the hangar to check out the trailers. They were tiltbed type, with full width extension ramps on each. The loading plate showed that they were rated at 3000kg gross and 764kg unladen, leaving 2236kg for load.

In their swept-back wing transportation mode the QuikR would fit within the trailer bed, sitting 1.75 metres above the flat bed. The tail of the microlight would extend over the flatbed by 360mm, so a warning triangle would be necessary. The take-off weight of the microlight was 270kg and so the trailer could take extra fuel, flying suits, spares and extra payload without any difficulty.

Felice and Lorenzo repainted the fuselage, the trike and other small components. They took delivery of the two new grey wings and set them all up again as a unit. They loaded them on to the trailers and set off for a trial drive around the Edinburgh bypass. All went smoothly and they returned to the hangar, unbuckled the transport straps, tilted the flat beds and winched the microlights back on to terra firma. They carried out their pre-flight checks and rose again into the sky, following the route to Jedburgh, after logging their flight with air traffic control.

On this occasion their flight path would continue over Jedburgh to Kielder Forest Park, the reservoir, the small valleys and hills that surround the forest. Their flying skills were honed, pitching into turns at the maximum sixty degrees, rising and dropping at maximum and minimum airspeed. They were testing the craft to their absolute limits of technical design. Both pilots proved that they could go beyond the QuikR's recommended data stated in the manufacturers safety manual.

....

Fatima spent the intervening weeks moving between the seats of power of the targets, The Ministry of Defence and The Home Office. Ardavan had arranged for two motor scooters and two delivery company driver bibs to be left for her in the warehouse. These allowed her to move around freely and switch around through traffic, whilst studying journeys or parts of journeys and work out some, but not all of the routine daily movements of the targets.

There were also changes in Ministerial appointments to consider, so that Fatima's hard work in tracking down targets was continually changing. Politicians came and went like geese from a field on a winter's day.

She wondered what Ardavan's final plan would be and how they would target the four British men on his hit list.

....

Paulo phoned Lorenzo again and said 'I want you and Felice to pack up the microlights and take everything with you to London. On the way there you'll receive another call, this time from my client, giving you an address you have to go to. You've to be there in 48 hours. Understood?'

'Yeah Paulo, understood. Will this client be our boss from now on or will you continue to be involved?' 'You'll have a new boss, Lorenzo. I'm no longer in charge so I'll see you when you get back. Ciao,' replied Paulo.

Lorenzo told Felice about the new schedule and they made a list of everything they would have to do before they set off. Felice was tasked with checking their route to London and he reckoned it would be easier to go straight down the A1 and then the M1 to the M25 orbital. They could jump off the orbital at any stage for whatever final destination was in store.

Lorenzo was working through the check list and a feeling began to gnaw at his guts. Why were they working for some other person. Why not the Neapolitans any more? Had it transformed into something more dangerous or more sinister? He wanted to get back at authority but not at any cost. His life did not really matter anymore but the lives of innocent others did.

They loaded up the trailers with the two microlights, fuel, spares and even the two old wings, hitched up the trailers to the tow units and were on their way within four hours. They arranged to stop every two hours to check their loads and take on board sustenance for their journey.

The following day, after an overnight stop near York, the two combinations were stopped at a service station for fuel and a break when they received a call from a woman.

'Hello, my name is Fatima. Paulo told you to expect my call, did he not?'

'Yeah, Paulo told me that someone would call. I'm Lorenzo.'

'I will meet you in the smoking area in five minutes. I will know you.'

‘How will she know me?’ thought Lorenzo, and told Felice to stay where he was and he’d be back shortly.

As he headed for the smoking area, he was bumped by a girl in a tracksuit, but thought nothing of it. He sat in the smoking area for a full ten minutes, getting more agitated by the minute, before his phone rang again. ‘Look in your jacket pocket. There is an address on a slip of paper. Go there.’ Said the woman’s voice. ‘That’s spooky. How did that get there?’, thought Lorenzo, as he took out the paper and looked suspiciously around him. Then he remembered the girl bumping into him. ‘Clever’ he breathed to himself, forcing himself away from the swirling cigarette smoke.

Back with Felice he explained that he had the address and that before they set off they would check the routing on his phone in his cab.

‘We’ve got to go to Wapping in East London Felice, so what’s the best way? It’s Atlantic Wharf.’

‘Well Lorenzo, my first thought was correct, carry on down the M1, then M25 and we’ll take it from there. We’ll be ready for another stop once we’re on to the M25 heading east, and we can check out the detail there, for the last piece of the journey.’

At the last break of their journey on the M25 around London they sussed out the route they must take and transferred the two way radios from their gear into the Hilux cabs, so they could check up on each other as they moved into the heavier traffic of the metropolis.

They arrived at the address in Wapping and were ushered in through a roller shutter door, which was closed behind them.

'I am Ardavan. You will operate to my instructions, or to that of my colleague, Fatima, who phoned you earlier. She will be here shortly. Did everything go okay?' 'Yes,' the lads said in unison and shook the offered hand.

They looked around, and apart from them and the combinations there was nothing else in the unit. There was a small office in the corner and a single door marked WC.

A few minutes later Ardavan's phone rang four times and he picked up the call, said 'Okay' and went to open the roller shutter door. A small city car pulled in and out stepped a very attractive dark haired girl, who also offered her outstretched hand, which the lads shook warmly.

'I am Fatima,' was all she said.

'Go with Fatima, to her flat and she will discuss with you some of the details which we need to iron out. I will join you later,' said Ardavan.

She drove to Riddell Court and all three went up in the elevator to the third floor. There had been no discussion during the journey and it seemed to take an age in the rush hour traffic. She showed them to one of the bedrooms and told them to make themselves comfortable. There was food and drinks in the fridge or they could choose something from the freezer and microwave it.

The two fliers tucked in to some pepperoni pizza and a couple of beers and settled down on the sofa. They found a sports channel with football and settled down to watch.

Just at that inopportune moment Ardavan keyed the lock and came in, flinging a wry smile at the two loafers. Fatima came out of the other bedroom, wearing a tracksuit, the one that had bumped Lorenzo in the roadside service station. Now Lorenzo was getting the connection. Had she been shadowing them since Gorebridge? He sat up to ask, but thought better of it and sat back into the sofa.

'Do you know why you are here?' Ardavan asked, looking at each of them in turn with his hawk like face.

It was Felice who spoke 'No, not really, but we do know that you need us to fly the microlights. It might, in fact most likely will, be dangerous, likely highly illegal and a way to strike back at the politicians and authority of this country, if not the wider world.'

'Well that sums up the logic behind all of us being here,' Ardavan replied. 'There is a basic plan, but before we can fully implement it, Fatima needs to find an airfield close to the city centre, which will be used for your takeoff. Fatima, have you progressed that glitch yet?'

'No. All airfields are too far away and would not give us any element of surprise. We've already discounted a ground attack so we do need to place that location.'

'Is it just the microlights that you are considering?' said Lorenzo.

'It is, that is what we agreed some time ago to use,' said Ardavan.

Lorenzo said, 'Well, in that case all we need is a piece of quiet road or a strip of grass. We would be restricted by width and length of takeoff, oh, and there cannot be any fences or wires overhead. The width of the wings is 8.45 metres. We would have to be prepared beforehand, as two microlights in the centre of London would raise a few stares.'

'Okay, Fatima, you research that a bit further with these two and hopefully between the three of you, you'll come up with an answer,' said Ardavan, as he rose to go. 'And, if there's further cash needed for anything, you know that I can obtain it. Call me as soon as you have a solution.'

....

Chief Inspector Victoria Douglas had gathered her team for the security meeting arranged for the 24th October to discuss the parade. Her underlings listened intently to what she had to say. There were no second questions asked at meetings under her chairwomanship. Everyone was tasked with individual operations and was expected to go away, armed with the information she had given them, and imagine the situation where they were the attacker and how they would deal with any threat.

In this way she could winkle out individual thoughts, new thoughts, historical failures and successes, but leave no stone unturned in her quest for total and utter security.

'I will start with the targets. In front of you is the list of attendees, some of a much higher rank or status than others. Some people think that the higher one is, the more secure one should be. I go on the basis that, if we look after the one at the bottom of the heap, then the one at the top stays safe as well.'

'In saying so, there will be different realms of security, this being dependent on when and where an individual arrives. We have to consider that the main threat to our democracy will come, not from within, but from outside of the people we are trying to protect.'

'In this regard we will start with the Bobbies on the beat, at four times their normal coverage, with riot squads, in transports, on side streets, ready and waiting. There will be a ring of uniforms to all accesses. There will be a line of police immediately to the front of the general public, no more than three metres apart. There will be airport style security detectors for the general public, bag searches and body searches. This will seek out hand held weapons, which would need to be brandished to effect an attack. Anything in a bag could contain explosive charges in any format, so any element larger than an airport clear plastic toiletries bag should be removed without question for later destruction. The articles will be put in the safe boxes adjacent to the security scanners. Place a notice in that vein in all media channels, and on site at two hundred metres and again at one hundred metres of the security scanner, in English, French, German, Italian, Arabic, Chinese and Japanese languages. Also add that any spectators must be in possession of their passport. No other photo ID will be acceptable.'

'All dignitaries will be issued with formal invitations, which will have photo ID attached and space for signature. These can be presented at any one of the four entry points to the parade and entry will not be granted without one. I don't care if the Prime Minister has forgotten his. He could have a body double and is therefore a threat. All entries must be signed by each and every dignitary.'

'There will be a pecking order in the line-up for dignitaries as usual, as we do not want a dose of people milling about. The invitees will therefore be timed to arrive and then allocated a place in the queue, so to speak.'

'Now let's go on to attack methods that we know about, which have happened to security details before and which are the favourites to happen again. Distant sniper...work out visually, on a nice quiet Sunday morning, all the vantage points which can be seen from your position on the ground, and by the ground I mean every single square millimetre of the extent of the parade. Then put a search and secure closure on each and every vantage point that could be used by a sniper. In this case take 1250 metres as the kill distance. We have to take a chance on the world's best long distance sniper not being there on the day, because that's over 3000 metres, people!'

'Then we go on to thrown armaments, such as grenades, maybe using sling shots or launchers. Work out the vantage points, seal off and then place two special armed response officers on the spot. Radio contact to be maintained at all times on the yet to be decided secure channel.'

'Then there is the vehicle attack. There will be concrete barriers placed at all entrances and exits to allow only personnel through. These will be placed at a distance apart where the individual has to turn through it to get in. They cannot hurdle it or run through it. There will not be enough room for two wheeled motor vehicles, or even a pedal cycle to get through. If practical, put in a secondary step over, but there may be a need to allow disabled persons through. Check thoroughly all disabled or handicapped persons equipment as you would a bag search.'

'Finally, attack from the air. There will be a 'No Fly' zone applicable on the day, with a range of five kilometres. London City will still be allowed to handle flights, as that is well outside of our exclusion zone. There will be no helicopter traffic to and from buildings within the zone. There will be two Police helicopters, fitted with the usual technology watching from east and west sides, both connected by radio on the same frequency.'

Vicky finished with, 'That's all people. Go away and think up some more ruses and come back to me individually. If a ruse has been done before I will not be pleased to see it again. I expect you to do your homework first. You may stand down.'

19 South London set up

The next morning, as Lorenzo opened the curtains, to be confronted with a dull late October morning, he had a brainwave. He hadn't noticed when he arrived in the darkness the previous evening. The third floor flat was on the end of a block that overlooked a public park. There were walkers, joggers, cyclists and buggies with infants being pushed. A network of paths stretched out in front of him, but his eyes were drawn to one particularly wide path. As he leaned out of the open window he could see from end to end. There was a roadway at one end and a pond at the other, but an uninterrupted wide tarmac path between the two. He reckoned it to be about two hundred metres in a dead straight line, cutting diagonally through the greenery. There were bunches of mature trees dotted around and some newly planted saplings which had been sporadically planted next to the main path.

'Felice, Felice, wake up man!' he cried and Felice woke with a start.

'What's wrong Lorenzo? You scared me!'

'Come here, quickly!' Lorenzo beckoned him to the window. 'What do you reckon? A ready made airstrip, on tarmac, in the city centre, or quite near at any rate! What do you think? Could we launch from there?'

Felice now stuck his head out of the window, surveyed up and down, took his head back in and said, 'I think you've struck gold. That's a great idea. Let's get Fatima, now!'

'Whoa. Hold your horses Felice. Let's do this right. I need coffee and some muesli first, then a shower to clear my head. Then we can do some measurements, you know, just by striding out, then, if it's fine, we can tell her and give her the full picture. At the moment it's only a hunch, right?'

'Yes, I suppose you're right, but I was dying to see what she looks like just out of bed. In fact, if truth be told, I'd like to see what she looks like in bed!' They both laughed a dirty man's laugh.

They went out into the cold of the morning and paced up and down the park, checking minimum dimensions, comparing them to what they knew of the microlights and concluded that the strip was fine, apart from a couple of newly planted saplings on either side of the main path, which looked like they would be closer than the wing span. Nevertheless, they took their idea to Fatima.

She was up and at breakfast when they came back. She asked where they had been and Lorenzo told her about his hunch and their visit to the Park. After some thought she said that it would be best to buy some tape measures or surveyor's measures, the long ones, and accurately check out the dimensions. She checked on line and found a seller of such equipment, not too far away in Brixton. She set off immediately in her small car and returned within the hour and handed the goods to the fliers. There was a flexible metal ten metre tape and a fifty metre roll out non stretch tape, with a winding handle. When they went back outside they found that the straight path measured one hundred and seventy-two metres and the width in the various places they'd selected was six metres of path.

They hit two snags, each with saplings, where the measurement between the branches was less than eight metres.

This was all related to Fatima, who wanted to go out with them and double check all their already double checked dimensions. She agreed with the length and agreed with the width checks and the issue with the saplings. She said to the two fliers, 'I want you to check these again tomorrow.'

'Check them again?' they wailed. 'We've already checked, double checked and triple checked. What good will a fourth one be?'

'I want them checked, okay? And another thing, how are we going to get rid of all these runners and cyclists?'

'Yeah, that's a bit of an issue all right. I'll work on it. I'll also have to work on how we remain undetected and not gather a mass audience around us, never mind the law,' Lorenzo stated.

‘Okay, till tomorrow then,’ and she turned and strolled off in the direction of the flat.

When the lads got back they noticed that she hadn’t returned, but went about their discussion as to how the place could be used or how another could be found.

The next morning the fliers went out to check their measurements again. She was nowhere to be seen. Everything was as measured the day before. Two policemen were checking out some vandalism that had seemingly occurred during the night. Four saplings had been broken and thrown about the park in small twigs. A small fire had been started and some beer cans were scattered around. The policemen took some notes and headed off in search of witnesses, or to look at CCTV.

The fliers thought it a tad opportune that their runway was now clear of obstacles for its entire length.

....

Fatima was already at the Parks Department of Southwark Borough Council, who was responsible for Burgess Park. She had made an appointment to arrange an Italian Day in the park. She put forward the proposal, without a date as yet, to show off all things Italian, in memory of the Italian losses under COVID19. There would be a number of marquees and smaller tents, each with stalls showing merchandise, holidays, regional specialities in food and some fast food stalls. All would be accessible from the main path running through the park, which would be cordoned off with tape on either side, at a distance of around ten metres, where they could. Where that couldn't be achieved, they would place bins for rubbish and recycling. She didn't have all information to hand as yet, as she needed to speak with others, who were awaiting the result of her chat with the Council.

The Council lady she spoke with was very sympathetic to her request, but needed to check the statutory requirements and would get back to her. Fatima responded by saying that she would not always be able to pick up a call, but she would call back the following day. The lady took her address as Riddell Court for the necessary permits, if the answer was affirmative.

Fatima called Ardavan and arranged to meet him at the warehouse in Wapping.

They both agreed that the opportunity was there to use Burgess Park as a runway. They could arrange for marquees and other gear, like generators, streamers, banners, knock in posts for tape and the rest.

They then sat for some hours discussing where and when and Ardavan came up with a solution. The location was ideal, the date was fixed and Burgess Park would be close enough to their target so as not to give much warning. He told her that the date would fall on Armistice Day and that all four targets would be together, out in the open.

Fatima would check out the rehearsal at the attack site and report back, just to ensure that all was as previous parades.

Ardavan put his plan into action for the alteration of the two QuikR's to take the weaponry. He instructed Fatima to measure up the exact course, scope out all the snags and possibilities and get the fliers training on a similar course, so that they could carry out the attack with their eyes closed.

Fatima returned to the Council offices and proposed dates for a Monday and Tuesday show, with the preceding Saturday and Sunday to set up and the following Wednesday to decamp and tidy the site. This was agreed and the Council lady said that she'd inform all relevant departments and advise the Metropolitan Police. The permits were signed and handed over.

Having been away for two days Fatima returned to the flat to find the lads to be a bit stir crazy. They told her they'd measured out the ground again and had seen the damaged saplings.

'You don't seem surprised, Fatima.' She smiled and said, 'Sometimes things just fall into place guys. It is the way of the world. Okay, listen very carefully. We have a final plan and this is what we must do.'

The fliers listened intently, whistled softly, went white, gulped, their mouths went dry and then Lorenzo said, 'If you get me the base materials I can make the adjustments to the QuikR's. I'm an Engineer. I can make anything, given the manufacturing tools and the raw materials. I've been doing this for years. I could set up a workstation in the warehouse and all could be done behind closed doors. We could fit all the attachments and make any final adjustments there. We haven't got a lot of time though Fatima.'

'Okay. That's a great idea. We'll meet Ardavan at the warehouse, all three of us. While you work on the manufacturing, Felice can work on the routing with me. Then you will both have to find a practice route to ensure that you can fly to plan.'

Felice broke in, 'I will need to find an airfield, a bone fide one, where we can launch from. Then we can find a quiet field somewhere to land and takeoff from again, timing the route, deciding on a flying altitude and speed of turns. Leave that one with me, Fatima.'

When they arrived at the warehouse in Wapping later that day Ardavan was already there and he had taken the packages from the top of the office unit down on to the warehouse floor. He explained that each QuikR would need an attachment on each side, which would have to be a stable platform to both support the weapon and also be hidden from prying eyes on the journey from Wapping to Burgess Park and to the airfield, which Felice would choose. The additions could not affect the flight stability of the aircraft.

Lorenzo said, ‘Show me the weapons and I will work something out.’

The packages were unwrapped and Felice was first to react. ‘What on earth? Is that what I think it is? I’ve only ever seen them in newsreels or films. They are deadly aren’t they?’

‘They are deadly, but only when armed. They are quite innocuous when just transported around. They’ve been adapted for just such an attack as this. They will be ideal. The effect will be catastrophic. We’ll hit our four targets. Now Lorenzo, let’s start on a design.’

Lorenzo picked up the various parts of the weapon and weighed them in his hands. ‘The first thing I’ll need is a fighting weight of each set. I presume that both sides of each microlight will have a support frame. The aircraft has a fixed payload, but as long as the payload does not weigh more than a 100 kg person, then I can make this work. The frames will have to be aerodynamic, otherwise flight will be affected. It can’t be too complicated either, or the mechanism of firing will be too much for us Red Barons to carry out while sticking to the task of flying. I am guessing, that when we fire, the after effects will not bring us out of the sky in a heap of tangled metal. If I’m going to die doing this I want it to be quick. I don’t want to be lying in a hospital bed somewhere as a blithering cabbage. That would be a sentence worse than death!'

'I agree,' said Felice. We do this and get away or we die in the attempt. I'd prefer to get away and read about what I've done to strike a blow at the society we live in now.'

Ardavan knew then that his main worry had been resolved. The two fliers could do the deed when it came to the crunch. They weren't Kurds. They didn't have the Kurdish national pride which would cause them to strike back against their enemy, but they had an enemy of a different kind. They wanted to strike back at a common enemy of uncaring billionaires and politicians, out for their own trading profits with their greedy, self-satisfying needs, with not a care for other less fortunate people around the world or family virtues. 'Yes, they have a need. They have a destiny. Just like us,' he breathed to Fatima.

Ardavan and Fatima procured the materials which Lorenzo had asked for, the aluminium sheet, rod and ingots. The stainless steel bolts and nuts, the lathe and formers, anvil and hammers and the screwing machine. Last thing to come was the matt grey spray paint. At the end of the intensive eighteen hour days put in by Lorenzo, with Ardavan's assistance, they had made two pairs of port and starboard aerodynamic torpedo shapes which were bolted to the frame of the Quick R's and looked a bit like long range fuel tanks.

Lorenzo had contrived to keep the weight well below the one hundred kilogram limit and had concocted a clever design to open the weapons from their shields and fix a remote firing mechanism, through a micro pulley system between the side of the fuselage and the triggers of the weapons.

Felice had sourced an airstrip near to Elstree Film Studios that had small aircraft traffic movements on a regular basis. They could also use the cover of filming for the changed shape of the microlights, just in case regular fliers of QuikR craft took an interest in what they were doing.

Ardavan and Lorenzo discussed the logic of firing distance. The side pods had been made adjustable so the firing tubes could be angled away from the aircraft or towards each other to a central spot. This became an extremely technical business. There were things like speed of the aircraft on approach, aircraft height, firing platform stability, target range, escape and the back blast of the weaponry to consider. They went to it with gusto and came up with a definitive setting for the firing tubes and ensured that they could not move with aircraft vibration.

Meanwhile, Fatima and Felice worked on the routing, the takeoff speed and distance to full flight, the exact route which would be followed, the speed of flight after takeoff, the speed into each turn along the way, the final turn, the attacking formation and separation distance. They also considered the escape route and the possibility of them being attacked along the way. Potential hazards would likely be met and countered and – if they succeeded – how they would all get away.

Fatima brought the escape plan to Ardavan's attention and they came up with an idea that would involve two other faithful Kurds, who would just come in and out of the plan, without knowing anything other than they would be couriers. They resolved that issue too, after a bit of rooting around.

Felice and Lorenzo loaded up the QuikR's onto the trailers, hitched up the Hiluxes and drove off to Elstree Airfield. As they arrived at their destination and headed along Hoggs Lane for the car park, they noticed quite a number of small aircraft through the wire fence, lined up on the hard standing and thought that they would blend in quite easily. Before they had left the Wapping warehouse they had fitted their peel-off aircraft identification numbers to both aircraft, so that no undue attention would be brought to bear.

The receptionist welcomed them with a ready smile and on enquiry advised them of the takeoff and landing fees and the car parking charges. She pointed out the fuel bowser and gave each of the fliers a token card for fuel payments. They opted for two hundred pounds Sterling each, to be debited from their own Gorebridge company credit cards. The receptionist then introduced them to the Security guy who hopped in to Lorenzo's Hilux and asked him to head around to the wire gates that they had just passed on their way in. He took them airside, to allow them to offload the aircraft, expand their wings and fuel up if necessary. He then pointed to the wind sock and the wind gauge on the side of the control tower, handed over their two identity passes and finally told them they could park the Hiluxes and trailers on the grass verges at the side of their chosen hard standing locations.

Lorenzo phoned Fatima and told her that all was well and that they would be ready to take to the skies that afternoon. Elstree would be their base for the next few days but they would return to the flat each night. They told the airfield manager that they would be carrying out trial flights for a low budget movie they were making and asked if there were any local farmers who perhaps had aircraft of their own and who would allow them to overfly at low level. He promised to ask around, as he was aware of two landowners, not necessarily farmers, who might be willing to assist.

That afternoon brought squally showers which limited their takeoff slots and visibility, so they decided to head out in one of the Hiluxes and check out the farmland that the manager had suggested to them. The landowner was away on business and they could have free run of his land. There were no animals to be concerned about except some horses that would be cooped up in the stables over the next three days.

Felice's plan of their attack route was such that he knew that they would achieve takeoff, acquire minimum flying height for stable flight, the time needed for the near four kilometres route from the start to the finish line, where the turns would occur in the timing and in which direction. He said to Lorenzo, 'I've noted all the timings down on a pad so you can see them while you're flying, without too much of a distraction. I've also fitted some weights inside the empty shells of the side pods, so that we're flying with the same operational weight as we will have on our attack flight. I've allowed a full load of fuel, so we can make our escape to a more remote location than the one we have already chosen if necessary.

Felice went on to say, 'The owner's farm is out from Elstree to the north west, just beyond Aylsbury and the land sits between Pitchcott and Hardwick. It's about fifty kilometres away as the crow flies and the land is quite flat, so field takeoff and landing should be quite straight forward, unless these showers have made the fields a bit soft. Only time will tell and in any case we can make allowances for takeoff time.'

....

Bernadette Bucheron made a phone call to Vicky Douglas.

'Vicky, I have some information for you, in relation to the three point plan we discussed some time ago. The guy who attempted to murder your husband's colleague is an Iraqui Kurd, Rohat Dilhan. He was in the PKK some years ago and was part of a Special Forces Commando unit, headed up by a guy, Ardavan Kamandi. In the squad was a Yusef Polat, whose photographic ID shows him to be the truck driver from Turkey. He was obviously travelling under a false Turkish passport, in the name of Behwan Fidan. Also in that squad, back in the day, was Felek (Lucky) Kinar and two others who have since died.'

'Ardavan Kamandi was the Kurdish representative at a secret meeting that my husband attended last year. This is no co-incidence Bernadette. This is serious and we must get to grips with all these people,' replied Vicky.

'Okay, Vicky. We know a bit more. Felek Kinar travelled on trains to and from Aberdeen and London. He also travelled on the overnight ferry, both ways, between Aberdeen and Lerwick. I've seen the ticket logs of all four journeys.'

She went on to say, 'I think that the truck driver, Yusef Polat, delivered something to Bergen, and that somehow, that delivery got from Bergen to Lerwick. Then Felek Kinar, maybe not so lucky now, was the courier from Lerwick to London.'

'Thanks, Bernadette, you are an absolute marvel. You must have a lot of resources behind you to get to where you are.'

'I wish! It's just my nose poking in where it shouldn't be and I play my hunches to the end. It may be logged out on the Interpol system but it's never logged out of my mind.'

'Yes, I get where you're coming from. I'll warn my husband on this one and push this all the way up to the top. I'll let you know what happens, if it happens. Incidentally, is there anything more on the link with the Bosnian?'

"No, not yet. We have interviewed him but he's giving nothing away and he's not broken any laws that we can bring to bear. We know that, before all this came up, he travelled to Albania for a short period of time, but what that has to do with the London thing is still a bit of a mystery. If we could track down the Kamandi fellow we might be on to something. We can try and find Polat in Europe or Turkey if you could concentrate on the Kinar guy. Maybe those men will lead us to Kamandi. He has been traced using his standard passport details on a flight from Iraq to Paris Charles de Gaulle and then onwards from Paris Gare du Nord railway station on the Eurostar to London St. Pancras station. That was in the first week in September. We have no leads as to his whereabouts since then, but he must have been seen somewhere in the last two months in your country, unless he has been using covert means of travel.'

'Consider it done Bernadette. I'll be in touch.'

20 Pre-planning

They got both QuikR's away in the early afternoon of the 5th November and were over Aylesbury within half an hour. Felice was in the leading aircraft while Lorenzo circled on his left. Felice tried a landing in the largest of the fields. It was good and firm and Lorenzo flew down to make a perfect, if slightly bumpy, landing. The two fliers went out to check the main frames, the attachments, the wings and their fuel loads. All ticked off as being in regular order, so they turned their craft around and taxied across to the other side of the field for the takeoff into the slight wind.

Felice went first again and radioed the other microlight, relaying everything he was doing. When Lorenzo engaged full power he was mindful of the need to exactly follow Felice's wheel marks in the grass and watch out for the occasional rabbit hole. When they were up in full flight Felice radioed and Lorenzo took the instruction to follow every move Felice made, flying just off his port wing at all times, in as tight a formation as was safe.

Felice went through the seconds count on the watch strapped to his wrist. They had targeted 120 km/hr flying speed, or thirty-three metres for every second they were airborne. They would time their takeoffs from the tarred surface at Elstree on other occasions to give the rehearsal a feel of the actual takeoff surface, as their overall timing for the final attack would be crucial.

They had allowed for clearing the first hurdle of the tall trees at the end of their Burgess Park runway within fifty metres of takeoff and forty metres of altitude, keep the climb for another twelve seconds, to one hundred metres altitude, ninety degrees to port, fifteen seconds straight, forty-five degrees to port, another fifteen seconds straight, starboard for twenty degrees, thirteen seconds straight, small jink to left, then right, same heading for eighteen seconds, ten degrees to port, another eighteen seconds straight, drop to forty metres in next seventeen seconds, ninety degrees sharp to starboard and one hundred and forty metres to target. Then it was just one hundred and ten metres until a sharp ninety degrees to port and escape route.

Their first attempt was a bit sloppy but Lorenzo had no difficulty keeping station with Felice, as he had to check all read outs as he handled the aircraft. They turned back to the original field, landed, ran through some tidying up they could do, checked their aircraft and rehearsed the whole procedure again. They took a rough count of the seconds to takeoff from their standing start in the grassy field, which they could extrapolate into a tarmacadam strip takeoff length in due course, to compare with the Elstree strip hard surface takeoff timing.

They were using a lot of fuel on each takeoff and so, after three full schedules, they retired and flew back to the airfield. While they were flying they went through things over and over on their hand held radios, in the knowledge that nobody could be listening in to their chatter. They were happy that they could get their takeoff to target time down to two minutes from the two minutes twenty seconds that they had managed on their third run.

....

Vicky Douglas made another call to Lyon and spoke quickly to Bernadette. 'We've traced Kinar, the musician. It was quite a simple task as he is featured to play in a number of venues as a soloist or as a member of an ensemble throughout Europe. We caught up with him at rehearsal at The Albert Hall in London and hurried him off to New Scotland Yard for interrogation. He admitted that he travelled to Lerwick from London, via Aberdeen, just as your records had shown. He said at the start that it was just to see a friend who had broken his leg, but he had cancelled a concert just to go there. That's not what you would normally do and after a bit of added persuasive tactics he further admitted to collecting two packages, described to him as definitely not containing drugs. The packages were quite heavy and were collected by Kinar from a Norwegian male, named Egil Hansen, who had sailed from Bergen. This confirms your hunch and why the trail ran cold. So now we have a package route from Turkey, across Europe by land, yacht to the UK and further couriered to London, where we believe the action will occur. We were getting closer Bernadette. Keeping on with the interrogation we found that the packages were no longer in his hands but had been delivered to an address not far from The Elephant and Castle but he either could not remember or did not want to give up the exact address.

“That’s great news, Vicky. We haven’t been able to glean anything on the Polat figure yet but we’ll keep plodding away until we dig something up. I’ll get my colleagues in Norway to trace down the Hansen contact. We’ll see where that leads us. Best of luck!’

Vicky cut the call and turned to her team. ‘Right people, this Kamandi chap should stand out in a crowd, just look at that great big snout of his. Start searching around middle-eastern or Arabian haunts in quick succession. That is where he would most likely fit in. His prominent features to us would not be so stark in that sort of crowd. He must eat, so try restaurants and small shops specialising in middle-eastern foods, especially Kurdish. Run off his passport photograph if you have not already done so and look into the eyes of all who you ask. The eyes are the most difficult feature in which to hide emotion. Anyone could be shielding him or covering for him. Go to it. Time is of the essence!’

....

Fatima was waiting for them when they got back to the flat in Riddell Court and the fliers explained the routines that they had carried out, and their thinking that the timing could be reduced. She replied that the exact time would not be strictly necessary, as the strike would have a window of opportunity in any case. But, she had added, they could not be early, or more than two minutes late.

In return she told them that the Italian Days had been set in stone with the Council and that they would set up the marquees in the weekend after next. The marquees were on order. There were various sizes and the largest was twenty metres long by five metres wide and three metres tall. This would allow the microlights to be stored inside, wings expanded and readied for flight inside the marquee. There were support poles all round, placed at five metre intervals. By removing two of the five front wall poles there would be room to roll out the aircraft through the openings together or singly, allowing for a bit of sag on the canvas.

'That's great Fatima, we should be able to open up the rear of the marquee and fire up the engines before they are powered out. They will be a bit noisier than generators, and we will have to screen the tail ends with the Hiluxes or vans or something that can't be blown down with the prop wash,' said Felice.

Lorenzo, without enthusiasm, voiced his approval and added, 'That timing will allow us to perfect our Red Baron work over the fields of Buckinghamshire.'

Fatima noted his slight change of tone and wondered what Lorenzo's thoughts were. She would talk to him later, in a quiet moment away from Felice and Ardavan.

Another day of flight exercises was carried out over the fields near Aylsbury and then the fliers headed back to the flat once more. Ardavan and Fatima were already there, beside a white van in the car park at the west end of Burgess Park. The weather was good and would stay calm and dry over the next few days. There were two other men beside the van and as the fliers pulled in behind it they reflected that they had not seen them before and they spoke to Ardavan in a language foreign to them.

Early on Saturday morning the two men began to extract canvas, stakes, poles, guy ropes and tarpaulins from the van. Fatima roamed up and down the park with plasticised notices and cable ties and stuck or tied them to various surfaces around the park. They depicted the words 'Italian Day' and various scenes of Mozzarella, Chianti, Rome, Vatican City and Sicily, declaring that the event would be on the following Monday and Tuesday.

Under Kamandi's instruction, the two men erected the large marquee while the fliers went off down the main path, striking metal uprights into the surrounding soil, at a separation distance of ten metres. They did this for the whole length of the path and then across the path at the end of the pond. The red, white and green ribbons were next, strung along the top of the stakes for the entire length and across the pond end.

Once the large marquee had been erected the men made a start on the second much smaller tent. Ardavan had spread some other tents at various spacings along the first part of the runway and these would be erected to follow. Fatima erected a sign at the large marquee with some more details of the event together with a copy of the Council Licence. A truck came and offloaded four portable toilet pods and the whole affair was beginning to look presentable.

There were some curious glances from passers by and some questions from an older couple. A passing police foot patrol checked the signage and asked to see the licence. After inspection they passed on their condolences to what was seemingly an Italian group by the sound of their accents, for their losses under COVID19.

By midday Kamandi gruffly told the fliers to take the two tarpaulins and some rope and go and collect the combinations from Elstree. They would have time for one last practice, then time their arrival at Burgess Park to coincide with dusk and offload the microlights from the trailers. The tarpaulins should be used to entirely cover their cargo and not draw attention to their delivery. They would have to arrive at the marquee and drive straight in and through, leaving the trailers behind, under the cover of canvas. They could then remove the microlights from the trailers and set them up into flight mode.

The fliers set off and by late afternoon the canvas village had been erected, as empty shells. The fliers had careered about the low skies above Aylsbury and had managed to drop their target time to just under one hundred and twenty seconds. The two extra men had left to complete another task that had been set by Kamandi.

As the last of the light dropped from the western sky, the fliers arrived with the combinations and went to drive into the marquee. However Fatima noticed a snag. The marquee was not tall enough! The height of the microlight had been checked but they had missed the lift height of the trailer. They would have to get the aircraft off the trailer and roll them in to the marquee, but there was a visual risk involved, which they firstly had to work out. She left both fliers to remove their loose equipment and find a lorry park somewhere close, to bed down for the night in their cabs. They would not look out of place under those circumstances.

Kamandi and Fatima went back to the flat and talked through the problem which had to be resolved overnight. She phoned Lorenzo and asked him to check the height of the trailer bed, which he did, using the edge of an A4 sheet of paper as a guide. The two Kurds worked out that they could raise the marquee poles on to bricks and gain the additional height, without anything being seen inside, apart from the wheels. When the microlights were offloaded they could then drop the canvas back down. Fatima set off in her little car to find a quiet building site and the requisite number of bricks.

She found what she was looking for a short distance away, at a Housing Association site with a brick façade. There was a security presence on site and a guy in a Portacabin. CCTV was also evident, so she walked straight up to the cabin and peered in through the window and saw the monitor and the recorder on the desk. The guard was looking at his phone and not paying any attention to the screen, but at any moment he could. So she decided to brazen it out and opened the door quickly.

She'd dishevelled her hair and smudged her make up, pinched her cheeks and neck and rushed in, sobbing hysterically. 'Help me, please help me, I've just been assaulted in the street, he got my bag but I managed to get away!' At that she pulled the surprised bloke from his seat and headed him out of the cabin, pushing him in front of her for protection.

'Look lady, this is none of my business, I'd better call the police,' and he raised the phone in his hand to see what he was doing. He never remembered what exactly happened next, when he related the story to the police, other than the fact that he woke up with a very sore head and a lump just above his ear. Nothing appeared to be missing apart from the CCTV recorder. He would not have missed a few bricks, which were piled up ready for the next lift, until the brickie foreman told him about a shortage of bricks the next day. He reported them stolen to the police and that went on their files, to add to the hundreds of unsolved thefts occurring on a daily basis in the Metropolitan area.

Fatima arrived back at the marquee and Kamandi helped her to get the brickwork supports readied and the marquee lifted, then they called Lorenzo. He broke from his uncomfortable and fitful snoozing, shook Felice awake and they drove the trailers back to Burgess Park. The marquee was open to the car park and they drove straight in, tipped the trailers and winched off the microlights, while inching out the Hiluxes out on the runway side, pulling the trailers behind. The microlights were perfectly placed, side by side, ready for the tarpaulins to be stripped and the wings set up for flight. The Kurds prepared for an uncomfortable few hours on the grass on watch over the kit. Lorenzo and Felice were glad to get back to the flat and grab a few hours in a real bed. They left the Hiluxes and trailers between the marquee and the second tent.

Kamandi finished his vigil and woke Fatima. Dawn had broken and he said that all was quiet, but he had to go in search of food and drink. In a short while he was back with a paper bag with hot food from a baker and two paper cups full of steaming coffee and they ate silently together. He said, ‘Fatima, go to the flat and take some time to gather your thoughts. Our big day will soon be upon us and we will need the strength of mind to look for anything that will, at the last minute, scupper our plan. I will stay here and work with the fliers. Send them down to me. I checked with our colleagues and our escape plan is in place.’

She went to rouse the two airmen and found Felice fast asleep and Lorenzo looking at his phone, with a worried expression on his face. 'What's up Lorenzo?' she whispered. Now was her chance to speak to him alone. She beckoned him into the lounge and closed the bedroom door behind him, isolating Felice from the conversation.

'Look Fatima! This is a video of the Armistice Day Parade from last year. I fully understand Ardavan's wish to take out the four British men and I would not lose sleep over them going and a few others as well, but look at the number of innocent bystanders, everyday Bobbies on the beat and the hundreds of others who would be caught up in the attack. There are even kids in the crowd! Is this what he wants to happen? Does he want to unleash the wrath of the world with this action? Did you know that this is what it was all about? What would your own Kurdish people say about this barbarous act, you included?'

He looked at her. She was visibly shocked by what she saw.

'Lorenzo, I honestly didn't know the extent of this. I thought it was a parade where a few men could be taken out in a close bunch, but not this. Our brothers and sisters in the KRG would not, could not, condone an action such as this. This is far too extreme. We have to put a stop to this and we don't have much time. We cannot let Ardavan know our thoughts though, as he might just get rid of us and get others to do his bidding for him. We'll have to go along with his plan as it stands at the moment and I'll work a way out of it. What do you think Felice makes of this? Is he also mad enough to carry this through? Does he even know what he is about to do? Can we trust him for the moment? I think you'll agree that we should keep this just between us and sabotage the mission in some way, but we'll have to find a way out for ourselves. We can't fall into the hands of the authorities, as they'll likely not believe that we were not involved in this mad scheme from the first instance. In any case we were both willing to take out a few men, so we'd definitely be held to account.'

'Okay, I'll go along with that, but if we can find a way out I'm ditching this mad plan and escaping the country as soon as I can, alone if necessary.'
'I'm with you on that one. Now please go and wake Felice and both of you head down to Ardavan. Thank you for telling me this,' she said as she leaned forward and kissed him full on the lips. 'Thank you,' she repeated, her brow creased with worry.

Lorenzo thought that he'd done the right thing, released his thoughts to her and her alone. He felt that she could be trusted. He opened the bedroom door and called to Felice. He didn't know if he could trust him for the present.

……….

The Metropolitan Police Headquarters at New Scotland Yard received a very short call asking to

speak to somebody in Special Branch and to phone back on a mobile number in two minutes. She gave the person on the end of the line a code word to use when they connected with the later call. The duty Inspector was alerted and he immediately moved it up the line to Chief Inspector Douglas, who originally baulked at the thought, until the Inspector told her that the code name to be used for the call was 'Armistice'.
She punched in the number given, finger poised over the green symbol, while shouting at anybody within range 'Trace this call!'

At the fourth ring a female answered the call and said, 'Let the parade go ahead. I have just found out what my boss is going to do and I can thwart it. Trust me and you will win.' The call was cut and there was a shake of the head from the tracing team. 'Get an all points out on the rough location. Stop all traffic in the surrounding area. Stop all people. Where roughly is the caller?' The shout came back as, 'Elephant and Castle! The caller could be on any one of four major arteries, a train or any one of the myriad of surrounding streets and lanes!'

'Shit, shit, shit! She could have gone anywhere. But it's The Elephant and Castle again – just where the other Kurd said he'd passed the packages! She knew what she was doing! We're dealing with a pro here and not some wacko! Start analysing the voice recording! Get a handle on her!'

In the next few moments she had made calls to her Head of Operations, MI5, MI6, the Prime Minister's office in Downing Street and her husband, who had been asleep at home.

21 Rehearsal

When the fliers arrived, Kamandi asked them to check that the aircraft were in their full attack mode and they went at their twin tasks, ensuring that the wings were in their final lock down and checking all their gauges and instruments, the battery levels, full fuel tanks and finally the adjustments and fixing of the weaponry, for the final firing range agreed. He asked them individually to repeat the flight timings and turnings and how each one would make their escape. In the afternoon the fliers set off individually, at hourly intervals, to walk the chosen route, while the two Kurds busied themselves around the marquee and fended off questions about the event. To all intents and purposes the Italian Days were on schedule and all the goods would arrive on Monday morning. Fatima brought a stereo system to the marquee and the small generator powered it up and blasted some Andrea Bocelli music from the speakers.

Kamandi followed on after the fliers and the last to go on the route walk was Fatima, after the fliers had returned. She'd changed her appearance with the addition of a blonde wig, jeans, trainers, a puffer coat and a woolly hat, with a back-pack draped across her front, in the touristy fashion. Her lithe figure could have been mistaken for that of a more rotund woman. Her disguise was enough to fool a search on any of the CCTV coverage along the route. The men wore jackets with hoods, pulled up against the cold air of the afternoon.

The walk there and back had taken around two hours and all four of them had taken photos on their phones, for comparison when they got back to the marquee. All four had picked up on something that they would have to avoid, look out for or mark as a beacon on the final attack. They had left nothing to chance. They'd talked over the presence of the normal Bobby on the beat and armed police with obvious handguns and automatic rifles. They'd noted the possible locations for security surveillance on roofs and they'd seen the security barriers being erected at the attack location.

The light morning rain driven in on the easterly winds had cleared and the sun was shining weakly through the fluffy clouds that followed. The fair weather was forecast to continue overnight and into the next day, the day of the attack.

The two Kurdish men had delivered two black Triumph Tiger XRx 1200cc motorcycles to Kamandi and had stored them in the second tent, complete with matching panniers and anonymous black bike leathers, boots, gloves and helmets with black visors and radio mikes. A second set of identical clothing had been delivered for Lorenzo and Felice, to wear while flying. A further element of the equipment puzzle had been solved. He had decreed that the bikes would be used to collect the fliers at the appointed escape route pick up point, after they had fled from the attack. The four of them would transform into everyday motorcyclists having a run out for the day.

The plan was for Kamandi to have Lorenzo as pillion while Fatima rode with Felice as hers, as the order of flying for the attack would be Lorenzo leading. He would lead the way on the first bike and she would follow with Felice on his chosen escape route.

'Where are we heading for Ardavan?' Fatima asked.

'Just follow me and you will find out,' he snarled back.

She noticed that his attitude had changed. He was becoming more sinister, showing more of his demonic emotions. Did he know about her chat with Lorenzo? Was she in danger? Had he been recording their every move at the flat? She remembered his words at the villa in Bled......

"***Only three of us will know the full extent of this mission. I will trust nobody so give me your sworn allegiance or I will know.***"

Rohat had already disappeared. Was that Kamandi's doing? Did her colleague somehow let the boss down or was it always his plan to get rid of the team? A chill ran through her and she felt the small hairs at the back of her neck rise.

Kamandi stooped to check the weapons and each explosive warhead was adjusted to give a fragmentation burst of twenty metres radius and the firing mechanism had been fitted within each, to give the required detonation time after launch.

The fliers would activate the firing mechanism that would trigger the grenade into the first eleven metres of space. The fliers would immediately lift their respective aircraft clear of the next stage, the rocket propulsion, which would accelerate the warhead to its target at three hundred metres a second.

The timer setting would be half a second, to take the grenade one hundred and sixty one metres after launch. The targeted epicentre of the explosion had been previously measured in Albania and the calculation was proven. The explosive warhead would ignite at a point just beyond the imposing pillar of The Cenotaph, above the heads of the main dignitaries standing behind the monument, the core of the Royal, Political and Defence establishments in the country. Ardavan Kamandi's year long quest to wipe out the four British men who had thwarted his nation's ambition to be an autonomous country was nearly at an end.

He was of the firm opinion that the death of the British Foreign Secretary, the Defence Secretary, General Sir Patrick Walsh Douglas and the very lucky General Russell Murdoch, who should have been taken out by the idiot, Rohat Dilhan, would soon be registered and a new set of people, more inclined to feel kindly towards the Kurds must emerge. They would take their seat at the United Nations as a certified State.

He gathered Fatima and the two fliers around him and painstakingly went through the whole process of the attack one final time. The steely glint in his eye, the almost maniacal look in his face, the great curving beak of his nose seemingly projecting even further forwards as he jutted out his chin chilled Fatima and Lorenzo to the bone.

'How the hell am I going to get out of this?' thought Lorenzo, as he caught sight of the automatic pistol in the shoulder holster beneath Kamandi's left armpit. 'Any false move now on my part could end up with me dying, but not in the way I thought I might.'

'Okay. I have done all I can here. Now I must go and see to the final part of our escape plan. Let's go Fatima!'

As Kamandi drew her aside Fatima spoke to him in a soft voice, 'Wait a minute Ardavan. I think it would be best if I stayed here and guarded the boys. I would not like to think that they would baulk from their task at the very last minute. You go on and I will see you at the agreed rendezvous in the morning. I will leave here at 10:00 and be with you by 11.00.'

Ardavan looked at her, into her very soul, she thought, before he acquiesced and with a small shrug said, 'Until eleven tomorrow then. Do it!'

Lorenzo and Felice had been on watch in the marquee with the aircraft throughout the night, with

Fatima overseeing them. After Felice had settled for the first watch at 19:00, Fatima offered him a steaming cup of coffee to keep him awake and asked Lorenzo to take over the watch in four hours. They could share the watch between them thereafter. Felice was fast asleep in a few minutes, helped along by the soporific drug crushed into his coffee. Lorenzo could now fully trust her. She told him to keep himself alert for any prying eyes and headed off on her motorcycle.

....

Fatima had a window of opportunity to be alone, away from the intensive stares and listening ears of Ardavan Kamandi. She had broken the Sim card on her phone after her call to Special Branch and thrown her phone in a bin. She had time as she passed the Elephant and Castle to purchase another 'Pay as you Go' handset and as she drew down the number memorised from the previous call her fingers tapped out the number for Special Branch again. She said, 'The code is Armistice, patch me through.'

Vicky Douglas took the call swiftly and again initiated a trace.

'An attack will take place at the Cenotaph but allow it to continue. You want Ardavan Kamandi and I will deliver. The attack will be a mock one but he will believe it is real. There is no other way to keep people safe.'

The call was abruptly ended and only fourteen seconds had passed, not enough to get a trace but again the area was The Elephant and Castle.

Vicky yelled, ‘All units to converge on The Elephant and Castle immediately. We are looking for a female!’ She then realised the futility of attempting to round up every female in and around the busy Elephant and Castle shopping centre, never mind the larger zone of the addressable area itself. The caller was gone. By the sound of her delivery over the two calls she appeared to be a good pro and would likely have fled the area immediately.

Vicky passed the information up the line and to all her usual contacts in a situation like this.

Moments later she received a direct call from the Prime Minister.

‘Whatever happens I want Kamandi. We need, and I will give you, all possible resources to thwart this attack. We will lock down the entire area around the Cenotaph. Can the female who contacted you be trusted to soften the blow? How is she to do this? Should this be a job for the SAS? I can have them on scene anywhere in central London within thirty minutes, using the V-22 Osprey Transformer. You likely don’t know about it. It takes off like a helicopter and flies like a plane, so it’s much quicker than the choppers that they have been using until lately. They can get two dozen fully equipped 22 Regiment lads into one of those!’

‘With respect Prime Minister, none of us know how the attack is to take place. We only have the date to work on, going by her code word of Armistice. This will happen during the Armistice Day Parade, or even during the ceremony before the Parade or the lead up to the whole thing. All we know is the description of Kamandi. We have no idea who the female is at this point, nor do we have any idea as to how many players are involved. We do have one thing. We are pretty sure that the attacker or attackers will use rocket propelled grenades and they have a range of nine hundred metres, in a clear line of view. There could be two or more RPG’s so they could attack from different directions. We can saturate the area with SAS but I have already been through a process with my staff to discover and eliminate all sniper positions, which cover a much longer range. We have to consider casualties in any case, which we have also done in our dress rehearsal. All emergency services will be on high alert as a result. We have to try to find him before he gets to the site of his attack, but he could be heavily disguised. We are really up against it if the impending attack is in fact real. The caller, and it was the same one on both occasions did not seem like a wacko and when her voice signature was analysed she appeared to be genuinely concerned and acting truthfully. Our whizz kids in this aspect are extremely proficient in what they do and I find no reason to doubt them now.’

‘Okay Chief Inspector, but it will be on your head if this all goes wrong. The consequences would be utterly unimaginable. It would be the end of the

Royalty of the Country and the line of heirs to boot. The cabinet, including myself would be wiped out and quite possible heads of State of our European cousins. Our opposition leaders will be there, but, frankly, I'd be glad to be rid of them. Heads of armed forces, countless serving soldiers, ex-service men and women and the public at large could perish. But of course, we're British. We cannot bow down to these terrorists. We must be seen to stand up to them. I will count down the hours.'

Vicky Douglas was left to consider the words of her Prime Minister, words which she had tossed around in her own head ever since she had received the first call from the phantom caller. She banked on a mistake being made and her luck to shine through. What else could she think of? What else could her team uncover?

....

Fatima had in the same time returned to the vigil at the marquee, having again crushed the Sim card and binned the burner phone. She held up a finger over her lips, as Lorenzo opened his mouth. It was 21:15 on the Saturday night. The vigil would continue and Felice's sleeping draught would wear off. They had work to do.

The pair looked through the equipment and found the trigger mechanisms for the launchers, disarmed the timers on the warheads and left the machines as they had found them. Lorenzo and Fatima knew that Felice would be none the wiser.

In the morning Felice had remarked that they'd both had a good sleep despite their rotas and thought it lucky that there had not been any incidents.

They sat in the brightening morning light, drinking coffee and snacking on their pastries in the marquee, passing the time until they would start their pre-flight checks. They had donned their motorcycle leathers and boots, had their black bandanas around their necks and their helmets, radio mikes and gloves lay by their sides.

The plan was that Lorenzo would fly lead and Felice would follow, in a tight formation. Lorenzo would fly slightly higher to enable his aircraft to rise and make the escape turn and also be above Felice's line of sight to the target.

They went through their simulation of the route for the umpteenth time out loud and in unison, so Fatima could hear.

'Drive the Hiluxes to the rear of marquee, to shield the prop wash
Open the back flaps of the marquee and secure
Start engines and wait 5 seconds for oil turnover
Switch off engines
Open the front flaps of marquee and secure
Switch engines on again
Lorenzo to taxi out of front of marquee on to pathway

Felice to taxi to follow only 50 metres behind and close up in flight, but lower to avoid backwash from Lorenzo's propeller

At exactly 10:58

Throttle to full power for 150 metres and takeoff point

Lift next 50 metres over the tree belt by the lake

375 metres to A2

90 degrees to port

500 metres to A2 / A201 interchange just past Stompie Garden

45 degrees to port

A201 for 500 metres

Turn 20 degrees to starboard

400 metres to Elephant and Castle

Jink around roundabout

A302 for 600 metres

Turn 10 degrees to port at Marley College

600 metres to Westminster Bridge south end

550 metres across Westminster Bridge, past Houses of Parliament

Turn 90 degrees to starboard into Parliament Street

The Cenotaph in sight at 140 metres

Fire weapons onto their planned 161 metre trajectory

Gain altitude quickly in the hundred metres straight

Turn 90 degrees to port over the archways on King Charles Street On to the flying route for the escape

'That's great guys. You have all the detail memorised. I have a hunch though and think that Felice would be better to fly in lead, as this is what you have been doing in your practice runs.'

Felice butted in, ‘But what about what Ardavan said? He expects Lorenzo to be on the bike with him. We really should not start messing about with the plans at this late stage!’

‘Don’t worry about Ardavan. I’ll deal with him when the time comes, but take it from me that you are in lead position Felice! Now I had better ready myself and go and meet him in the escape rendezvous. I wish I knew where he was taking us on the bikes though. I don’t care for loose ends.’

‘I overheard him talking to your comrades who delivered the motorbikes about somewhere. Let me think for a minute……oh I remember…..I think……The Schooner Restaurant…… yes, that’s it …..The Schooner Restaurant car park! That’s where he will dump the bikes.’

‘The Schooner Restaurant where, Felice? There could be hundreds of Schooner Restaurants!’ exclaimed Lorenzo.

‘It doesn’t really matter where it is,’ said Fatima, not wanting to give her game away. ‘Suffice to say that he has a final destination in mind. He’ll let us know at the rendezvous.’ At that she donned her leathers and the rest of her biking gear and headed off. It was 08:46 on a quiet Sunday morning.

22 Retribution

Fatima was astride the big Triumph and thinking fast as she rode away from the marquee. She had to give up Kamandi somehow but she could not endanger herself or Lorenzo. She couldn't let the authorities know about his location yet. The pair of them had to get far away first. But she decided that she could let them know about The Schooner Restaurant. They could find him from that, wherever it was, or how many there may be. She could whisk herself and Lorenzo, dear Lorenzo, away from the scene on the bike and get far, far away from the scene of the action. It was only about an hour till the ceremony started. Time was against them, but she had to make an attempt.

She had no phone and an early Sunday morning did not allow her to shop, so she halted at the first available phone kiosk that she came across and phoned Special Branch for what she expected to be the last time.

'Armistice' is all she said and within seconds she was speaking to the familiar voice. Vicky Douglas said, 'Help me, please.'

'He will be at The Schooner Restaurant, I know not where, at some time after eleven fifteen. There will be an RPG attack, but I have disarmed the warheads, so they will just crash at some distance away. This is all I can do. This is not what Kurds wanted. We only wanted freedom. He has gone rogue. Good luck.'

She remounted her bike and whisked away to meet dear Lorenzo.

Vicky looked at her watch. Nearly ten o'clock. One hour to go. She immediately shook all her contacts into the hunt for a 'Schooner Bar or Restaurant'. Her team came up with four.

Bournemouth, St Catherine's Road
Gateshead, South Shore Road
Penarth, near Cardiff, Wales
Alnmouth, Northumberland Street

'Get units to them all – local forces – how far away are these from The Cenotaph? And we are looking for a middle-eastern man with a large hooked nose. Get on it!' It was 10:15.

……….

22 SAS Regiment at Hereford had been at Action Stations, since the call the previous night. As soon as they got the call at 10:03 their Director informed the caller from the Ministry of Defence that they could be on station at Horseguards Parade within thirty-five minutes. That was where the delay started, as the men in command who could make quick decisions were all at the Armistice Day Parade.

By 10:31 local police forces had descended on all of the locations, including the rural one near Cardiff. All of the investigating officers found all of the premises closed, but with staff inside preparing for their Sunday opening hour.

The man they had described to them and which appeared to them in the form of a passport head and shoulders photograph, not really showing his spectacular nose in the head on shot, was nowhere to be seen. They were all instructed to hold station until told otherwise, so a variety of uniformed constables had a long stand in store.

A sixteen man SAS troop and an additional four man sniper squad lifted off from Hereford at 10:35, heading for Horseguards Parade.

The Parade had commenced. Kamandi had known that it was always held on the second Sunday of November, as the calendar year on year had it closest to the eleventh day. It was one of the very few days if not the only day where his four targets could definitely be found together.

Rows of the general public stood ten deep on every vantage point they could get. Boy Scouts and Girl Guides circulated among them, handing out information leaflets. In front of them stood the thin line of London Bobbies with their iconic rounded helmets. Standing ahead of them were three ranks of service personnel and emergency services, resplendent in their dress uniforms.

The Director of Music for the Guards conducted the mixed bands of the Grenadier Guards, Coldstream Guards, Scots Guards and Welsh Guards in front of his podium. Behind them were the Highlanders of the Fourth Battalion of The Royal Regiment of Scotland. The Royal Marines buglers waited in the wings.

The Life Guards formed a hollow square, then at the pre-determined time the bands struck up Rule Britannia, Heart of Oak, Isle of Beauty, David of the White Rock and Oft in the Stilly Night. The bagpipes continued with Flowers of the Forest and on followed Nimrod, The Hunter, from Edward Elgar's Enigma Variations.

The Clergy and the Choir were first out, their silver cross held high. The choirboys in red and then the Bishop of London followed, past the row of Buglers of The Royal Marines now assembled. After a short pause the leaders of all the religious denominations within London followed the Bishop.

Then it was the duty of The Major General, Chief of Staff of the Household Division, The Queen's Guard, to assemble, with the ADC Captain.

The Chief of Defence Staff, General Sir Patrick Walsh Douglas, The Chief of General Staff Russell Murdoch, First Sea Lord Admiral Robert Anthony and Air Chief Marshall Alan McIntosh took up their positions opposite the monument.

....

One of Vicky's subordinates in Special Branch had come up with a diamond in their search. He had trawled though Council papers in each of the London Borough Councils and found the thoroughly legitimate process of an Italian event in Burgess Park. He had cross-checked with the local beat Bobbies and all seemed to be normal. Something niggled away at his brain and on looking further he noticed that the event was scheduled for a Monday and Tuesday, which he thought to be odd, as these were usually weekend events, to draw the crowds.

He had double checked his possible link and then, at 10:48 tried to bring this to Vicky's attention but she was at the Parade vicinity and dealing with a host of other associated matters.

....

Then came the Prime Minister and Leaders of the Opposition, The Foreign Secretary, The Defence Secretary and the Home Secretary, The Ambassadors of Nepal and Ireland and The Heads of State of Italy and France. Other Members of Parliament spilt from the building followed closely behind by High Commissioners and Representatives of The Commonwealth and Crown Dependencies.

Next it was the turn of the Merchant Navy, Fishing Fleets, Air Transport, Auxiliaries and Civilians of note.

Prince Charles, The Duke of Cambridge, The Duke of Sussex, The Duke of York, The Earl of Wessex, The Princess Royal and The Duke of Kent all marched out of the Foreign and Commonwealth Office, while the Queen, The Duchess of Cornwall and The Duchess of Cambridge looked on at the continuing spectacle from the first floor balcony overlooking Whitehall. The hundreds of ex servicemen who packed Whitehall below the towering TV platform all watched, in their Maroon, Green, Blue and Tartan headgear. Some bare headed balding pates shone below the sun and the Guards' shiny helmets glistened.

The two Police helicopters had been instructed to move off station, away from the parade site, for what was to happen next, removing their invasive noise from the scene. One headed East towards London City Airport and the other towards Heathrow.

....

At exactly eleven o'clock, just as Big Ben started to chime, Kamandi rose from his seat in a small house in Richmond, Surrey, killed the television set and was heading out to his waiting motorcycle to meet Fatima at the rendezvous. All his planning had worked and his actions would take out his four targets and quite a number of others besides. In his mind his work would be revered, lauded throughout Kurdish territories. He would be their hero!

....

An artillery gun fired a one-gun salute from nearby Horseguards Parade and the one minute of silence started to count down, to mark the eleventh hour of the eleventh day of November, on which The Armistice had been signed, marking the end of World War One.

As the sh... descended upon the massed bands, warriors of all types past and present, bowed their heads in remembrance. Nobody looked up past the Cenotaph, standing ready to take the poppy wreaths. There was a noise from the South end of the street, then a WHOOSH from something at the end of Whitehall.

None of the gathered dignitaries or veterans first realised what it was.

Then those on the ground who were more alert, who had seen active service more recently and had witnessed it before, started up the chorus.

'INCOMING!'..... 'INCOMING!'

General Russell Murdoch, ex SAS Director, was the first to notice it as he glanced over his left shoulder in the direction of the engine noise, which shouldn't have been there. He saw two movements on the low horizon between the buildings in Whitehall coming from Westminster Bridge. In the milliseconds he had, he saw two airborne machines, a smudge of grey against the background of sky and open buildings.

Then he saw the bright explosion from the twin muzzles and his thought process took in what he had just witnessed. Hundreds of ex servicemen at the other side of the Cenotaph, waiting in lines to pay their respects to the fallen dead of wars since 1914 had lifted their eyes a fraction skywards and also took in the sight. Some saw the rocket motor kick in and others dived for what cover lay around them, which was very little.

General Russell Murdoch realised that the RPG's, for that was what they were, were on a trajectory which would fly over their heads and he rushed at the bewildered figure of Prince Charles, standing out of sight of the danger, immediately behind the pillar of The Cenotaph. He knew that he would not reach him in the time it would take the rocket to arrive but it was part of his DNA. He had to make what defence he could on the heir to the throne.

The RPG's whooshed over the heads of all the Royalty, visiting politicians, members of the armed forces, serving and retired and flew on before ironically burying themselves in a wall of The Banqueting Hall, the home of The Royal United Services Institute. A couple of bystanders were showered with building debris when the four rockets chipped away at the stonework. There was no explosion.

Felice and the following Lorenzo had gained altitude from their firing position, the lead microlight just clearing the trajectory of the second pair of rocket propelled grenades as they swept to port and their escape over King Charles Street. They never saw the warheads hit the target. They rose further to fifty metres altitude and headed out over St James' Park, over Green Park, Hyde Park and Kensington Gardens, whizzing over the treetops and scaring all and sundry along the way. They were flat out at 150 km/hr and were just a blot of grey against the cloudy sky. Most observers were unsure as to what they had seen. Microlights were not the sort of thing you expect to have over central London parks.

....

It was 11:10 before Vicky managed to speak to her sergeant, aghast at what was happening around her. She was extremely relieved that the female on the phone had been true to her word but cutting across all of that was the absolute need to catch the perpetrators, especially Kamandi. She immediately escalated the action to a fully armed action on Burgess Park.

....

On they flew over Holland Park, The Botanical Gardens and to Richmond Park, where they scattered a herd of fallow deer and landed on the open grassland just to the south west of the Disabled Only Car Park beside Peg's Pond Gate Public Toilet. They ran the hundred metres to the waiting Triumph motorcycles at the junction of Ham Gate Avenue and Queen's Road.

Felice was the first to land at 11:05 and as instructed by Fatima, he ran towards the larger figure of Kamandi, sitting astride the big motorcycle and jumped on as pillion. Behind the dark visor Kamandi was not aware that he had Felice aboard, until he spoke to him on his head mike. The grip of fury took the Kurd but he realised that time was of the essence and that the pair had to make a fast getaway. He would deal with the insubordinate female and the other Italian later. In his wing mirror he saw the pair mounted and following as he started on his journey to freedom, blissfully unaware that his plan was in tatters, not knowing that the biggest manhunt in British history was about to unfold, and that the target was known to be him.

As he roared along the back roads Kamandi screamed, ***'THAT WAS RETRIBUTION!'***

The three other leather clad bikers heard the shout in their helmet headsets as they headed out of Richmond Park along Queen's Road, past Kingston Hospital and headed for the A3 South. As he glimpsed in his wing mirrors again he noticed that the following Triumph was no longer in sight, but he would see them again on a straighter piece of road.

They kept close to every speed limit but overtook any slower cars, trucks and buses along the route. Then they were on to the A240. As they joined the A24, around Horsham heading to Goring-By-Sea, they were just like any other two up motorcycle heading to the seaside for a jaunt. They struck off on the A283 and the second Triumph was still not in sight. Kamandi made for Shoreham-on-Sea, cut left onto the A259 and on to the Ferry Inn (the old Schooner Restaurant, but renamed after the COVID lockdown lack of business some months previously) on Albion Street overlooking the marina. He reckoned on Fatima and Lorenzo arriving within moments. There was no radio traffic from her or her pillion passenger. He popped the bike on to its stand in the car park and they headed towards the marina, removing their leather jackets, gloves and helmets as they made their way.

He noticed that there were no police in sight but a sizeable crowd was gathered around the large television screens above the bar area and a noisy muttering from the gathered viewers, as the newscaster related the big story of the day. It was 12:30.

Still no sign of Fatima, but maybe she'd been caught, or had a fall off the bike on their speedy journey south. 'She will just need to take her chances,' he muttered to Felice. 'Come on, we must go before the tide turns!' Unhurriedly, they sauntered to the waiting twin engine fast RIB sitting at the end of Pier 2. The two courier Kurds were waiting for them as they stepped aboard. One cast the moorings and the other handed over the wheel to Kamandi before leaping ashore.

He reversed out into the River Adur, swivelled and headed for the lock gates at the harbour entrance joining the craft that were already there. In a few minutes the RIB was in Shoreham Outer Harbour, out between the breakwaters and heading as fast as they could towards the coast of France.

The abandoned microlights were being pored over by detectives after a member of the public had phoned in. Lorenzo and Felice's experience, that of owning a Flying School and flying like Red Barons had indeed happened, but had been short lived.

....

Vicky Douglas had the sense to carry the hunch through to the end, just as she had discussed with Bernadette. Both astute members of their respective Police Forces, Special Branch and Interpol, were convinced that Ardavan Kamandi, an Iraqi Kurd, was involved in this, and at the head of it. The paths all led back to Turkey, or their ties with organised crime in Albania and Bosnia. Vicky had also the attempted slaughter of Russell Murdoch to consider, also carried out by an Iraqi Kurd. There was the link with the possible weapon shipment from Romania, via Norway to Great Britain, again by a Kurd. The searches had also picked up on an Iraqi travelling from London to Lerwick, in Shetland. That one had been a lucky break, but yet another Kurd. Felek Kinar had confirmed that packages were transported across the North Sea and that he had couriered them to London.

It was unfortunate that luck struck against the authorities. The Police helicopter to the East was too far away to do anything, having cleared the area for the obligatory minute's silence. The Police helicopter to the West had to return to base with a fuel warning light issue. The SAS operation was diverted to cover the airspace to the west, but the microlights had been ahead of their movement.

The vehicles on the ground could not determine the actual route of the fliers' escape. The aircraft could outrun vehicles on the ground and avoid all traffic. The radio communication was good, but sight lines were not. The microlights had simply disappeared for a while.

Both Bernadette Bucheron and Vicky Douglas wanted the elusive head of the operation. They wanted to flush him out, even if there was collateral damage to a few innocent bystanders. The window of opportunity had been very tight. They had missed him and they had missed the two pilots of the microlights. From the equipment serial numbers of the aircraft they determined from the Civil Aviation Authority that they were the property of Gorebridge Flying School, near Edinburgh. From that nugget of information they had discovered that the business had been purchased in the previous September, for persons unknown, by a law firm in Edinburgh. In turn they discovered that an Italian legal firm based in Nola, near Napoli in Italy had instructed Strachan and Fraser to make the purchase on their behalf. The British authorities had acted very quickly, considering that it was a Sunday. Vicky had all this information by 13:08. She immediately telephoned Interpol Headquarters in Lyon.

'Bernadette, it's Vicky. You'll no doubt be aware of the incident we had this morning. It was just as you and I had predicted. We got lucky though, as a female gave us a warning and even told us of a location where the Kamandi fellow might be, but we either missed him or she set us up with a red herring. He used two microlight aircraft to fire a total of four rocket propelled grenades at the high and mighty of our country at the Armistice Day Parade this morning. The rockets worked as intended but the grenades had been disarmed in some way, maybe by the female.'

'Well Vicky…'

'Hold on a minute, we reckon that there are four of them in this group. Kamandi, the female and two pilots.'

'Vicky I must…'

'Hang on a bit Bernadette, the aircraft were flown by persons with a knowledge of a Gorebridge Flying School, in Scotland. But there is a link, we think, to Nola, Napoli, Italy. There's an involvement with a legal entity there in the purchase of the School. We don't yet know who the purchase was for, but it's our guess that it was for Kamandi.'

'Well, Vicky, I was going to say, when you first mentioned microlights, my heart skipped a beat. When you added the bit about Napoli it skipped another one. This may be a long shot, but it might be yet another hunch. Interpol has an undercover operative working on Mafia connections in Italy and his particular location is Napoli. He disappears from our radar for periods of time, due to the nature of his work, but when he can he sends us a coded signal to let us know that he is okay. His last signal to us was in mid October, when he told us he was onto something very big. I'm putting two and two together here, but maybe, just maybe, he is one of the fliers, as he uses a tourist flying experience company as a cover, coincidentally in a microlight, flying out of Salerno Airport, which is close to Napoli. Maybe he disarmed the grenades. Maybe we have a handle on Kamandi. And even better, on the inside.'

'Well you do come up with some beauties, Bernadette. I must go and tell my seniors.' She glanced at her watch…13:12.

……….

In the RIB, as it left the south coast of England and headed at full speed across the English Channel towards its plotted destination of Boulogne-sur-Mer, Kamandi looked back in the cold autumnal grey day at the receding coastline and at the outlined figure of Felice Capasso behind him, clinging to the safety rail. His thoughts were centred round the missing woman Ardalan and Russo, the other Italian. What had happened to them? What was he to do with Capasso? He had to disappear. His quest was complete and he could afford no witnesses. He still had to take his Nation forward in the quest for autonomy. Nobody must know what he had done.

The welcoming coastline of France appeared over the horizon and the port drew near. Large and small vessels dotted the sea on the course in front of him. Kamandi's concentration homed in on all the marine dangers around him and he was too late in realising that what flashed in front of his eyes was one of the mooring ropes which dropped around his exposed neck.

Felice Capasso pulled the evil fiend towards him, using the seat backrest as a lever, throttling him. Kamandi's feet flew up, pulling the kill cord on the RIB from the console, his hands grappling for the man behind him, trying to grip the wet surface of his assailant's sailing jacket, his eyes bulging over the great beak of a nose, seeing stars as he started to lose consciousness. All Felice's strength was concentrated on choking this animal to death, to stop him repeating what he had just engineered some hours ago. At last the kicking and struggling diminished and ceased. The RIB lay dead in the water and his quarry was also dead.

As he loosened the kill switch cord from Kamandi's leg and tied it around his own, he thought about what it would be like to get back to France. It was a lucky break to hear the conversation between Fatima and Lorenzo as he feigned sleep in the bedroom of the flat. He powered up the engines and sped towards the harbour, to Lyon and the wonderful Bernadette, back to his life as Philippe Bucheron. He had a lot to explain.

Acknowledgements:

To David Robinson, whose expertise in the field and extensive comments made a difference to the whole novel. Eternal thanks.

Thanks to Fiona Hall at Camban Studio for the cover artwork.

To all the real people, who might discover a part of themselves in this novel, my heartfelt thanks for knowing you and giving me the inspiration for some of the characters.

Printed in Great Britain
by Amazon

64268924R00194